This book is a work of fiction. Names, characters, places and incidents are either products of the author's imagination or are used fictitiously. Any resemblance to actual events or locales or persons, living or dead, is entirely coincidental.

ISBN (pbk) 9781648716300

Flaming Light Publishing
A Division of Wonderment Records.

Pap Dockin
By Royal Wade Kimes

Author's Note:

Over the years I've met one or two Pap Dockin's. A breed of their own, in a time of their own.
One of those was a true cowboy by the name of Butch Johnmeyer who is featured on the cover as Pap Dockin.

Dedication
To Times Gone By

Thank you to all involved in making this work of love happen.

Royal Wade Kimes
(The Gentleman Outlaw)

Edited by Nona Wilke
Art & Cover Design by Debbie Brooks

Pap Dockin
By Royal Wade Kimes

Pap Dockin
By Royal Wade Kimes

Prelude

Franklin Dockin was more than a West Texas cattleman and landowner of thousands of acres. He was a pioneer, a leader and tough. He loved his land, his high caliber horses and cattle. But life was not easy for him and had dealt a difficult hand many times. The results led him to believe having a family of his own wasn't an option. His ranch hands were like family and no doubt were the reason he was good natured about their starting to call him "Pap" on his 40th birthday. The nickname stuck. But nobody, nobody, had better call him "old man" or they would surely regret it.

Pap's large spread was partially separated from his neighbor Zell Davis, by a patch of land belonging to an absentee owner in Kansas City. Zell was a consistent festering thorn in his side. The two of them once ran a cattle operation together but had a serious falling out and hadn't gotten along since. Zell was full of contempt and anger, but he always backed off before starting a range war.

In the absence of nearby lawmen, Pap had enforced the law to its full extent for years. In his own way he was fair, but he pulled no punches. If the Saint Maker didn't resolve it, a gun did. Unfortunately, things were about to go rapidly downhill. Pap was going to be seriously challenged by not only Zell Davis, but the arrival of the owner of the patch and his pregnant wife. Hired guns would drift in making their presence known, employed by Zell. The beautiful female owner of a transport and freight company comes to town with news Pap would never have dreamed possible, which would dictate a new way of approaching some situations. Renegade Indians, stolen cattle, a widespread fire, and an idiot marshal would plague Pap Dockin. That, combined with increased Zell Davis treachery, his patience would surely run out.

Pap Dockin
By Royal Wade Kimes

Chapter 1

"Ease along here old son."

Pap Dockin always talked to his blue roan gelding when riding him. This time he had a reason. "You be quiet. I smell beef cookin'."

Pap rode another fifty yards and came upon a camp with two hard looking cowboys sitting around it. They were wearing worn out boots, sweaty dust covered hats, and needed shaves. Nice holster rigs were strapped to their sides with six-guns filling them. There was a hind quarter from a steer roasting in the fire, and one of the cowboys was sitting near the carcass. Pap rode in with his right hand close to his own six-gun. He spoke to them in a rather quiet voice. "Evening."

A yellow-headed cowboy squatting by the fire slowly stood up. The second cowboy, sitting by the half-butchered steer, tore at a chunk of beef with his teeth. Neither one answered him or seemed all that concerned about him.

"You boys hungry?" He elevated his voice just a smidge.

"Was... ain't now." The yellow-haired cowboy snickered at his partner's comment.

"Did you say you was... but ain't now?"

"Yeah, yeah... that's what I said."

"Good... that's good. I hate to see a man die hungry."

That was the first time either one of the cattle thieves acted concerned. The cowboy sitting by the beef eased his right hand down beside his gun while he held the fresh cooked meat in the other.

"You fellers aren't from around here... are you?" Pap scanned the camp, making sure there were only two of them.

The yellow-haired cowboy stuck another piece of meat, with his long-bladed knife and answered with his mouth full of beef. "Nah, up Kansas way."

"Up what?"

"I said... up Kansas way!" The cowboy raised his voice rather loudly.

"Up Kansas way you say? Well, I don't know how things work up Kansas way, but down here around the Texas Panhandle, you don't butcher another man's steer unless you pay for it first."

Pap's gun came from its holster before the beef eaters knew it was there. Though he had the drop on them he was concerned. He had the cattle thieves covered, and way too easily. They were both eating his beef and wearing guns. He couldn't figure why they didn't draw and go to shooting. It was a puzzle. He decided to play it out and see where the trail led.

The yellow-haired cowboy stopped eating. "Fast for an old man." He looked around at his partner and then slowly back to Pap. "Now what?"

"Does the brand on that steer mean anything to you?"

"Not particularly."

"That's the Dockin brand... belongs to me. The Dockin ranch takes in several sections north and a few sections south. It runs east and west about the same."

The one sitting by the beef spoke up. "According to a map at the courthouse in Mason City, there's an elbow of land that joins the Dockin property line along in here somewhere. It runs along beside the Dockin spread for a good distance. Belongs to your once upon a time partner, Zell Davis. There's another hundred acres belongs to somebody in Kansas City, Missouri, whoever the hell that is. That little patch separates part of the Davis Ranch elbow and the Dockin Ranch for a short distance. It pinches in right between the two ranches. Dockin name may be on a large chunk of land but has close neighbors in a place or two... old man."

Pap realized they knew way too much about his boundaries, which made them a different caliber of cattle thief. "Well I know you know, but I'll say it anyway. Name's Dockin... Pap Dockin. 'Old man' won't cut it when addressing me. A good cattle thief ought to have a little respect for the man whose beef he's chewin' on, especially when there's a forty-five pointin' at him."

"I've heard your hands call you, 'old man', I figure I can. I'm not afraid of you. You ride around feeling like a stud rooster, and I understand that. You own some ground. What you're overlooking is the 'over the hill factor' that has set in on you. You're damn near double my age. You've slowed down and don't know it." He grinned and glanced at the yellow-haired cowboy. "Do yourself a favor and move on. It beats hell out of me why you're out here worrying over a beef and two cowboys anyway. Head that nag you're riding towards home and think back on how it used to be. Fond memories are all you have left... old man."

"Say again? I missed half what you said. You need to speak up a little. My hearin' ain't what it was. I did hear the name Zell Davis, and you boys seem to know the lay of the land." Pap wasn't saying, but he'd heard most of what was said, which he didn't think amounted to much. Hearing his old partner's name... that meant something. Now he knew who the boys worked for and why they were here. They were hired guns, hired to kill him. "You fellers throw your guns down on the ground there in front of you, real easy like. Might need to know, I'll kill you dead if you move sudden."

The yellow-haired cowboy was easing his gun out slow, but the one by the beef would have none of it. "Old man... you can't hear it thunder, let alone shoot."

Pap smiled. "You want me to send your body back up Kansas way or bury you down here in Texas? You pull iron on me and I'll kill you dead as last year's daisies." Pap smiled at the young cowboy. "You can try your luck, like you say... I'm past my prime. It'd be a surprise if you do. You youngsters comin' up these days ain't much on nerve, but big on mouth."

The young cowboy turned red from anger. "There ain't no over the hill old man going to flush me up. I see your game. Nah, I'll leave it for another day. You got the drop on me now."

Pap Dockin
By Royal Wade Kimes

"Say again? Did you say you was scared to death?"

"Hell no! I didn't say I was scared! I'm not afraid of nothing!" The cowboy shouted as loud as he could as he went for his gun.

Pap fired and a forty-five-slug hit the gun for hire in the chest. The impact of the large lead bullet knocked him flat of his back. Pap's eyes left the fallen man and went to the other gun hand. "You not scared either?"

The yellow-haired gunman already had his gun in hand to drop it like he was asked. Though he was afraid to move, he for sure would comply. His partner was lying badly wounded or dead, and he was staring at the end of the gun barrel that had shot him.

"Son, I'm feelin' boar hog mean right now. I'll shoot that little dinky of yours off, and you'll have to find a job at an Opera up Kansas way singin' high notes."

"I'm dropping it." The cowboy slowly dropped the gun. "You went too far old man."

"Say again?"

"Too far... you went too far."

"I'm not done yet, Dinky."

"Name is Watts, Ben Watts."

"Why don't you check on your brave friend?"

He ambled over to his partner and felt his pulse. "He's dead. Shot through the heart. Are you that good... or that lucky?"

"He'd still be alive had he had any sense."

"The hell you say! You goaded him into making a move... drawing on you!"

"You both made a move, a wrong one when you killed my steer." Pap stepped down from his horse and stuck a chew of tobacco in his mouth. "Dinky, I wasn't getting through to him like I was you. He kept callin' me, 'old man', showed little respect for his elders."

"You shot him for calling you an old man?"

Pap cut a chunk of beef off the roasted hindquarter. "You

happen to have any salt?"

The gunman couldn't believe he asked for salt. "Yeah, there on the rock wrapped in brown paper."

"Say again?"

"Paper, in the paper!"

"Much obliged." Pap sprinkled salt on the beef and waved it around on his knife a bit. "You want to know what I'm doin' here, Dinky?"

The gunman looked around like he wanted to run, but he knew that was crazy. Pap Dockin had already proved he could shoot. "Not really."

Pap chuckled. "I'm gonna tell you anyway." He took a long spit towards the campfire and wiped his mouth. "A man ought to be able to do two to three things at once. I'm tryin' to cool this beef off a little while my chaw runs out. I think they both should come together about the same time. The other thing I'm doin', is getting ready to enjoy a nice steak you boys cooked up. No sense lettin' my beef go to waste. Now let me see, where was I? Oh, I'm also tryin' to figure out if I hang you here for stealin' my steer and eatin' it, or do I take you down to the ranch and hang you? Hard decision I have to make. Takin' you to the ranch would require havin' to watch you the whole time. Don't like the idee of that, but I guess I could do it. A hired gun needs to be strung up where the man that hired him can see what happened." Pap looked towards the fire and spit in it. He then took his finger and pulled the tobacco out of his mouth and threw it in the fire. "A proper hangin' might discourage anyone else from killin' what don't belong to them."

"You knew we were hired guns? You knew and tried us anyway?" The gunman could hardly believe it. "You ain't nothin' like Zell said you was. He said you were old and feeble, talked to yourself a lot and took rides alone. He said you were always getting lost."

Pap didn't answer. He was too busy enjoying his prime beef.

When he finished, he wiped his mouth with his handkerchief and cut another chew of tobacco. "Load your friend on his horse and mount up." Then out of the blue, Pap asked a question. "Dinky, do I look old to you?"

"Well, no, not really."

"Well, is forty- five old?"

He thought about it for a second and then cut his eyes to Pap. "Well, I'm thirty-one. That don't seem so old... but in my line a work, thirty-five is old. Not many live in my game to see thirty-five. So, I..."

"We're not talking about you, damn it. I asked if forty- five is old?"

"Well, I was getting to that. No, forty-five ain't what I'd call old. I know a few men in their seventies. It is a fact though, ain't many get past forty-five these days. Illness or something gets us." He glanced at Pap, trying not to get caught doing it. "To answer your question. After what I've seen here... no you're not what I'd call old. But I'd damn sure call you savvy."

Pap thought about that for a few seconds. "Well, you sure went around the damn house to answer me." He tilted his head at the gunman. "I appreciate your answer. It was long on coming, but it seemed honest." He shook his head as he looked at the campfire. "Man kills and eats my steer and I call him honest. I must be old... or I'm losing my mind early in life. Well, I don't guess it makes any difference. Get your friend loaded on his horse.".

The yellow-haired gunman did as Pap told him and then turned and asked a question. "What do you plan to do with me?"

"What's that?"

"I say, what are you going to do with me?"

"Well, Dinky, we hang rustlers here in Texas. Don't they hang rustlers in Kansas?"

"I told you my name is Ben Watts!"

Pap Dockin
By Royal Wade Kimes

"Dinky, here's the truth of it all. I'm law on my spread. There ain't any other law... not for a lot of damn miles there ain't. It's up to me, and others like me to take care of law and order here in the Texas Panhandle. I try to be fair with my lawin'... try hard. I don't bend it, twist it, and for damn shore I don't break it. Now I know the verdict on you already. Guilty as charged. No question about it. I caught you in the act. What the punishment will be, that's a whole 'nother thing. I figure you'll hang. If you don't, you may wish you had."

The yellow haired cowboy had a frown on his face. "Is someone else handing down sentence?"

"No... no, that'll be me too. I do all my handin' down of sentence." Pap spat at a cricket and just missed him.

Ben Watts, alias Dinky, was bewildered by his captor.

"Dinky, we're going to head out to my place. I'm not goin' to tie you up. You run, that's okay. I won't have to go to all the trouble of hangin' you."

They mounted up and rode for about ten minutes when Pap pulled off the moonlight bathed trail. He dismounted and pulled back some bushes and other brush.

Ben could not believe what he was looking at. In front of him were two of the best-looking horses he had ever laid eyes on. They were high dollar colts, and few people he knew could afford one or even knew where one was of that caliber.

"Dinky, I'm gonna get those lead ropes and tie these colts off to my saddle. If you're feelin' like a rabbit, this would be the time to take off."

"Pap, you said you don't break your law, but you shot Beal dead, and in cold blood. I'll not run."

"You're a tad smarter than your deceased partner." He motioned for his prisoner to move out. "I'm guessin' you know where the ranch is, lead off."

Pap was leading two of the finest horses he'd ever owned, and he had owned some good ones. He turned forty-five not more than a month ago. Franklin Wayne Dockin was a five-foot nine-inch man with broad shoulders. His hair was a sandy color and had begun to turn white along the temples. Pap had a rugged but handsome look about him. Over the past three years after he turned forty, the younger ranch hands began to call him Pap in fun. It kind of caught on around the ranch and soon they were all calling him 'Pap'.

He had to smile at the marvel of it. Dinky was right, not many men live past forty on the High Plains of the Texas Panhandle. If the heat and rattle snakes didn't get you, a longhorn bull or a Comanche just might. Then there were always unsavory characters running around causing trouble. They had to be dealt with from time to time.

It was untamed country for the most part and took the Pap Dockin's of the world to conquer it. He had money, but he didn't go in for spending much of it. The boots he wore needed polish, and the heels were half worn out. He liked boots that were broken in good. He always wore spurs and a hat with a sloped crown. Pap Dockin was all cowboy and proud of it. He might be forty-five, but he carried his age and stout frame like a twenty-year-old.

Pap Dockin
By Royal Wade Kimes

Chapter 2

Chalk Cranfield was almost to his destination. He was standing at the counter of a hardware store, purchasing forty-five caliber shells, in a place called Mason City. He'd never been in Texas before. The dry dusty street and the high plains of the panhandle were a far cry from the streets of Kansas City.

"I'm much obliged for the information. You say I keep due west three miles and I'm there?"

The store owner was a tall slender man bent over a little from a lot of hard work over the years. He peered over his glasses and smiled. "Yes Sonny, that's what I said. You'll know you're there when you see a big rock with a smaller rock sitting on top of it. You really can't miss it. Turn by the rock and head due north for a half mile and you're there. Sonny, there ain't nothing but an old run-down shack out there. It's not any place to take a wife, especially one in her condition."

Sarah Cranfield was expecting a baby in a month, if not sooner. She had been in the store and went back outside to the wagon.

"It's not more than a dim trail right now, grown up a bunch I suspect." The storekeeper stood with both thumbs under his suspenders.

Chalk and his wife Sarah moved from the hustle and bustle of Kansas City, Missouri, to live on a hundred acres in Texas, willed to him by his mother, Paula Cranfield. She had passed away a year prior to their trip. He wanted to be a rancher and the piece of ground willed to him was giving him a chance to do so. A chance to live his dream. He noticed the store owner kept eyeing him while he was explaining how to get to his land.

"Sir, if you don't mind me asking, why do you keep looking at me funny like?"

"Well, it's a given you don't know what you're getting into."

"Oh?" Chalk stopped sacking up the canned peaches and shells he had bought. "Go on."

Pap Dockin

By Royal Wade Kimes

"Son, you're moving in between two of the most stubborn and feuding men in the territory. There's been hell out there on those plains for twenty years. I can't imagine what is going to happen when you show up."

"Why is that?"

"Because both Dockin and Davis run their cattle on your patch of ground."

"Well, I guess they'll have to stop." Chalk was curious. "You call a hundred acres a patch?"

The store owner laughed. "I'm afraid so. Dockin and Davis own thousands of acres, biggest spreads in these parts. Son, those two are a couple of hard men. They grew up tough and kept getting tougher. They live tough and they are tough. Pap came to Texas by way of Alabama after the war. Zell Davis did too come to think of it. I believe I heard Pap say Zell lived in a little town about ten miles from where he was from. They were partners for a while, but things went bad between them early on in the deal. Seems it happened on a cattle drive. Pap came back without Zell." The storekeeper was enjoying the telling of the story. "Ole Zell, he came dragging in about two weeks later as I recall in pretty bad shape. I was a young feller then always nosing around."

"You seem to have a talent."

"What does that mean?" The storekeeper crossed his arms in an expression of displeasure.

Chalk smiled. "Nothing, nothing at all." Suddenly, Chalk heard Sarah's voice outside the store. He turned and hurried out on the boardwalk where two men were standing by her at the end of the wagon.

The store owner walked to the door. "That's Ted Davis, the bigger one, and his brother Huey. Be careful. They can be mean."

"You alright honey?"

Sarah was a young twenty-year-old blond with blue eyes and

a smile bigger and brighter than the Texas sky. "I'm fine."

Chalk noticed one of the men eased his hand from out of the back of the wagon. The other one was standing closer to Sarah. He sized them up. Ted was the big burly slow type. Huey was not as big and might be considered nice looking. He figured Ted to be on the slow side with his hands not to mention his mind. "You boys find something in my wagon you'd like to have?"

Ted grinned. "Hell no! You ain't got a thing in there I'd have. I'd shore take a round with your woman there if she wasn't carryin' a pup."

Chalk stepped down in the street and walked around to the end of the wagon where he could face Ted. "You got a mouth full of vile corruption." Before he could answer, Chalk pulled a singletree from the wagon, and with one motion came around and caught Ted across the face and head. He was knocked out cold and halfway out into the middle of the street.

Huey acted like he was going to take it up, but then relaxed. "This here was all Ted's doings. I told him not to mess with you folks. This is not my way."

"You pick Ted up and get out of here before I decide to lay you out beside him."

After the Davis boys were gone the store owner brought out a small cloth sack with a tiny hemp string that pulled the opening to the little sack shut. It was peppermint candy for Sarah. "Son, you might just have a chance out there on your patch of ground, but you sure started off on the wrong foot. I hope you can use a gun. You'll have to."

"Why is that?"

"Those boys belong to Zell Davis, one of the men I was telling you about whose land happens to join you."

Chalk climbed up on his wagon after he had helped Sarah up. "Sir, one question for you. If Dockin and Davis have so much land, why do they need to run their cows on my patch?"

"Good question." He grinned and then chuckled. "You should

take that up with them."

"I plan to. Be seeing you."

"I hope you can handle what's coming."

He picked up the check lines to his team and faintly smiled. "Get up, Bill, Fred." The wagon wheels picked up dust as he headed out of town to see his little patch of ground.

Chalk Cranfield was born in Dodge City, Kansas, but moved to Kansas City, Missouri, at the tender age of eight. He was an only child and in six short years he became a tough boy scraping it out on the streets. Later, at twenty-one, he had become a smart, tough man. He grew up with one parent. His father left his mother before he was born. They were never married, and she never spoke of him.

Sarah looked at Chalk as they rode along on the wagon. "How far?"

"A ways." He had been quiet ever since they left the mercantile.

"Chalk, are you thinking about your mother?"

"Yeah... I suppose. I wish she could have been a part of this."

"Though she isn't here, she is in spirit." Sarah smiled for him.

Chalk looked over at her. "Sarah, Mom left a lot unsaid. She never once said my father's name in front of me. The one time I asked his name, she broke down and cried. Mom spent two nights with the man and then he left her. I think he was some drover from a cattle drive. She loved him despite him not marrying her. She never married because she could not get beyond him. The man doesn't know what he missed in her."

"I'm sorry, Chalk."

"Awh, my cross to bear. I remember when I turned eight, she came into some money, a good sum of money. She moved us to Kansas City, and to this day I've never figured the why. The money was a mystery. It came by way of a carrier in a plain brown twine weaved sack. There wasn't a name, no address and no explanation. Then a few years later a lawyer came to the house with some papers and when he left, Mom was the owner of a hundred acres near a town called Mason City in Texas. Right away she made a will leaving everything to me. That was one year before she died with her tuberculosis. She spent very little of the money other than maybe the price of the land. I thought she bought the property for us to live on, when in reality she purchased the land for me to have a place to go. She wanted me away from the city. She knew she would not be on this earth long. What I can't figure is why she chose Texas, and why the High Plains of Texas. It's dry, hot, and... hot and dry." The both of them laughed.

"Maybe the lawyer that cut the deal for her happened to be familiar with the high plains part of Texas."

"Could be. Mom didn't tell me anything. It doesn't make sense her buying land she never even saw. Well, anyway here I am. Hello Texas."

Sarah smiled. "I love you, Chalk."

"I love you, honey."

Chalk Cranfield had a way about him unlike most. He was quiet and calm, always in charge of himself and a handsome man head to toe. He was just under six foot and blessed with a big stout pair of shoulders. He was known for his big wide fists which were his working tools on the streets of Kansas City. As a boy in Dodge City he helped the big boss at the stock pens. He carried water and ran messages from the yards to wherever a message was supposed to go. He liked that life. His dream was to be a rancher. The idea of owning cattle and a ranch was exciting and pulled at him. The big cattle drives would come in and he would sit and watch the cowboys herd the cattle in the corrals. He loved the horses, the punchers, the ropes, the bedrolls, saddles and the smell of it all. He didn't know if he would ever make sense of it all... especially his mother owning land in the panhandle of Texas. A smile formed. Maybe he didn't have to. It might would all come out on its own one day, or maybe he would never know. Whether it did or didn't, he bought a team, a good wagon and headed to Texas where he would become a cowboy.

Pap Dockin rode into his ranch at near two in the afternoon. A gold sun blazed bright from a big wide blue sky. Speck Jernigan, the foreman of the ranch met him in front of the house. Speck was eyeing the stranger riding with him and noticed he didn't have a gun in his holster. He had an idea what happened to it.

"Speck... have one of the boys take these two colts to a corral. How's things been while I was away?"

"Damn nice colts."

"I say, how's things?" Speck never dodged questions and Pap knew that to be the case.

"Quiet, nothing happened, 'cept Duke treed a big coon in the barn rafters."

"Did he handle him?" Pap was grinning.

"Duke took him on when he finally bailed out onto some hay. Damn good fight. Ole Duke held his own, but the coon shot through a hole in the wall and got away." Speck laughed and slapped his knee.

"How's the roundup comin' along?"

"Coming along tolerable." Speck looked off towards the west.

"Say again? What's wrong with the roundup?"

"Nothing." Speck didn't want to talk in front of the stranger, and Pap figured that out after a few seconds.

"Well, fill me in later."

"Who's your friend?"

"What?"

"Who's the empty holster?"

"Oh him... well Speck, he's a lost and misguided kind of a feller that run onto some bad luck. The man was caught eatin' one of our steers. He's not got one ounce of sense or remorse about it. I brought in a verdict of guilty early on. I didn't even get to retire to chambers. I caught the rascal red-handed, had to kill his partner."

"You didn't have to kill him, you just did."

"See what I mean, Speck, no sense whatsoever. Verdict is in and I think I know what the sentence will be. I had time to think on it while we rode in together." Pap looked around at Ben and then at Speck. Suddenly it was like he was another man. His voice changed. It was stern, business like, and the smile that had been there earlier was gone. "Gather the hands, judgment has got to be dealt out." He looked at Ben. "Mister, you killed one of my beeves. You acted like you didn't give a damn and me standin' there. You snickered at me. You're a hired gun, nothin' more, nothin' less, just a killer for hire, and for what? Money. Well, maybe up Kansas way they abide by such, but down Texas way... we don't."

Ben began to sweat. "Pap, I... I... sure would like another chance. I can't see me doing anything like this again... I."

"Say again?"

"I said I will never do anything like this again!"

"No, you surely won't." He looked around for Speck. "Bring me the Saint Maker."

All the hands who worked for the Dockin Ranch gathered around. Speck had four of the men pull Ben Watts, nicknamed Dinky, from his horse. They drug him cussing and kicking over to a snubbing post where they normally snubbed rank horses.

"Dinky, ordinarily your crime would call for hangin' straight up. I've give it careful consideration and the sentence will be... the Saint Maker. Twenty lashes ought to get your attention and others like you. So, toughen up here and take your medicine like a man. I hear you whimper... I'll add a lash each time you do. When I'm done you'll be a saint, or lookin' to be soon as a preacher makes an altar call. Cut his shirt off of him!" Pap slung the bull whip back behind him and let the end of it lay on the ground while he stuck a big chew of tobacco in his mouth. "Dinky, your friend paid the big price. I'm goin' to let you live.

Consider this a lesson on how to get along in this country. When I'm done, like I say, you'll be a changed man. If it don't take on you, then hell will have you soon enough."

The Dockin hands tied Ben to the post and ripped the shirt from his back. Pap went to work from there.

Pap Dockin
By Royal Wade Kimes

CHAPTER 3

Zell Davis was having a bad day. His two boys, Ted and Huey, came in from town telling about some squatter setting up out on the hundred-acre corner that separated the Sliding D from the Dockin Ranch. Zell didn't take the news well about squatters, and Ted taking a whipping was not to be tolerated. His boys didn't take whippings. He expected Ted to redeem the Davis name.

Later that evening, Ben Watts, Dinky as Pap had called him, rode in slumped over his saddle horn and fell off in front of the Davis house. His back was a bloody mess and he was extremely weak. The two Davis boys, along with a couple of the Sliding D hands, carried him to the bunk house.

"What happened here, Ben? Who did this? Where's Beal?"

"Dead." Ben looked up at Zell and then fell unconscious.

"Huey, you ride into town and bring Doctor Zimmer. If Watts here doesn't get some medical attention he could die. Hurry about it, hear?"

"I'll hurry, Pa!" Huey bailed out of the house and rode for town.

That night after Doctor Zimmer left, Zell sat down beside Ben who was in a bunk lying on his stomach. "You gave me quite a scare. Thought you had lost too much blood. Doc says you'll pull through." Zell asked the rest of the hands to step outside. "Boy, who did this thing to you? Your back is chewed up worse than if a mountain cat had gotten hold of you."

"It might as well of been. When Pap Dockin gets through with you, there's not a lot of difference. He came ridin' in like you said he would, bold and proud. What he didn't do was lose his nerve or sense about him. You said he was senile, Zell. He's not at all what you told me and Beal. Pap Dockin is a hand with that gun of his and mighty damn good with a bull whip, too." He paused and stared Zell dead in the eyes. "You lied to us."

Zell looked towards the door. "Well, I figured you'd find out how he was once you run onto him. I didn't want that old man running you off before you started."

"Zell, that old man is anything but an old man. As for running... Beal and me don't run. Beal would still be alive if you had given us the straight of what that old man was like. Hell, Pap's tough business. He's the kind of man that gives more'n he gets." He gave Zell a disapproving look before continuing. "I ought to kill you for what you did, not telling us the truth about him."

Zell stood up. "Maybe I was wrong. I'll admit to it. But you go to threatening me and I'll plant you."

"You're a hard man. I'm laying here near dead and you want to finish the job." Ben took a deep breath. "You need not worry. I'm sticking around for the party myself."

Zell smiled exposing a wide gap between two front teeth. "That's more like it. I guess I should have been a little more forthcoming about Pap. I'll shoot straight with you from now on. By the way, I've got another gun hand coming. Since you know the lay of things, he can follow your orders."

"Zell, I sent for my partner. When he gets here, you won't need anyone."

"Who is he?"

"You'll see. He's from Kansas. He's one of the best."

"Alright then, you get some rest and I'll talk to you tomorrow. I think me and the boys will pay Pap a visit."

Zell left Ben alone and gathered up his two sons along with five of the ranch hands.

Ted was excited as he strapped on his gun. "Where we going?"

"We're paying a visit to Pap Dockin. No one whips my men like dogs."

It was near ten o'clock at night when Sarah woke Chalk from his sleep. They had taken the bed from the wagon and made the rundown shack of house do to sleep in for the night.

"Chalk, wake up. Wake up."

He awoke with a start. "Sarah, you alright?" His first thought was the baby.

"I'm fine… but listen. Can you hear that?"

He lay quiet listening and then heard what Sarah was hearing. "Yeah I hear it. Sounds like gunshots and lots of them. It sounds like a war."

"What do you think it is?"

"Well, it could be something to do with the Dockin and Davis bunch. The storekeeper said there's bad blood between the two ranches. The shots are coming from the direction of the Dockin place. If I was betting, I'd say that's it."

"You don't think Indians? Comanches?"

"No, Sarah. It's okay. Lay back down and go to sleep. I'm going to get up and have a cigar. Get some rest."

"Okay, if you're sure." Sarah turned over and before he could say a word, she was asleep again. She felt safe when he was close by.

Chalk got up and slipped out onto the front porch, what there was of it. The floor was almost gone. The house was near collapsing in several places. He knew he would have to build a new house. He figured to ride to town tomorrow and pick up building materials and supplies.

He walked out to the top of a small hill north of the house where he could look across the range for a ways. He was surprised that he could actually see flashes of light in the distance from the gunshots. The hill was all that kept the Cranfield patch and the Dockin spread from being in sight of one another. He turned to go back when the shooting suddenly stopped. He waited and listened. He started to walk back to the house when he heard horses coming at a dead run. They sounded like they were coming right up the hill, when they turned suddenly and went the direction of the wagon road.

They soon were out of hearing. He didn't know what happened, but someone was getting out fast. He had moved in beside some very loud night owl neighbors. He finished his cigar and went back to bed where he fell into a deep sleep.

Pap was up at daylight the next morning. He had ten riders with him tracking the men who attacked his ranch in the night. They ended up in front of Chalk Cranfield's shack. Pap pulled his pistol and fired in the air. "Wake up and get out here!" He was angry and lacked patience.

Chalk came to the door with a rifle to his shoulder. "I've been awake for some time. I've had this rifle on your head since you rode up. In fact, I've had it pointed over your right eye."

Pap's posture changed from a range bull looking for trouble to more of a stranger asking for directions. "I think I caught all that. I don't hear so good. Sorry if I come at you a little strong. We been trailin' a bunch of men and one of them came here. We tracked his horse to your wagon over there. He's not in the wagon and he's not on the horse... I figure he stumbled inside the shack. We found some blood a ways back." Pap eyed the boy standing on the front porch with thoughtfulness. There was something familiar about him. "If you happen to have the ambushing cutthroat, maybe you'd like to bring him out for us to all look at."

"Sir, my wife and I are the only two residing here. If I did have a wounded man, I wouldn't let you have him. If he's hurt, I'd first tend the wound and then I'd take him to town for the doctor. The law could look into his reason for bleeding after that."

Pap was still in thought when he began to smile. "Good words, good intentions, but they ain't any law in this part of the country but our own. Each man deals out his own law. Nearest judge and lawman are clear to maybe Amarillo or Dodge City. They're way too far from here to be worrying on any of us. Mason City doesn't have a lawman and I've never seen one even ride through our part of the world. Since this is my affair, you might want to rethink the handin' over. What's your name, boy?"

"Chalk, Chalk Cranfield. And it's not, 'boy', and I'm not just talking. Like I say, if I had him you wouldn't be getting him."

Pap's demeanor changed abruptly. He was anxious acting and his color changed from flush to a pale look. Speck noticed it. He too took note of the boy standing on the porch. He looked very familiar. What Pap said next was perplexing, because he knew Pap had never been to West Kansas.

"I knew some Cranfield's in West Kansas near to the Nebraska line. You happen to be from there?"

"No, I'm from Kansas City, born in Dodge City. We moved to Kansas City when I was eight years old. I've never heard of any other Cranfield in the area."

Pap took a big deep breath and collected himself. "Well, maybe I'm mistaken about the name. I'm hard of hearin' and... well, that's all I guess."

Speck's boss was acting mighty peculiar and he thought he knew why.

Chalk eased the gun down and let the hammer off. His gruff neighbor had backed off his tough way for the moment. "I'd invite you in for coffee but we ain't got any made quite yet."

Sarah came to the door. "Maybe you all could come back sometime, and we could have a cup. We'd surely admire company now and then."

Pap removed his hat, turned to his men and glared at them to do the same. He saw the little lady speaking to him was heavy with child.

"Yes, yes, that would be right neighborly. Maybe me and ole Speck here will take you up on that sometime. My name is Pap, Pap Dockin. I own the ranch over the hill from you." Pap placed his hat back on his head as did the rest of the men.

"Mister Dockin, this is my wife, Sarah. She makes a great cup of coffee."

"Pleasure ma'am." Pap looked around at the men riding with him. It was obvious he felt a little awkward. "Well, boys... huh... I guess we might as well ride on to town. The rest of the tracks hit the main road. We're not goin' to be able to track them now, not once they've mixed with all the other riders that come down the road. We'll nose around a little in town."

Pap and his men turned and rode off. He looked back one time as he rode away.

Sarah and Chalk looked on as the band of men rode down the hill to the main road and out of sight. Sarah didn't say anything, but she noticed resemblances between Chalk and Pap Dockin, big ones. They had the same eyes, features, build, and the same hands.

Chalk turned with Sarah to go in the house when she heard something under the porch beneath her feet. She squeezed Chalk gently and pointed down. The boards were broken out in the floor. She could see a man lying underneath. Chalk got down under the porch and pulled him out. He had been shot in the right shoulder and had lost a lot of blood.

"You hold on partner, me and the little woman will get you going."

"Thanks. Name is Troy Howell."

The bullet passed through and missed the bone as best Chalk could tell. He and Sarah cleaned and bandaged the wound and got some water down the man. Chalk made sure he got rest by taking his time fixing breakfast. Sarah prepared the coffee while Chalk did the cooking. He wouldn't let Sarah do much if he could help it.

After breakfast, he loaded the wounded man into his wagon and left for Mason City. Sarah elected not to go. She didn't want to ride in the wagon if she didn't have to. She had ridden for days and needed a break from the rough ride. The wagon was enough to start a woman with child into labor.

Chalk waved to her as the wagon rattled out of sight.

Pap and Speck, riding in front of the men, rode towards town at a slow gait. Speck kept looking over at him.

"Somethin' on your mind, Speck?"

"Might be a little something. You haven't asked me yet what's wrong with the roundup."

Pap smiled at him. He knew that wasn't what he was after. "You're wonderin' about the lad back yonder. Well, I'll tell you what I know. I met a gal twenty-one years ago in Dodge City on one of my cattle drives and spent a couple nights and days with her."

Pap took a big chew of tobacco and stuck it in the side of his mouth. He made an extra big wad this time. "I took a real shine to her. Had feelin's come on me for her." He leaned forward in his saddle trying to get comfortable. It wasn't the saddle making him feel uncomfortable. It was the subject he and Speck were discussing. "Truth is, I asked her to marry me. She turned me down. I guess I couldn't blame her. Hell, she'd only known me for two days and most of that was on her back." He paused and spat tobacco juice to the side of his horse. "I don't mean that to sound as if she was a... a common... well, you know, a bad person so to speak. She was a hard-workin' woman. She sewed and washed clothes for people in her neighborhood. It just happened that me and her hit it off mighty fine, and... well we spent time... making love." He looked over at Speck. "Yeah, even Pap Dockin has known love. You ever known a woman in that sort of way?"

"I have."

"You have?" Pap was surprised and cut his eyes at his old friend. He had known Speck a lot of years. He'd never known him to spend time with a woman or even talk about women for that matter.

Speck smiled at him but said nothing.

"Well?"

"Well, what?"

"Well… who was it? Hell, I've known you for… well I've never seen you with a woman."

"Fell in love with a lady by the name of Rue Hendricks. Married Her. She was something fine. I got to spend three good years with her. She was killed riding her horse one day from town. A storm blew in and before she could get home, lightning struck her horse and killed them both. I drifted after that, from town to town, until you hired me. I never have had the desire to have another woman since. Now that we shared that news, let me have the rest of the story about the gal you were with for them two days."

"You know, Speck, just when you think you know all there is to know about a man, somethin' will happen to prove you don't know anything at all. I'm sorry things didn't work out for you."

"It worked out. I fell in love and I'm still in love. I'll always love Rue."

"I know what you mean. I… I loved Paula. I think me and her could have had a good life together… but." He looked off out across some blue stem grass mixed with some spots of brush. "Speck, I had planned to be with Paula the next day, but I had to go see the cattle buyers to get our money."

"Our money?"

"Yeah, me and Zell Davis was partners on three hundred head of beeves. We were goin' to get in deeper on the cattle business, but somethin' happened to cause us to dissolve our business dealings all together. Zell didn't show up for the signin' off on the beef, or to pick up the money with me. I figured he was laid up with a… a woman of the night somewhere. That didn't turn out to be the case. It turned out he paid a visit to Paula while I was at the cattle exchange office. He knew I would be there. I saw him leavin' her place as I came around the corner of her boardin' house."

"The dirty…" Speck threw his hands up in exasperation.

"I went in and found her cryin'. She asked me to leave. Before I left her place that morning things was fine. I didn't know what Zell said to her, but he sure messed things up. I finally found him and confronted him about his being at Paula's. Well, he thought Paula had told me exactly why and what he was doing there. Things came out that caused us to settle permanent on everything." Pap glanced at Speck. "Settlin' got a little rough."

Pap pulled up and spit tobacco juice out. "I guess I never told you, but I knew Zell back in Alabama. Me and him left together after the war, drifted from town to town. We got in a card game and had the dangdest streak of luck a man could have. Fact is, me and him shot it out with the ole boys we won the money from. Later we ended up with us a ranch a piece, and we were goin' to partner up. Zell always did have a mean streak of sorts, and a hot head to boot. Anyway, the thing with Paula Cranfield dissolved our business relationship along with our personal one. I went back to see her and found her gone. I hung around for a week, but she didn't come back. I wrote several times. I never did get a response. Well, a little over a year later I trailed another herd of mine up there. I went by to see if Paula came back and got a hell of a surprise."

"Oh?" Speck was leaning towards Pap not wanting to miss a word.

"She had another man in her life... a little boy. I asked her if he was mine. She said he wasn't and that she had been seein' someone else for near to a year. I figured it was a lie. I looked at the little feller, but who can tell about a baby? I wondered if he was mine, but wonder was all I could do. I tried to get her to come back with me to Mason City... I knew she loved me. I didn't believe her story about another man. It didn't matter what I said though, she wouldn't come with me."

"Maybe there really was someone else. Women can be sly?"

"Say again?"

"I said sometimes you can never know the why?" Speck knew

he nearly messed up. That was the woman Pap loved. It wouldn't do to cast doubt or speak out of turn about her.

Pap spit again and looked over at Speck. "I figured it out."

"You did?"

Pap frowned. "You've got to speak up. These damned ole horses make too much noise. I can't hear you."

"I say... you figured it out?"

"That's what I said." Pap eyed Speck over. "You can't hear a damn thing."

Speck shook his head at Pap and grinned as they eased on up the road.

"I figured she had more than one reason, but the main one was that she didn't want to bring shame to me in my home. You know... a bastard child and all."

"Makes sense. A good woman is like that."

"I tried to tell her it didn't make a tinker's damn to me what people said or thought, and I was glad it happened. I loved her and nothin' could change that. I told her I had a hand in the makin' of that baby, same as she did." Pap spit his chew out. "I guess there was one more thing that eat at her hard. She still claimed she had been seein' someone else and that she wasn't sure the boy was of my blood. She said, "I can't marry you, Franklin. I'd rather live apart as to live always wondering. One day you might start having doubts, what then? People are cruel. There'd be eyes watching and whispering behind our backs. I won't put you through the trial of it, nor the child. You said Mason City is a small town. Small towns know everything about everybody." She loved the boy with all her heart and didn't want anyone saying anything to him about being an out-of-wedlock child. A child she wasn't sure as to his true blood. She said rumors can become blown up fict... fict... tion."

"Fictional?"

"Yeah, fictional, fictional facts."

"She sounds like she was a hell of a woman."

Pap looked over at Speck and held his gaze. "She was. She was honest with herself and who she loved. There was another reason she didn't want to come here... but that one lives with me and will die with me." He leaned back in the saddle and checked the reins to his horse. "Whoa up, son." He looked at the riders behind him. "I know you big-eared cowboys are doin' your best to listen in on the conversation between Speck and me. In case you didn't get it all, that boy back there stands a good chance of havin' Dockin blood running through his veins. He looks like me, doesn't he?"

The men looked at each other and then agreed he did look like Pap. Pooh Smith, the ramrod of the men spoke up. "Pap, the truth is I thought he was your spitting image, but I would have lied and took your place in hell if you had asked me if I thought he did." The whole bunch broke into laughter including Pap.

"That's what I thought. You boys know how I am; don't keep nothin' much a secret. Now that we have that settled, we'll ride into town." He picked up the reins but then stopped. "Pooh, you think I'm goin' to hell?"

"Hell no, I don't think you're going to hell. You'll miss it by one small horsehair and that's shore close, but close is good enough." Everyone laughed. Pap liked Pooh.

They had only gone a short distance when Speck asked the obvious question. "Pap... what's the boy doing here you reckon? I mean... there seems to be some missing pieces, him showing up all at once and."

"What?"

"The boy. He seems to be the new owner of the hundred-acre patch. At least I got that feeling."

"Me too."

Speck looked over at Pap as they rode. "We going to look into this situation?"

"Do what?"

"We're going to look into this... right?"

"I think we ease along, mind our own business and let the answers come to us. We might do a little invite to supper one night, maybe encourage the information."

"Alright, but one thing I'm real curious about. How did this Cranfield boy end up with the hundred acres, the exact hundred acres that cuts a corner out of one of your sections?"

Pap looked over at Speck without a hint of a smile.
"Wonderin' that myself."

Chapter 4

Pap and his men tied their horses in front of the Prairie Grass Cafe and walked over to where Zell was standing in front of the Dry Rock Saloon. Zell had been watching Pap and his men as they rode into town.

"You short a man this mornin', Zell?"

"Don't think so. I heard your barn caught fire last night. Do you have any idea what happened?"

"I might. Zell, I catch any more of your men butchering my steers, I'll be lookin' to you for payment. If my place comes under attack again... you'll be lookin' at somethin' you don't really want... a war."

"Pap, those are mighty hard words."

"You and me been goin' at one another for years, until now it has been kept in Texas. Now you've brought in hired guns. That changes things. I'll not whip the hide off the next thief I catch... I'll hang him. You best back off, or they'll come a time I'll come for you."

"Why don't you do that. I'll tell you now, Pap Dockin doesn't run me or tell me what to do. You killed a man in cold blood. There wasn't any hanging. Killed a man and then took a bull whip to another one. Those two boys thought they were on Davis land."

"Say again?"

"Those boys thought they were on my land! You killed one of them in cold blood!"

"They knew where they were. The one that died told me exactly where we were standin'. He knew my boundary lines as well as me. You're fair warned of how things are goin' to work from here on. You bring in gun hands, blood will flow, and it won't all be Dockin blood." Pap turned and walked to the cafe.

Chalk delivered the wounded man to Doctor Zimmer without incident but wasn't that fortunate while walking to the courthouse. Zell spotted him and immediately ordered his sons to set things right.

Ted met him in the middle of the street with Huey hanging back. He felt it wrong to harass the newcomer again. Ted didn't feel that way at all. "Mister, you got lucky yesterday with that pole."

Chalk stared at Ted for a short second. "I hit you with a singletree you idiot."

Ted's neck and face turned red. "How good are you with that gun hanging on your side?"

"I don't know. Never shot it. I purchased it a few weeks ago. Traveling I never had the time to practice. However, I have great eye to hand coordination."

Ted smiled. "Do you now. Why don't we see if you can take me with that shooter... city boy?"

"What makes you think I'm from the city."

"Written all over you."

Chalk looked around and realized quite a crowd had gathered. "Look, I came here to start a ranch. I'm peaceable for the most part."

"Looks like you're yellow for the most part, too."

"Ted, I may not be a gunfighter but I'm so much faster than you. I could shoot this gun empty before you could clear that long barreled piece you carry."

Ted stood there amazed. "You funning me?" He went for his gun.

Chalk drew and fired five times. The bullets hit within inches of both sides of Ted's left foot. "I've got one bullet left. I can place it between your eyes, or you can walk away. Your gun is still in its holster. If I had wanted to kill you, I would have. I've made my way with quick hands since I was a boy. I know guns. I said I wasn't a gunfighter... that doesn't mean I can't handle a gun. I'm older now and confident of what I can do. What will it be? You walking or dying?"

"I'll walk." Ted started to leave.

"Not with the gun, drop it."

"The hell!"

"Now!"

Ted dropped the gun and hurried into the saloon; red faced with embarrassment.

Chalk reloaded his pistol and started towards the Prairie Grass Cafe. Zell stepped in front of him. "Hold up, you hold right there! Who the hell do you think you are?"

"Chalk Cranfield."

"Well..." Zell was about to say something else when the name Cranfield stopped him cold. "Cranfield?"

"Yeah... Cranfield."

"Never heard that name in these parts."

"I'm from Kansas City."

"Well, Chalk... it is, Chalk?"

"Yeah."

"I'm sorry you and my boys haven't hit it off so well. Maybe we can make it up to you some way in the near future."

"No need, we're just finding our pecking order."

"Yeah, well, have a nice rest of the day." Zell turned and disappeared in the saloon.

The storekeeper came running out to Chalk. "I can't believe what I saw. I just can't believe it. No one has stood up to Ted, and for sure Zell Davis. He acted like he was going to take you on, then suddenly backed off like you had skunk on you. Can you explain that?"

"No, I have other things to do."

"It's not normal, it's not like Zell." The storekeeper stared after Chalk. He just saw Zell give the young stranger a pass, and that was hard to imagine of Zell Davis.

Pap and his boys watched the whole thing go down between Chalk and Zell. They had left their table inside the Prairie Grass and stood just outside the door of the establishment. Speck leaned over into Pap's right ear. "That settles it for me. The boy is yours. Not only does he look like you, he handles a gun like you with those big hands."

"Yeah." Pap stared after the boy. "Yeah, may just be."

They turned to go back inside when they heard the stagecoach coming. Being the nosey cowboys that they were and liking to see and know who was coming to Mason City, they stopped long enough to find out.

Once the dust settled and the stage driver climbed down, the first passenger climbed off. He was a tall well-dressed man wearing a black leather gun rig with silver Conchos on the side. He sported a well-groomed mustache with shoulder length hair. Cold black eyes took in the town from underneath a wide brimmed hat. The next passenger was a man dressed in a suit. He turned and helped a lady step down from the stage. She obviously was with the man in the suit. She looked to be thirty-five to forty years old and well kept. She wore an expensive full gown the color of the bluest sky. She was remarkably beautiful from all indications. She wore a small hat with a black net coming down in front of her face, so it made it hard to see what she really looked like. She and the man in the suit disappeared into the Lazy Day Hotel. The tall man followed behind.

Once again Speck leaned over into Pap's ear. "The tall man comes to town maybe looking to cause trouble, but damned if I don't think the one wearing the dress is the one to watch, she's deadly. I know she's trouble."

"Some trouble makes for an interestin' day." Pap smiled, and they went back inside the Prairie Grass.

As he was tucking his napkin inside the top of his shirt, he looked across the table at Speck. "The tall man looked like a slinger. I'll bet Zell sent for him."

"Things are getting interesting. First Chalk Cranfield comes to town, two new gunnies show up eating Dockin beef, and now these three get off the stage."

"Yeah." Pap had just begun cutting up his sausage when Speck pointed out the window with his fork. They all turned to see the lady who got off the stage coming towards the Prairie Grass Cafe with her companion and the Cranfield boy. "What do you make of that?"

"What?"

"I said what do you make of that?"

"I make it to be two men and a woman." He winked at Speck. "Things are sure not dull around here today. I'd like to see her with that bonnet off. Can't tell anything about her."

"I meant, what do you make of her and that Cranfield boy being together?"

"I don't."

"Sometimes I wonder why I even talk to you, and I might have known you was looking her over."

Pap grinned. "You been with me so long you wouldn't know how to act or talk if I wasn't around. You do repeat yourself a lot though."

Speck shook his head. He cut a piece of his sausage off and swallowed it whole. "I repeat myself because you can't hear good enough to hear a train whistle blow."

Pooh spoke up. "There goes another interesting thing." Again, they looked out the window. The tall well-heeled stranger was crossing the street from the Lazy Day Hotel to the Dry Rock Saloon.

Pap watched and said nothing.

Zell Davis was setting in the corner of the Dry Rock Saloon alone sipping on a beer. He was in deep thought. Something had happened out in the street he hadn't counted on. The man that outdrew Ted was not supposed to be in Mason City. He knew who the boy was instantly when he heard the name Cranfield. The question Zell was pondering, why was he here? He was finishing off his second beer when the tall man from the stage walked in. He ordered a beer and then made his way over to the table where Zell was sitting.

"Zell Davis?"

"You must be Quint Hobbs."

"At your service." The tall man sat down and smiled.

"Service? You ain't nothing but a gunny. I'm not real proud of myself for hiring you. Don't come in here acting like you're something special. You're nothing but a hired killer, and you wouldn't make a wart on Pap Dockin's backside. He's a better man than ten like you, and he's proving to be a better man than me."

Quint had a surprised look on his face. "Look, you sent for me, I didn't ask for the job. Pay me and I can leave. You're the one wants the rusty old man killed. Sounds like you've changed your mind. I get paid for a service, it may not be cleaning rooms at a hotel, but I'm mighty damn sought after."

"I didn't say I wanted him killed. I sent for you to help me put him out of business. We kill a few of his men and the rest will high tail it. I already made a blunder and got one man killed. I got Ben Watts laid up over it, too."

"Watts' here? What happened?"

"I thought if Pap saw what he was facing... I thought he might start to think maybe this was getting out of hand. I figured Ben would get the drop on him and work him over real good. Instead he got the drop on Ben and Beal. Hell, I've known Pap Dockin pretty much all my life. I should have known better. I knew he wouldn't back away from a fight. There could have been ten men eating his beef, and he would have taken them on." Zell gulped the rest of the beer down. "I guess if I've committed to this thing I might as well see it through." He laid a dollar on the table for the drinks and stood up. "We take Pap down, but we don't speak disrespectful doing it, hear? We'll kill them that shoots at us and we'll stop his roundup. If he can't get his cattle to market, he'll be in trouble trying to feed everything. I want his hay and corn fields burned to black ash. I want him to have to buy every grain he feeds. It'll be slow and painful, but he'll go down." Zell stared at Quint for a moment. "We kill him after he's lost everything... not before."

"It's your fight and your money. You sure seem to have a burning hate for him. What did he do to you?"

"That's my business. Let's get out of here." The two of them walked out onto the boardwalk in front of the saloon. A man was riding down the center of the street and rode over to the cafe.

"Well, I'll be."

Zell looked at Quint. "Do you know him?"

"That's the Checkered Kid. Is he riding for Pap Dockin?"

"I don't know. If he is, Pap lied to me about bringing in guns. I've never known him to lie. It'd be hard for me to believe he hired a professional gunman. Pap's the kind to handle his own trouble."

"If the Kid is against us, the money you're paying me ain't enough. I don't fight the Kid for less than five thousand."

"If he's hiring out to Pap... five thousand it is. You hungry?"

Ted and Huey were sitting outside the saloon and fell in behind Zell and his new friend. They were headed for the Prairie Grass Cafe. When they walked in, they found a table across from Pap and his men.

The Checkered Kid was sitting at the back of the cafe with his back to the wall. He recognized Quint Hobbs right away. He was ordering breakfast from a waiter while his gun hand hung by the handle of his six-gun. The hotel clerk entered with the town barber and the storekeeper.

Chalk and the two strangers sat off to the left of the Dockin and Davis tables. He hadn't been around cowboys much, but he had been in many places in Kansas City that loaded up with tough men like this. It normally meant one thing... hell was about to break loose. Even so, business was booming for the

Prairie Grass. The hotel clerk and his two pals sat near the door. The table was handy to let them get out fast if trouble started.

Chalk addressed the lady who had removed her veil to reveal a face of porcelain skin and ruby lips. "Ma'am, I don't really know why you have asked me to breakfast. I was heading over here anyway, just needed to make sure my wagon was okay. I mean, you don't even know me and you for certain don't have to buy my breakfast."

The lady smiled. "My name is Vivian. You can call me by my name. No, I don't have to buy your breakfast, but you and I have something in common. Let's order and then we will talk. Waiter."

Maybe it was the long wagon ride, maybe it was the stress of the bleeding man and the men wanting to take him though he was helpless. Whatever it was, Sarah Cranfield felt a strong contraction. She hoped it wasn't her first labor pain, for she was all alone. She decided to lie down on the pellet Chalk and she had made. Maybe rest was what was needed. She had just gotten lain down when there was a noise outside the shack. She rose up enough to peep through a crack in the wall. What she saw frightened her half to death. She didn't know what to do. There wasn't a place to hide. She didn't have a gun or knife and was completely defenseless. She could only hope Chalk hurried.

Sarah was crying silent tears, for right outside her door stood three muscular Indians. They were going through a couple boxes that Chalk had taken out of the wagon making room for the wounded man. One of the Indians found a top hat Chalk had won in an arm-wrestling contest. After each one had found something they wanted, they started toward the house. Complete fear ran through her.

Chapter 5

"Speck, it seems to be gettin' a little crowded in here." Pap smiled as he looked around.

"I noticed."

Pap was enjoying the tension in the thick air. There were two gun hawks staring at one another, the one Zell was with and the one in the back of the establishment. Then there was the woman sitting with the dude and Chalk. It made things interesting. "You ever seen any of these newcomers, Speck?"

"Not a one. There's only one worth getting to know."

"I thought you weren't interested in females, Speck."

"Well, I had rather talk to a beautiful lady than an ugly man."

Pap grinned. "Sometimes you prove smarter than I think you are."

Speck smiled and winked at him.

Pap casually looked around the room again. "Things could get to heatin' up in here, crowded as it is. Folks don't get along well when cooped up in a chicken coop very long."

Speck signaled with his eyes across at the table where Chalk and his two friends were sitting. When Pap looked in that direction the beautiful lady was staring at him.

After the waiter took Vivian and her two companion's orders, she reached over and touched Chalk on the arm. "If it would be alright with you, I would like to invite another party to the table."

"Well... Vivian, this is your table. I'm a guest. You can invite whom you like."

She turned in her chair and stared across at Pap. When he finally turned and looked in her direction, she addressed him. "Excuse me, I don't mean to take you away from your friends, but would you like to join us for breakfast?"

"Me?"

"Yes... please."

Pap looked at Speck nervous like, picked up his coffee cup and then made his way over to the table where the woman and Chalk sat, along with the dude in the suit. "Howdy do, I'm Pap Dockin."

"Yes, I know. I came here to see you."

"You came here to... is that so?"

"Yes. Would you like some more coffee?"

"No... yes. I believe I will."

"My name is Vivian Martin, of Martin and Jones Transportation and Freight. We are headquartered in Kansas City, Missouri. This is Ellison Jones, my partner."

Ellison reached across the table to shake hands, but Pap didn't reach back across. "Mister, I never tie up my gun hand when other folks are around. Glad to meet you anyhow."

"Likewise." He smiled faintly as he slowly drew his hand back. He wasn't used to the crude tough crowd of men he was beginning to meet.

Vivian began, "This young gentleman."

Pap interrupted her immediately. "We've met." Pap and Chalk smiled at each other across the table in acknowledgement.

"I see. Well then, let me give you a little of my history. "My late husband was Peter Martin, who was half owner of the Transportation and Freight Company with Mr. Jones here. He left the company to me along with a hundred acres of prime grazing land he acquired as an investment. It joins your property I believe."

"Yes, it's the hundred-acre patch."

"Yes, my husband bought the land from a Mister Mills."

"That would be the man alright. Your husband made a bad deal. He gave three times what it was worth. Then I offered your husband ten times more than what he gave for it. He told me it wasn't for sale at any price and never would be."

She was looking Pap in the eyes and smiling as she did so. "My husband bought the land for me. The bad deal, if there was one, would be my fault. However, if it was such a bad deal, why did you offer him ten times the amount he gave?" There seemed to almost be a twinkle in her eyes as she took a sip of her coffee. "Something that might be of interest to you. I asked my husband to buy the land no matter what the price. Money was no object. I had plans for it." She smiled again.

"Well, my reason for offering more than the patch was worth was to square up my place. The land joins me." Pap took a swallow of his coffee. "I guess I'm confused. He said the land would never be for sale. You said you wanted it no matter the price... you had plans for it. If you had plans, why did you sell it to Chalk Cranfield?"

"I didn't sell it to Chalk Cranfield. I sold it to Paula Cranfield, Chalk's mother."

Pap turned pale in color when he learned she knew Paula. The strange lady was a mystery. "Miss Martin... I don't..."

"Call me Vivian."

"Okay then, Vivian. I guess you knew Chalk's mother in Kansas City? You must have liked her. You sold her a patch of land you didn't really want to sell?"

"I did like her. She was a wonderful and beautiful lady."

"Would you mind me asking how much you sold it to her for?"

"Not at all. I sold it to her for one dollar."

"One dollar!" Pap's voice was heard all over the cafe. "You gave it to her! Why? And why her?"

"She asked for it."

"I asked for it! Didn't do me much good." Pap's face turned red with heat.

"You weren't Paula... and Paula isn't just anyone, is she... Pap Dockin?"

Pap was baffled by Vivian Martin. She knew Paula and by that remark, a lot about him too.

Chalk had been sitting quietly while the two of them carried on a conversation centering on his mother. He didn't like it. He was asked to breakfast and excluded from the conversations thus far. He realized Vivian was right about one thing; they had plenty in common, his mother for one. He wondered how his mother and Vivian became friends. What was the connection between the two? Chalk learned a long time ago you learn more by listening than talking. He decided to listen longer. The same big question Pap was asking was on his mind too. Why did she sell the hundred acres to his mother for one dollar, when she said it wasn't for sale at any price?

"You won't mind if I continue to call you, Pap?"

"No, with the way this conversation has gone so far, I wouldn't be surprised to find out we've known one another from a past life."

She laughed, and Pap found it to be a very pleasing thing. "Well, Pap, you have plenty of land. You really didn't need a little hundred-acre patch, now did you? I know it would have been nice to have, square up your front section so to speak. Truthfully, I too really didn't have a need for the land. Paula was the only one who did. She was dying and had a son she wanted to get out of Kansas City, Missouri. I could help her do that. Since I'm in the transportation business, land has not been that much of an interest to me. So, what better reason to sell a spot of land than to help someone out who needed it." Vivian looked across the room at the table Zell Davis occupied. "There is another reason, however."

"What other reason?" Pap saw her look at Zell.

"You know very well what that is, Pap Dockin."

Pap suddenly felt a little uncomfortable. He didn't like her take-over attitude, her know it all way, and he didn't like her having him at a disadvantage. In his way of thinking she needed a dressing down. Pap looked at her as a woman busting it right along beside the men with her freight business. She needed to be talked to the same as a man. "Look, you need to simmer down. If you were a man, I'd tell you to shut-up."

"If I were a man, I would have already whipped you. Since I'm not, my alternative is to tell you the why and way of things."

"Lady, that'll do. My time at this table is up." Pap started to leave, when the table across the room and the small table in the back suddenly became center stage. He couldn't hear them plain, but he recognized when two bulls were about to get together.

"Whose side you with, Kid?"

"Well, Quint, it really isn't any of your business. I can tell you it's not the one you're hired on with, and it doesn't make any difference which one. I wouldn't work for a man that would hire the likes of you. I'd have to kill you before I could go to work for him. You see, Quint, I don't want to be watching my back constantly. With you around that's exactly what I'd be doing."

"You sure haven't changed much, Kid. You're still as mouthy as you always were."

"You might not last the day, Quint, talking like that."

"Kid, this conversation turned ugly. You calling me out?"

"I didn't know anyone could call you out. The way I hear it, you walk away, and the poor devil is found shot in the back later."

The smile had vanished from Quint's face. The Checkered Kid had gotten to him. There was no letting that go. Someone would be carried out of the cafe with a bullet hole in him.

Pap saw the need to stop the ruckus before someone besides the two gun hands got hurt. In one motion he stood and cocked his gun. The barrel of his pistol was pointed at Quint. "Mister, you ease on out of here. We don't need two bulls in here pawin' and lookin' wild-eyed at one another while the rest of us are pulled up to the trough."

Pap looked over at Speck. "Boys!" All the Dockin riders along with Speck and Pooh slapped leather and drew on the Checkered Kid. "Boy, those guns aimed at you belong to the Dockin Ranch. I didn't hire you, so that makes you and this other killer workin' for the same man." He looked at Zell with a hot glare. "You can go outside and kill one another if that's what you want to do. But gunplay won't happen in here unless I'm doin' it. Boy, this tall man is leavin' now. He'll either be outside when you're through grazing or he'll be gone. I don't care what happens to either one of you when you're clear of this fine eatin' establishment."

The Kid answered. "Sir... I'm the Checkered Kid. I can wait."

Then Quint answered. "I can wait too... old man."

The riders of the Dockin Ranch knew the tall man made a big bad mistake. Calling him Pap was one thing, but no one called him... 'old man'.

"You can wait, can you? Well then, you wait outside. I'll be along."

The tall man smiled. "It'll be a pleasure to take you first."

"Saunter on out of here then. I'm enjoyin' a cup of coffee, and conversation with friends."

Quint got up slowly and was starting to walk outside, when Pap held him up. "Say, before you go. Do I really look like an old man to you? I mean... for real? I sure been worryin' about it."

"You're kidding... right?"

"Well, I don't guess it matters who kills you... if it's an old man or that kid back there with his back against the wall."

Quint glanced at the kid and then smiled at Pap. "Cute... real cute." He left but in no hurry.

Zell wasn't happy with the current events. "Pap, you got no business poking your nose in where it don't belong."

"You brought this trash here. I guess it will be up to me and the boys to rid the town of it. You need to hire a little better quality of gunmen. These aren't making the grade. They sure aren't the pups me and you were when we were their age."

"Well, Pap, I have to give you that. We got our schooling in the war. I may have to kill you myself."

"You have an open invitation to try." He smiled. "Zell, you turned out to be a worthless coward, half a man at best." Pap's voice was quivering. "You won't face me straight up, but then you never could face anything head on. A man would call me right now, but you won't. Slapping women around is more your style. You can handle them. If it's a man, you'll wait till dark or bring in hired killers." Pap stepped back to the table where the three newcomers were sitting.

Zell got up with his fist clinched staring at Pap. "I'm no match for your gun, but I don't need a gun to take you." He turned and went back to the back of the room to talk with the other gun hand.

Pap smiled as he watched Zell take a seat with the gunman called the Checkered Kid.

"Hello, Mister Davis."

"You come here looking to hire on?"

"I have a partner that works for you, Ben Watts."

"Yeah, he does… come to think of it he did mention he had someone coming to help him out with this job."

"Ben said it's a range war of some kind."

"You might call it that, but it's a private damn war. I want that old man over there run off this range. I'm paying top dollar to run him and his whole bunch into the ground."

"I don't mean to rub you wrong, but you look as old as him, maybe older."

"Yeah, well I am. Fact is I'm older by a year or so. People around just got to calling him, 'Pap', making fun of him turning forty. He's forty-five now. Mostly his own men call him Pap."

"I see. Sounds as if they like him."

"Are you hiring on or not?" Zell showed his impatience.

"I'd sure like to help you but like I said, I don't work for anyone that hires Quint Hobbs for a job. He's good but he's also dangerous. If he gets drunk or feels threatened in any way, he's slapping leather, and it's always from the back. I'll hire on but only after I kill him."

Zell had never met a colder blooded killer. The Checkered Kid was all business when it came to killing. He realized he was going to see firsthand how good the two of them were real soon. He would be left with the better of the two. He couldn't lose. "Well… I guess if that's the way of it."

"It is. I'd like to thank you in advance however for the job." The Kid smiled and went back to eating.

Pap sat back down at Vivian's table. "I'm sorry about all the commotion, Vivian. Sometimes the young boys get a little rowdy."

"That is quite alright."

Something was different about her. He heard it in her voice, and he saw it in her eyes. He wondered what changed from the time he left the table until he sat back down. He recognized her attitude had changed towards him.

"If it would be to your liking, why don't we talk about our situation over supper tonight?" She smiled and waited for an answer.

"I didn't know we had a situation, but supper sounds good. How about my ranch?"

"I thought I would buy supper here in town. However, I would love to see your ranch."

Pap smiled at her as he asked Ellison Jones a question. "Mister Jones, do you think you could find my ranch?"

"Most certainly."

"Then why don't we plan supper about six thirty this evenin', if you like. Speck over there is the best cook this side of the Arkansas." Pap had suddenly forgotten anyone else was at the table and so had Vivian.

"Six-thirty is fine. I look forward to it. Oh, one thing if I could take the liberty, I would like to bring my friend Chalk with me?"

Pap was caught a little by surprise. "Well… that would be fine. It's his mother and his land we were talkin' about."

Chalk spoke up. "Well, up until now I wondered if anyone cared. I might have something to say about this supper. Maybe I should be asked. Maybe I..."

"You're asked." Pap smiled for the first time.

"Well... alright then." He looked at Vivian. "There are lots of things you haven't told me and Pap, and I expect to find out what they are at supper."

Vivian smiled. "So it will be."

Chalk started to get up when Ted Davis spoke up from across the room. "City boy, I'm not through with you, not even close to through."

"You've been fortunate today, Teddy. I wouldn't push it. I could have killed you instead of knocking you out. Your head is soft as butter and you're slow as an old maid heading home from church. If you come at me with a gun again, I wouldn't want to, but I'll kill you. I guess I'm having a hard time figuring things out here in this town. It doesn't seem like anyone gets along. I thought I left the fighting and killing back in Kansas City, but it seems you people aren't much easier to get along with than that bunch. Difference is, Ted, your mouth is the fastest part about you, and it's always shooting off."

Ted's face became bright red. Suddenly he jumped up and ran towards Chalk, but he never got there. Speck stuck his foot out causing him to trip and fall. The cafe erupted, even the hotel clerk, the barber and storekeeper were laughing. Ted jumped up and ran outside.

Zell was enraged at the town citizens laughing at his son. "You people think you're damn smart! Why don't you try me on for size? You push a boy around. Well how 'bout pushing this old man? Do I have any takers?"

Pap spoke up. "Is that what it takes to make you find your nerve? Let it go, Zell. The boy was out of line. You saw it. Otherwise, I'm a taker."

"Yeah, well, what would you know about family? You've never acted like you had any. The only boy you ever had was left to fend for his self."

"Zell Davis... I've killed men for less than that." Pap's voice took on the same tone it had just before he took the whip to Ben Watts. "I killed 'em, but they were better men."

Zell looked around the room at all the staring faces, and then left the Prairie Grass Cafe in a hurry with Huey following behind.

Chalk could not help but ask the question. "There's a lot of bad blood between you two. What caused it?"

"Blood, what blood?"

"No, I asked what caused the bad blood?"

"None of your business." Pap flushed with momentary anger.

"Are you sure, Franklin?"

Pap was taken aback when she called him by his given name. She asked to call him Pap, but then she called him Franklin. How did she know his first name? He didn't give it out to her. There was a lot more to her than he was even close to knowing. He would learn more at supper.

She stood, and the men at her table stood instantly. "I'm looking forward to supper." She smiled and left, being escorted out of the Prairie Grass by Chalk and Ellison Jones. The hotel clerk and the barber left behind them.

Pap was still sitting at Vivian's table pondering her. She knew his name, she knew Paula, and she knew Chalk. It was beginning to bother him a little. She knew everything about him, and he knew nothing about her, and that... he didn't like. He came out of his thinking process and looked over at the table where his boys were sitting.

"What the hell you all lookin' at? Order me another round of eggs. I didn't get to eat my breakfast. Soon as I get my eggs and bacon we'll see if anyone's waitin' outside for me. If not, we'll ride for the ranch."

The storekeeper walked up beside Chalk. "You know since you hit town, and it hasn't been twenty-four hours yet... things have really gotten rather exciting. I don't know what exactly is going on, but it sure seems like it centers around you and that patch of land you own."

"Patch of land? Mister, a hundred acres is a little more than a patch."

"Not really, but it sure must be some patch."

The storekeeper left, and Chalk climbed up on his wagon and headed home. He was full of questions that might be answered at supper... and he didn't like his land being called a patch.

Pap ate his breakfast and then sat talking with the owner of the Prairie Grass for a while. The owner had bought breakfast for the Dockin party in appreciation for stopping the gunfight. After another cup of coffee, he and his men left the cafe heading for the hitching rail where his horse was standing.

"I waited... old man!"

Pap stopped and then looked over at Speck. "Did you hear somethin' pass gas?"

Speck chuckled. He and Pap turned around slowly and faced the tall man by the name of Quint. He was standing in the middle of the street some fifty feet from them. Speck slowly moved out of the way.

Two young cowboys across the street were dismounting from some tired looking ponies when they heard the loud voice calling out to an old man. They eased over towards the men that rode for the Dockin spread.

Speck saw them as harmless cow punchers. One of them spoke to him. "What's going on here?"

"It seems the tall gunslinger wants to make a play on Pap."

"You mean that old man standing over there?"

"I mean Pap Dockin. I'd advise you to call him Pap and leave it at that."

The cowboy had a funny look on his face. "My name is Fayet Billings. This here is my partner, Johnny Walls. We rode a long way looking for a job. We heard the Dockin spread was hiring for roundup. I sure hope that old coot doesn't get killed."

"Fayet, if you don't figure out how to call him Pap, you ain't going to be around much longer than that slinger out there."

"You think that old... ah, you think Pap can take him?"

"Pap didn't get hard of hearing from someone talking to him too much. He's worn out many a pistol. Pap may not be twenty-five, but he ain't over the hill yet either. That slinger is just whistling past a cemetery if he thinks he can take Pap Dockin in a gunfight. He'll be in one if he goes for that gun of his."

People were gawking through windows and stood in the doors of their businesses awaiting the outcome of the gunfight. Pap and the tall stranger wearing the slinger rig on his hip were seconds away from drawing.

CHAPTER 6

Chalk slapped his team hard with the check lines when he saw three Indians in front of his shack. Two were on the porch, and one was out in the yard. His heart raced faster than he had ever known it to. They had set fire to the shack, and one had a quilt in his arms. When they saw Chalk coming, they ran for their ponies and galloped off due west.

By the time he made it to the front porch it was engulfed in flames. He tried to go inside, but the roaring fire wouldn't let him. He ran back to his wagon, pulled a buffalo rug from the back and wrapped it around himself. Then he turned and ran into the burning building.

"Sarah! Sarah!" He couldn't see through the heavy smoke. His eyes immediately begin to burn and tear up, and it was hard to breathe. "Sarah!" The roof began to cave in on the left-hand corner. "Sarah!"

"Chalk! Help me! I'm under the floor! I'm stuck, I can't move! Hurry!"

Chalk was beginning to be overcome with smoke. He fell to the floor trying to get his breath. He couldn't see anything, and the shack was beginning to collapse around him. The buffalo rug was beginning to let the heat through. He flattened out on the floor and crawled to where he could hear her calling his name. When he got there, he could feel the hole in the floor. He reached through and felt her back.

"Sarah, hold on honey, just hold on!"

A burning board fell from the ceiling and landed across his back. It wasn't heavy, but he had to get it off. The rug was all that saved him from being severely burned. He knew he had to pull the floor loose. He grabbed the flooring on each side of the hole Sarah had slipped through and pulled with all he had in him. He was lucky. The whole side of the floor came up. It was half rotten. Just as the floor let loose, the ceiling came down all around him.

"Sarah, move over if you can... fast!"

She moved enough that he dove through the floor onto the ground.

"Sarah, you okay?"

"I think so."

Chalk was beginning to see again. The smoke had not gotten under the floor. "We've got to get out of here. It looks like we can make it if we crawl to my left. You grab hold of my boot when I get beyond you. Stay hold of it. You have to follow me... can you do that?"

"I'll try. I couldn't move past the board in front of you." He saw the floor joist she was talking about. It was two thirds rotten from the looks of it. He took his elbow and hit it as hard as he could. It splintered easily. He moved it out of the way and looked back at her. "Can you follow me?"

"I'll follow."

He was scared for the first time in his life... not for himself, but for his Sarah. He had to get her and the baby out of harm's way. He began to pray quietly as he crawled. "God, I know me and You, we've not had a lot of conversations, but we need to have one about now. I'm probably not worthy to ask anything of You, but this woman that loves me sure is. Sarah's with child and it was You who seen fit for her to be. You got her all the way from Missouri to Texas on a damn hard wagon seat... sorry, Lord, about the swearing but I'm kind of in a situation here. If You can't save me, then get her out of here. Make this crawl space big enough to get her belly through here. Lord, I'm asking, You're bigger and tougher and a whole heap smarter. I'm begging, Lord, please spare my Sarah. "

Suddenly he could see daylight straight ahead. He could also see plumes of smoke and drops of fire falling through the floor ahead of him. But then there was a crash from above. The floor caved in ahead of him. "Sarah, turn right! Can you turn right?"

"Yes... I can."

"Go, now!" He felt her let loose of his boot and begin to turn. He then crawled around in front of her. "You okay, baby?"

She began to cry. "I'm okay. I'm just scared. What if this little fellow doesn't get a chance to see this great big world?" "He will see it! He will! Now follow me, honey." He had not crawled ten feet when he came to what looked like where an old cellar had been half dug. He crawled down in it and helped Sarah down. They both could almost stand up in the hole. "Follow me." They walked not more than twelve feet out into the open.

Chalk looked towards heaven. He was thanking the Lord for sparing them. He was sure God had dropped the floor in front of him to force him to turn the right direction to get out.

He sat down beside Sarah and made sure she was okay. That was when she saw the burned spot on the back of his leg. "Chalk, you've been burned!"

"It's nothing."

"It is something. We have to take care of that." Sarah got up and went to the wagon. He laid there looking up at the sky as the shack cracked and popped from the fire. His hands and face were black from the smoke and charcoal. She came back with a hand full of hog lard. She cleaned the burn and gently applied the lard. Chalk didn't wince one time. His days growing up on the streets of Kansas City made him one to never show pain or weakness.

"That should do it." Sarah was relieved. "I don't think it burned deep."

"The buffalo rug saved me. I guess it's no longer with us." He looked at the shack as the walls collapsed inward. "Makes me glad we left most of our things in the wagon last night."

"They're just things. I'm glad we got out and the little one gets to see this world."

"I wasn't saying I wasn't thankful."

Sarah put her arms around him, and they lay down on the grass looking up at the blue sky as puffs of smoke from the shack dotted it. "You know, Chalk, we'll have to live out of the wagon awhile."

"I know. We could get a room at the Lazy Day."

"No, I wouldn't hear of it."

"That may be, but if the little guy needs a better place to stay, he's getting it."

Chalk stood and left for a few seconds and came back with a pail of water. He took the dipper and gave Sarah a drink first. It was cool and sweet. "You know, Sarah, that well has real good water. It looks to be deep. I think we'll have plenty of good water on this place." The fatigue and excitement of getting her out from under the house suddenly hit him. He lay down beside her and dozed off for nearly an hour.

She sat there beside him rubbing his temple and holding his hand. She was thankful they had survived.

Pap had eased away from his horse at the rail and stood facing the tall man with the gunslinger rig. "I guess I kind of forgot about you. I think I heard you called, Quint, not real sure. I am sure you're goin' to die if you pull iron on me. I may be slowin' down a tad, but not enough to worry on. I'm still faster and more accurate with one of these shooters than you young pups."

"Old man, I don't scare. I said I could wait. Here I am." He walked to within thirty feet of pap and stood ready.

"I can't hear what you're sayin' but whatever it is, it probably don't amount to much. If you want to use that piece there on your hip, get to it. Me and the boys got cattle and a ranch to see after."

"Who the hell do you think you are, God?" He went for his gun immediately. He saw Pap draw and shoot before he got the hammer pulled back on his pistol. The bullet hit him in the chest, knocking him backwards a couple of steps. He stood staring and then fell backwards. As he stared up at the sky, his grip around the handle of his gun relaxed.

Pap walked slowly to him and Quint smiled. “So… this is it. Quint Hobbs, taken by an over the hill rancher… not much of a showing.”

“To answer your question, I’m not God but not over the hill yet either. The Bible does say to listen to the elders. I told you I was faster and more accurate, even in my possible slower years, than you new gun hires.”

“You said that… alright.” He stared at Pap. “Elders.” His smile slowly faded, and he was gone.

Pap turned, walked to his horse and mounted. He didn’t like killing a man, but when they’re hired to kill you, then you do what needs be done. He noticed the two new cowpunchers standing by their horses. “You boys lookin’ for work?”

Fayett glanced at Speck first and then looked at Pap. “We are.”

“If Speck here nods to it… guess you’re hired.”

The storekeeper walked out into the street and stood over the tall gunslinger. Pap rode up beside him. “Get him off the street. This is a pretty little town. Don’t need any unsightliness dirtying it up.” He then whirled his horse around facing his men. “We ready to ride?”

Pooh spoke up. “Hell yes, we’re ready to ride!”

Speck looked over at the two new cowpunchers. “You boys mount up. You’re hired.”

“Alright!” The two punchers mounted with enthusiasm, and the Dockin riders rode out of town in a slow lope.

“Mister Davis, I believe I can work for you now. Things seemed to have worked out suddenly.” The Checkered Kid smiled as he looked from Quint Hobbs to Zell.

“I’m glad to have you on board.” Zell glanced in the direction Pap and his men had ridden out of town. “Ole Pap, he ain’t lost much in that fast draw of his, not much at all. I remember a time down in Texas me and him got called in a poker game, said we was cheating. We weren’t, but we were having a run of damn good luck. They was three of them sitting at the table and another one standing at the bar. One of 'em went for his gun. Pap killed three of 'em while I killed the one."

"Three?" The Kid was questioning the truth in that.

"I said three. On the same trip, we was bringing back three hundred head of prime beeves when two gunnies came up on us. We had ridden on ahead of the herd checking for water. These damn cowboys liked our horses better than their own, and somehow thought they could take us. Well, I guess they thought that because one of 'em had a rifle pointed at me. It didn't make Pap a damn. He drew and killed that cowboy before he even knew he was shot. I winged the other one. We hung the sonofabitch for attempting to steal another man's horse, and the fact they planned to kill us. Pap said he figured if we didn't hang him, he'd pull the same thing on someone else. It was better to rid the country of him."

The Checkered Kid had a puzzled look on his face. "I thought you wanted to take this old man down?"

"I do."

"It sounds like you like the old coot."

"What was and what is ain't the same."

"What turned you on him?"

"None of your damn business. You're hired to do a job, not collect knowledge."

Zell turned and walked a short distance from the Kid. "Mount up, we're heading to the ranch."

Chalk awoke suddenly as he heard horses running. It was Pap Dockin and his men. They came riding up at a gallop.

"Seen the smoke... anyone hurt?" Pap's eyes were wide as he searched the perimeter.

"No, we're alright. The shack went up though."

"Well, it's for sure you've lost the roof over your head... for what it was. You can stay over to my place tonight."

"Are you asking or telling?"

"I guess I'm askin' if that's what works for you. You sure rile easy."

Sarah spoke up. "Don't pay Chalk any mind. We'd love to, Mister Dockin." Sarah smiled at him and then Chalk.

"I'd be obliged, Mister Dockin."

"Nonsense boy, I'll enjoy the company. Only one I got around to talk to is ole Speck. We've been tellin' the same lies to each other so long, we've come to believe 'em. You stop callin' me Mister and call me Pap." He was all smiles. "One question, what started the fire?"

"Indians. I saw them leaving the place as I came around the bend of the road."

Sarah confirmed what Chalk was saying. "There were three of them. I lay quietly until I saw them coming to the door. I slipped through a hole in the floor. Mister Dockin... Pap, it near scared me to death. I've never seen Indians before."

Pap looked around at his boys. "You heard her. Post some guards starting tonight. We stay alert 'til we see what this is all about. May be nothing more than some bucks scavengin' around... we'll stay watchful. You never know about Comanches. They're good people... but they are damn good warriors, too. We've always gotten along with them. They've been peaceable. One or two renegades can stir up some trouble though."

Chalk and Sarah had very little to do but get on their wagon and head to the Dockin Ranch. They had quite the escort with Pap and his men following along on all four sides of the wagon.

Pap rode along on the right-hand side. He had something on his mind. Normally he was just out with it, but Chalk was different. It would be Chalk that would give him an opening.

"Pap, I sure appreciate you putting us up for the night. I wasn't liking the idea of Sarah sleeping in the wagon."

"You can stay as long as you like. Fact is... I was thinking that the two of you should stay until the baby is born." He looked over at Chalk to see how he felt about it.

"I don't know. I sure don't want to be a weight around your neck."

"Son, I would be overjoyed to have you. That's enough talk. It's settled. You and Sarah can stay at my place until you get tired of me and want to leave." He smiled and then spit some tobacco juice to the right-hand side of his horse.

"Well, alright then." Chalk looked at Sarah who was smiling big. "I see you like the idea."

"I'm for it, yes. What woman wouldn't want two men fussing over her?"

Pap laughed and rode on ahead.

The Checkered Kid unsaddled his horse and carried his gear to the bunkhouse where his partner was laying.

Ben Watts was all smiles when he saw the Kid. "It's about time you got here. That must be a slow walking horse you're riding."

"I've ridden faster. I ran into a little cutie on my way down. Ben, what happened to you?" The Kid saw his back.

"I ran into what's called the, 'Saint Maker'."

"Did you become a saint?"

"No, but I sure cussed like the devil. Pap Dockin gave me this whipping and he killed ole Beal."

The Kid smiled. "Beal wasn't any count anyway. I didn't meet Pap Dockin, but I did see him handle Quint Hobbs with ease."

"Pap Dockin took Quint Hobbs?" Ben was stunned.

The Kid drew his gun and made a blowing sound. "Like blowing out a candle."

Ben shook his head. The news of Pap taking Quint was big. "Kid, that means he could have taken Beal any way he wanted to. I didn't know he could handle a gun. He already had his out when he shot Beal."

"Trust me partner, he could take ten like Beal, two or three at a time."

Ben sat up in his bed. “I guess you got the lay of things by now.”

“I believe I do. Zell doesn’t seem to want the old man killed. He wants him run off, busted and then killed. I’m not sure he wants him killed even then. He sure has a powerful hate built up inside him for that old man... to respect him, too.”

“Yeah, it’s a peculiar thing between those two.”

“Ben, he wants to see him suffer before he dies, which seems to out-weigh the respect he has for him. Make sense?”

“Yeah, it does. Me and Beal didn’t care if he suffered or not. We figured on killing Pap soon as we met up with him. We were going to feed Zell a line that the old coot left us no choice. He fooled us though. Came in, said little, drew and then shot Beal. That old man is nothing to fool with, Kid. There is one thing I can put you wise to... he doesn’t like being called an old man. He shot Beal dead for it.”

“How did you and Beal come on to ride together?”

“We didn’t exactly. I run on to him on my way here at a little trading post back up the way. The conversation led to one thing and then another. Well, the short of it was he wanted to tag along, see if he could hire on with me.”

“I see. Well, I’m going to put a bullet in Pap Dockin. He ain’t horsewhipping my partner and living to tell about it. I don’t care what Zell Davis says.” The Checkered Kid was all smiles.

“I appreciate it, but I can put a bullet in him myself.” Ben looked at the Kid with a dread of what he was about to say. “You know Kid, I kind of like the old coot.”

“You what? He must have done more to you than give you a whipping. The man cut you up for God’s sake.”

“Yeah, I know, I can’t explain it. He just seems different than them church goers. He has sand, backbone. His kind is fading away.”

The Kid had a funny look on his face. “I don’t know what to make of it. Zell was talking like he was bosom buddies with him, hated to see him turning up daisies. The man wants him brought down, but he wants it done careful like. I can't figure it. I don't know if I'm supposed to love the old bastard to death or slowly drain the blood out of him."

Ben shot the Kid a worried look. "Kid, I've taken some jobs I didn't like and this one here, it's the lead steer on all of them. I don't like any part of this deal. I'm telling you there is something in Pap Dockin that don't exist in this country anymore. He's got courage, toughness, savvy, fairness, and he's stubborn enough to back it all up. That's hard to find these days."

"I'm hearing you, but I ain't letting that get in the way of my money. Zell Davis pays well. You get some rest. I'm going over to the big house and parlay with him. I'll be back a little later. Need anything?"

"Yeah, bring me a shot of his best." Ben smiled and turned over on his other side. He still couldn't lie on his back.

Chapter 7

Vivian Martin and Ellison Jones arrived at the Dockin Ranch around six fifteen in the evening. When Pap came down the stairs from his room, he was dressed in his Sunday best. A white shirt, maroon vest, black bow tie, frock coat, and his best boots.

Sarah made sure she told him how good he looked. He smiled and then licked two fingers to get an unruly hair to lay down in the front. He always wore a hat, but he was inside and had company. He had taken a bath and splashed on some perfumed lotion that smelled something like lilac flowers. Chalk thought he looked spiffy, and Speck was looking at him like a wide eyed mule. Pap saw the look right away.

"You have somethin' to say?" Speck shook his head and went back into the kitchen to prepare dinner.

Speck didn't cook every day, but he did prepare the meals for company. Pap had a lady that worked until five each day, baking bread, and preparing dinner and supper through the week. She always had the weekends off. Today being Saturday, it was Speck at the stove.

Pap had seen Vivian's carriage coming from his bedroom window and was hurrying to the front door. Before he could greet them, Sarah, Chalk, and Speck had to voice how swell he looked. Well, all but Speck.

Pap opened the door as they were stepping onto the front porch. The house was rather large, and the porch practically wrapped around it. Beautiful flowers hung between each porch post. They looked to be rather fresh. That's because he had his men digging flowers and putting them in pots all afternoon as fast as they could.

The house was white with yellow trim and had a feeling of warmth as soon as anyone entered it. Pap lived alone, except for Speck having a bedroom in the house. Between the two of them and the hired lady, they kept the house very nice. There were three bedrooms upstairs and two on the main floor. He always thought he would have a big family one day, but love had been a dry riverbed for him. He used the big house to entertain guests from time to time, cattle buyers and businessmen mostly. Speck had the bedroom at the end of the hall on the second floor. It had been decided that Chalk and his Sarah would stay in one of the bedroom's downstairs. They picked the one with a large brass bathtub. Sarah thought she had died and gone to heaven.

"Good evening, Vivian, Ellison. Welcome to the Dockin Ranch. Please come in."

"Good evening." Vivian smiled ever so softly as Ellison nodded.

There was a large half-moon shaped flat rock entry to the main room. Pap took her by the hand and held it until she made the three-inch step down. He was being the perfect host and gentleman. "Supper is almost ready. I hope you like Dockin beef. That's what we raise around here. I picked the cuts myself."

"I don't know about Ellison, but steak is my favorite."

"Yes of course, I like steak or anything else that is beef."

"Franklin... Ellison and I came by Chalk's place and the house was smoldering. Do you know what happened, and where he might be?"

Pap smiled at her. "I might. They had a little problem. I'll let them tell you about it over supper. They are already here. In fact, they'll be stayin' here until Chalk can build a house for Sarah, and the baby is born."

"I wasn't aware she was with child."

"Oh yes. I'd say in about three weeks we might have a little one runnin' 'round here. You know that might be the first thing you didn't know anything about."

"Now, Franklin." She flashed him a smile and batted her eyes. She caused Pap to blush, something no one had ever done to him. He stood there for a second thinking back to the Prairie

Grass Cafe. He remembered when she took the veil from her face. He felt like a spooked colt looking for a place to run. She was one beautiful looking woman.

The supper was superb, and the dessert was unbelievable. Cherry pie, with a crust that melted in the mouth, served with coffee. Everyone had two pieces except Vivian. When the dinner was over, coffee was served in the living room with a dash of whiskey. It was during coffee that things began to get interesting.

"Franklin, how much have you told Chalk?" Speck was bringing in a tray with a fresh pot of coffee when she asked the question. He almost spilled the pot in the middle of the floor.

"Well... I..." Pap turned three shades of red. He hadn't told Chalk anything. He hadn't even considered telling him anything. Things usually take care of themselves sooner or later.

"Franklin?" Vivian looked over her cup of coffee at him.

Chalk was beginning to get irritated. It was like he wasn't even in the room, yet the conversation was about him. "Begging your pardon, but it seems like everyone knows some kind of secret about me and my mother except for me. I'd like to be let in on it... or pick another subject. Mom taught me it wasn't polite to talk over folks."

Vivian smiled at him. Pap had a little more serious look about him.

Sarah felt a tingle run up her spine. She was sure as to what it was they were about to tell her husband.

Speck was wondering how his boss was going to circle the wagons if he didn't spill the mystery to the boy. He was enjoying watching Pap squirm, so much so he lit himself a cigar while peeking through the kitchen door. He had gone back to the kitchen, but he wasn't missing this. He was laughing while trying to hold it in.

"I agree there's things need to be talked about and thrashed around some."

"Will you stop stalling, Franklin?" Vivian smiled at Pap and casually looked at Chalk.

Pap liked her calling him by his name. She could say it so soft. He was wishing Ellison would take his ragged butt back to town. He felt he could talk to Vivian all night long.

It was at that very second a horse came in hard and fast. A strong knock hammered the door. Pap got up quickly and answered it. Pooh was standing there very excited. "We got trouble Pap! Indians hit us tonight! The boys counted upwards of three hundred head missing! That's the third time since you been gone, we've had cattle missing! We found one bunch but never did find the others."

Pap looked around for Speck. He had come out of the kitchen when he heard Pooh at the door. Pap looked at him with a hard eye. "I guess I've been a little preoccupied. You mind tellin' me what's been goin' on with this roundup?"

"I was going to get around to it sooner or later. You're right, we've been a little busy with other matters. Truth is we lost about fifty head in the first bunch. It rained hard that night and we lost the trail. I got my suspicions about who took 'em but that's all."

Pap scoffed. "I know where they went... Zell Davis. Pooh, did anyone get hurt?"

"Tanner got a flesh wound, not bad though. Hurt his pride worse. He stuck that knife of his in one of them. We found a blood trail, but it played out."

"Change horses, Pooh. We'll leave in about an hour and see if we can tell anything in the dark. Moon is near to full. We might get lucky. Lay out some fresh rope... oh and lay out the Saint Maker."

"I'll do it." Pooh turned and disappeared into the dark.

"I'm sorry about this, Vivian. Things can happen on a ranch this size in a hurry. It's not like havin' a small patch you know."

Chalk heard the small patch comment. "Pap, what is a small

patch?"

"Oh, I don't know... somethin' about like you got."

"Must be."

"What's that mean?"

"Storekeeper in Mason City called it a patch and I felt insulted. I guess maybe he's right. My hundred acres stacks up to be a patch. I can raise cattle on it, can't I?"

"You can, just not so many."

"How many would you say?"

"Well, that place you got ought to run twenty or so head fairly easy, a few more in wet years. Problem is, we don't have many wet years. Damn near none."

"That's not near what I had on my mind." He felt like the greenhorn was showing in him. He also knew there would be no way to add to his patch. He had the money to buy more, but he was smack dab in the middle of two ranches feuding over what they already had.

"Out of curiosity, Chalk, how many head did you think you could run on that place of yours?"

"I didn't know."

"I see." Pap gave that a second of thought and then turned to Vivian. "Would you like to go for a walk? I would sure like to show you a couple of fine breedin' stock horses before I leave. I've not had them long."

"I would love to."

Pap took her hand inside his arm and the two of them walked out to the barn. There was a burned-out spot in the left front corner where a lantern had been thrown from the attack the night before. It didn't do much damage, but it needed to be repaired.

When Pap opened the door to the barn, Vivian was totally surprised. The barn was very clean and well put together. It had eight spacious stalls plus six standing stalls. The hay loft smelled of fresh stored hay and the horses were making that noise they can make when crunching it. It smelled wonderful to her. Pap walked her over to the young horses he had purchased.

"Oh my, they're beautiful, just beautiful."

"I hoped you'd like 'em."

"The only thing I see wrong with those stud colts is that you don't have anyone to leave them to when you leave this world."

The smile left his face. "I ain't leavin' here."

"Franklin." She half scolded him.

"Okay, let's get it out of the wagon. I know business wise you're Martin and Jones Transportation and Freight, but who are you besides that? I mean, you know Paula Cranfield, you know Chalk, and it seems you know me. Would you tell me how you come by knowin' so many people I am connected to?"

"Of course, all you had to do was ask. I'm Paula's half-sister, Chalk's aunt."

He stood stunned for several long seconds at that revelation. "I... I didn't know Paula had a sister... or half-sister either."

"She did. Our father was married one time before. My mother died, and he remarried. Paula and I were three years apart in age. I went off to college and ended up getting married. Paula stayed in Dodge City for a while, then later moved to Kansas City. She was a hard-working girl and had the gentlest soul I ever knew. She loved you, Franklin. Now I see why. You're easy to love."

"Me... an old sly fox like me?" He stopped and stared at her for a brief few seconds. His mind was processing the last part of her comment. She said I was easy to love. Is she having feelings about me?

"You're a man, a real man, and Franklin, there's not many. Paula could only love a real man. I should have known what you were like before I came. I'm afraid I'm following in my sister's footsteps. I'm feeling things I didn't expect to. I think I am falling for you. I hope that doesn't seem too forward. I've lived and worked in this man's world until finally I learned to just come out with it."

"Well... well now... I guess I don't know how to respond to that. Ah... well maybe, maybe I do. I guess I never thought I'd ever be saying this to a lady, especially at forty-five years old. But I'm findin' myself thinkin' about you more than anything else. I didn't think I could ever think on another woman like I did Paula. I'm not twenty anymore. Chances of a woman in my life was next to none. I've been ok with that. Accepted it. But I'm findin' it mighty pleasin' that you have those kinds of feelin's' towards me. Maybe it will make it easier to call on you tomorrow."

"Oh?"

"Well, I was thinkin' that maybe tomorrow you might like to see some of the Dockin Ranch. I was hopin' to pack a small lunch and take a buggy ride across some of it."

"That would be nice."

Vivian then got her first shock as Pap Dockin awkwardly pulled her close to him and kissed her unexpectedly. She first started to pull away, but then relaxed into a long passionate kiss. When they broke apart, she was trying to catch her breath and regain her composure. "Pick me up at the hotel around ten if that is desirable." She smiled at him as they looked each other in the eyes. "Franklin, don't you think we should be getting back to the house? The kids are bound to be missing us."

They both laughed as he took her arm. As they neared the front door, he looked at her without her knowing. He wondered how this could be happening. Pap Dockin was falling in love with a beautiful woman that seemed to be having the same feelings. He hoped God wasn't playing a trick on him.

Chapter 8

Ben Watts stood at the entrance to the bunkhouse watching as Zell Davis, along with the Checkered Kid and half the Sliding D men, rode out at four in the afternoon. He didn't know where they were going, but he knew it would have something to do with Pap Dockin. The Kid was supposed to come back with a shot of whiskey, instead he rode out with Zell. Ben was having second thoughts about things. Up until this job he had never questioned anything he and the Kid had done. He smiled and spoke aloud. "Maybe the Saint Maker has done more to me than cut my back up. I've not turned yellow... but something has changed with me. Pap puts me in mind of a man I met in South Texas. He was younger but the two of them could have been kin. I think Dockin has a little more hardness about him, and he's not the kind of man I favor going up against."

Ben slowly walked back to his bed and eased into it. He had time to think about it all. One thing he knew already, he would like to know just what the quarrel between Pap Dockin and Zell Davis was all about.

Chalk rode in silence beside Speck. Pooh was leading the way to where the cattle had been stolen by the Indians. Pap was riding up beside him. This was a first for Chalk. He was being introduced to the way cowboys take care of things in the West. His heart was pumping fast from the sheer excitement of it all. For the first time in his life his hands were sweating, and he felt nervous. The horse he was riding was black as a chunk of coal and had an easy gait. He was a fine one.

Suddenly the Dockin riders brought their horses to a halt. Pap got off with Pooh and they began checking the ground. Speck dismounted and threw his reins to Chalk. The two new punchers rode up beside Chalk and watched the three men on the ground ahead of them. Fayet Billings slowly looked over at him. "Reckon they found a track?"

Chalk glanced at the puncher. "Don't know. They found something."

"Ole Pap, he's all business ain't he?"

"What do you mean?"

"Well, I watched him take a gunfighter in town, and now we're out here trying to take someone else down."

"I would think when someone steals your property, that would be the thing to do, go get it back and arrest the ones that took it. I don't know anything about the gunfight."

"I'm Fayet Billings. I was just talking... Pap is fast with that shooter. I'd sure not face him alone." Fayet looked around himself for a second. "From what some of the boys told me, Pap don't arrest anyone, he deals out his own judgment."

Chalk looked from Fayet back to where Pap and the others were. "I wouldn't know about that."

Pap was in a hurry when he came back to his horse. "Boys, these cattle are headed due east. I can't tell much about it yet, we'll track awhile. Let's see where we end up."

Pap and his men had ridden out leaving Vivian, Ellison, and Sarah alone at the ranch. Pap asked them to spend the night and Vivian took him up on it, under some protest from Ellison. It gave her and Sarah a chance to visit and get to know one another. At first it was just chit chat until Ellison went to bed.

"Sarah, how do you like Texas so far?"

"It's a change from Kansas City that's for sure. A lot fewer people, plus big and beautiful. I like it."

Vivian studied her for a moment. "Sweetheart, you do know that Franklin 'Pap' Dockin is Chalk's father?"

She smiled. "Yes, I know. They look too much alike not to be, same actions, everything. I don't think Chalk has figured it out. I'm not saying anything. I'm letting Pap tell him. I thought he was about to when the cowboy came in with the rustling news."

"Yes, he was, and he will tell him soon."

"I think Chalk will be pleased to learn he is Pap's son. I know he has harbored a certain amount of resentment about not knowing his father and feeling he ran out on his mother. Chalk is easy going and forgiving mostly... he'll be pleased once he has time to think about it." Sarah paused. "Vivian."

"Yes."

"I'm excited for him. Isn't it wonderful he finds his father just as he is having his first child? His child will have a grandfather and will grow to know him."

"Yes, it is."

Vivian gave some thought as to whether to take the conversation further than what Sarah was aware of. She decided to venture out. "There's more than Chalk finding his father." She waited for Sarah's reaction.

"Oh?"

"Yes, first let me tell you, Franklin didn't run out on Chalk. Paula ran out on Franklin. She had her reasons. We all handle things differently." She touched Sarah on the hand. "Paula went through a time of mental blues. The doctors call it depression."

"How do you know that? Chalk never mentioned it."

"Chalk was a baby. No one knew anything about it. As I said before, there's more to this than Chalk finding his father. You know there is bad blood between Zell Davis and Franklin, don't you?"

"I've been hearing and picking up things, yes."

"The bad blood between them is not over ranches and range."

"What then?"

She stared at Sarah for a moment. "It's over Paula. Sarah, she was my half-sister."

"Chalk's mother is your sister? Why, that makes you his aunt!"

"Half-sister and yes, his aunt."

Sarah was bewildered. The news that the fight between the two range bulls, Pap and Zell was over Chalk's mother was mystifying. She stared at Vivian for a moment. "Zell Davis, was he in love with Paula, too? Is that what the quarrel is about? Why didn't Chalk's mother tell him of you?"

"I can only tell you the fight does have to do with her. If the why of it all comes out, it will be Franklin Dockin who brings it out. It will be up to him. That said... you and I must keep what we have talked about to ourselves."

Sarah looked at her for a long moment. "I understand, but I don't understand Paula not telling her son about you."

"Paula was a very quiet girl. She was a loner to say the least. We always got along, but she felt... I don't know, kind of odd I think about being a half-sister. She was proud and never but one time asked for anything from me. The last thing she wanted to be was a burden to anyone."

"What was it she came to you for?"

"She came and stayed with me for a while. She was going through the depression like I said, and she was also pregnant with Chalk. She needed someone then but only then. Paula was a beautiful, gentle, kind person, but she was also the strangest girl I ever knew. She didn't make friends easily and she never wrote more than one letter a year, if that."

"I hope you and I will be friends for a long time." Sarah smiled at her and Vivian returned it.

"How's forever sound?"

"Just fine." The two of them giggled at one another and hugged.

Pap and his men trailed the stolen herd to a small creek. Clouds had moved in and made tracking impossible. They decided to wait until morning to start tracking again, so they made camp and sat around the campfire. It wasn't long before drinking coffee and telling lies began. Normally Pap would have been in a foul mood, someone stealing his cattle, but he had his boy with him, and things couldn't be better. He kept looking across the fire at Chalk. He thought he was his spitting image but for being a couple inches taller.

Chalk listened to story after story, and finally had to ask a question himself. “I can’t tell which one of these tales is true and which ones aren’t, but I want to know how Pooh got his name.”

All the hands began to laugh. The two new punchers didn’t know either, so they sat listening in silence.

Speck wanted to tell the story. “Well son, I’ll tell you about ole Pooh here. You see, he’s quite a lady’s man. He has a woman in Mason City that thinks he’s the one that hung that ole yeller moon up there. Her name is Sitting Dove, a full blood Comanche. And you know how Indians like to give white men Indian names?”

“No but come on with the story.” Chalk was fascinated by the tale being told. Pooh pulled his hat down over his eyes and ears.

“Well, it so happened that me and the boys was coming out of the Dry Rock Saloon when we heard something in a wagon sitting at the corner of the saloon. We noticed the wagon a rockin’, and you know how it is with cowboys, how they always like to know what’s going on. They like to be included in the fun being had.”

Speck stopped and looked around at the group of men. He was grinning with glee as he paused with the story. The men were spell bound with the tale. Most of them already knew what happened, but they liked the way Speck could tell the tale.

Pap sat back and grinned as he watched the men being drawn into the story.

“Well, we snuck up to the wagon, tippie toein’ mind ya, being extra quiet. That old wagon by this time was rockin’ like a baby carriage. Now there’s one thing I left out of this story. Ole Pooh back then was known not to take a bath but once a year, whether he needed it or not. He has improved to four a month, makes us all feel a whole heap better.”

Everyone laughed and shook their heads.

“Well anyway, here we are hugging close to the wagon trying

to hear what's going on. Finally, we look inside from each end. It was too dark to see anything, but we knew what was going on. The little Indian gal was talking really fast in her native tongue between licks, and the only thing we could understand was Phew Bear, Phew Bear, Phew Bear!"

The cowboys including Pap laughed so hard they were shaking.

Speck continued. "Since we knew she had given him an Indian name, we tried to soften it up some. So, we took it to Pooh Bear. The little Indian gal has been calling him Pooh ever since. It was the least we could do for our ole buddy, Pooh."

Everyone was laughing and having a good time until Fayet, one of the new punchers made a blunder. "Well, I'm new here and don't know all of you boys yet. I met Chalk and I know Speck, but I have a question." Fayet looked over in the direction of Pap. "Is Chalk your son or kin to you in some way?"

Silence filled the camp. Fayet didn't know how, but he knew he messed up.

Chalk looked up from his cup of coffee at the new wrangler and then over at Pap. He wasn't sure what Fayet said, but it sounded like he asked if Pap was his father. Chalk looked at Pap with a different eye this time. He began to put things together. Pap knew his mother, and he suddenly realized he and Pap favored in looks. It then came to him that his mother might have bought the patch of land so he would discover his father. His next thought was a question, why didn't she just tell him who his father was? He stared at Pap thinking to himself that his mother was a great lady and Pap was a hell of a man, so why did they not marry? His mind was racing with questions.

Pap sat across from the new puncher staring at Chalk and at the same time thinking the new man a damn fool. The last thing he wanted was for Chalk to find out who his father was before he told him. He was afraid Chalk would hate him before he could set things to right.

The silence continued. Pap was about to speak when Chalk spoke up.

"Yes, Pap is my dad, why did you ask? Surely you can tell by looking."

"Yeah, well, yeah I can."

"Pour me another cup of coffee, Speck." Chalk held his cup out.

Pap reached his cup in from the other side nearly touching Chalks. "Pour me one, too." His cup was outstretched, but Pap and Chalk's eyes were locked on each other. They stared at one another from across the campfire. At first it was intense, neither cracking a smile nor showing any kind of expression. Then slowly they both begin to form a smile, and gradually began to laugh. Speck started laughing as he poured the coffee. Then Pooh and all the old hands began to laugh and reached their cups out for a refill beside Pap's and Chalk's. The two new cowboys didn't know what to make of it all. They were beginning to wonder if the Dockin bunch wasn't about half crazy.

When the cups were full, Speck called for silence. It became deathly quiet. "I propose a toast. To Pap and his son, Chalk, may they have a long and prosperous relationship." The men all clanged their cups together and took a drink.

Chalk was looking at Pap in silence. He had a father. He was sitting across in front of him. He was Pap Dockin's son. Pap was looking at Chalk while in deep thought. He had a son. He wanted to talk to him in private as soon as he could. He decided to nod to him. He wanted him to follow him out to where the horses were tied. The two of them got up and walked out into the dark.

"Chalk, I'm sorry it was broke to you like it was. I planned to tell you back at the ranch."

Chalk nodded his head it was alright. "I'm kind of confused but maybe tomorrow we can talk, I..." Chalk's part of the conversation was cut off when two rifle shots were fired and then a short volley of gunfire followed. They ran back to camp to find one of the new puncher's, Johnny Walls, lying dead and Pooh had a bullet in his leg. Pap dowsed the fire with the last of the coffee.

"Boys, fun's over. Stay in your bedrolls and don't light any fires. You do, you're a dead man. If they don't kill you, I will."

Pap carefully made his way to Pooh. "How bad you hit?"

"A scratch is all. It went through the outside of my leg. I'll be alright."

"Speck... watch the east side of camp. Chalk... take the north. One of you other boys take the south."

Luke Tanner who had been wounded when the Indians stole the cattle spoke up quickly. He wasn't letting an arm wound hold him back. "I got the south, Pap."

"You up to it?"

"I'm in better shape than Jim Bowie was when Santa Anna took the Alamo."

"Alright then, I'll take the west. Anything moves out there in front of you, shoot your rifles dry. Reload and ready for another round. I figure they've already high tailed it, but they could come back."

Chapter 9

The Comanche braves delivered the beef to the Sliding D Ranch, at near midnight, for ten jugs of whiskey. Zell's men took the cattle while the Indians went on their way whooping and hollering.

Zell had sent two men back to keep Pap penned down if he tried to follow. Then he took the cattle a mile down a small creek. He drove them back and forth across the water making it hard to tell what was going on. The final deceptive trick came at dawn. He had half of his men standing by with five hundred head of the Sliding D cattle. He drove the stolen cattle for two miles down a grassy valley and then went up a big canyon. It was big enough to hide ten times what he drove into it. He had his men drive his own cattle over the two miles, and then bring them halfway back. It wiped out the trail of the stolen cattle completely. Zell then made camp. His men started a couple fires to heat branding irons, making it look like they were getting ready to start branding cattle after breakfast. It would be next to impossible to find the stolen beeves. Zell made camp in an obvious location. They were sitting on the back corner of Chalk's hundred-acre patch which cornered with his Sliding D Ranch. The opposite side bordered and cornered with the Dockin spread.

Zell knew Chalk was Paula Cranfield's boy and he knew Pap thought Chalk was a Dockin. But the father had not been proven or named as far as Zell knew. He was sure Chalk belonged to Pap after seeing him, he looked just like him.

At daylight Pap and his men began trailing the stolen cattle. Chalk was given the job of getting Pooh to a doctor and Johnny Wall's body back to the Dockin Ranch. Pooh's leg was swelling and it looked worse than first thought. He decided to take Johnny to the undertaker in town and while there, get the doctor to come out to the ranch and tend to Pooh. That should have been all there was to it, but it wasn't. Chalk ran into some trouble of his own.

He had left the doctor's office, when he saw two men ride in on hard ridden lathered up horses. They dismounted and went into the Dry Rock. It was late morning, a little early to start drinking but cowboys sometimes haven't any recollection of time. He decided to snoop a bit. Chalk walked over to the horses and talked to them easy like.

"You little guys are mighty hot. You could use a drink worse than the two that rode in here on you." Chalk started to go into the saloon when he noticed one of the rifles sticking half out of the scabbard. He reached to shove it back in when a voice came to him from behind.

"You touch that gun and you'll not touch another."

Chalk turned slowly. "You're correct. It's not mine to fix."

"Fix?"

"Well, the gun is half out of the scabbard. I was..."

"Don't lie to me. You know damn well who we are. I figure you trailed us here while your boss rode after whoever took his cattle." The two men walked out in the street and spread out.

"So, you're the ones that shot Pooh and killed Johnny Wall. To be perfectly honest I wasn't trailing you. I brought Pooh back to the ranch to be tended and Johnny to town for the undertaker to bury him. Until you opened your big mouths, I was none the wiser. I was going to tell you that you've rode the hell out of them horses and they could use a drink."

The cowboy doing the talking moved over another couple of steps to Chalk's right. "I guess maybe I learned a lesson. I need to hold my tongue until I know who I'm talking to, in this case a fool."

Chalk stood quietly while sizing up the two cowboys.

"If you were coming to tell me to water my horse, I'd a probably just pistol whipped you. Now that you know too damn much, I'm going to have to kill you. Ain't that a hell of a thing?"

Chalk smiled. "Yes, it is. Another hell of a thing is to learn something new and not be around to use the knowledge."

The cowboy looked puzzled. He looked over at his partner as the wind kicked dust up in the street. "I'm not following you."

"Well, you're going to learn you are too slow to be drawing on me. However, by the time you learn that you'll be graveyard dead."

The cowboy broke for his gun. Chalk drew and shot him through the chest just as his gun cleared the holster. The man's partner raised his hands when he saw that Chalk already had his pistol on him. He had never seen anyone so fast.

"Drop your gun or I'll drop you."

The cowboy eased his pistol out and dropped it in the dusty street. Chalk then walked over to the man lying on the ground.

"I'm done."

"Looks like. I'm sorry, but ignorance has killed many a man."

The dying man looked up at him, and with his last breath gasped. "Hell of a... thing."

Chalk turned to the other cowboy. "Mister, you mount that worn out pony you're riding and ease along with me. We're riding to the Dockin Ranch after you water him."

As they rode away the storekeeper came out of his store. The barber ran to where he was standing, very excited. "That Cranfield kid is as fast as Pap Dockin and he favors him, too."

The storekeeper looked around at the barber. "I guess I better roundup a burial detail. I took care of the one Pap left lying in the street yesterday, now I guess I'll get this one planted Cranfield left me." He looked back the way the two riders went. "You know... he may just make a go of it... and he seems to favor Pap."

The barber looked in the direction the two cowboys were riding. "Danged if he doesn't. Yes sir, danged if he doesn't."

Pap Dockin and his riders rode into the camp Zell Davis had set up and surveyed the lay of the land so to speak. Pap sat easy in the saddle while his eyes roamed.

Zell came out from around his horse with a saddle blanket in his left hand and a pistol in the other. The Checkered Kid walked in beside him. The rest of the men fell in behind them. "Well, what brings you out here, Pap?"

"I think you asked me why I'm here?"

"I did."

"You well know why I'm here. I'm looking for my cattle, the one's you took."

"Those are strong accusations. Now why would I do that? I have plenty of my own cattle. Get down off your horse, have a cup of coffee, we'll discuss your missing cattle."

"I didn't come for talk. We had ours a long time ago." Pap stared hard at him.

Zell stared back as his fake smile faded away. "Yeah, I guess we did. I remember you done all the talking, if you could call it that."

"I want my beeves."

Zell casually gazed around the camp. "I don't see any cattle with the Dockin brand on them. If you have a few steers missing, you're welcome to ride through my herd and maybe see if any got mixed in with mine. How many did you lose?"

Pap didn't answer him. "Speck, take a couple of the boys and see if any of our cattle are here."

"Will do." Speck and three of the Dockin men rode out to the herd while Pap sat staring at Zell.

"I'm sorry to hear of your loss. We were fixing to brand some of ours. Now that you lost some, I'm damn glad we're doing it. At least I'd be able to claim 'em if some did come up missing."

"Zell, what happened? There was a time I thought you were goin' to be alright. Me and you should be able to get along, but you keep a cockle burr under your saddle blanket, especially where I'm concerned."

"Yeah... well, mister high and mighty big shot, I didn't grow up with two parents like you did. I had to scrap to make it. I didn't have a horse or much of anything else. My mother and me done the best we could, while you lived down the road in a house that actually had walls. I could throw a pig through the cracks of the house we lived in. Me and you fought in the war together, but we ain't never had more than that between us. I partnered up with you because I figured you owed me. All those years you had a plenty, and I had little to nothing. Well it ain't like that anymore. I have same as you. The only thing bad that ever happened to me was the name Dockin! I said that loud enough for you to hear! If you missed any of it, I'll repeat it. Otherwise get off my land!"

"It's not your land." Pap smiled. "This land is in the family now. So, once we're through lookin' your herd over, you drive them off this land. The name Dockin owns it."

"You claiming this ground? I don't see the Cranfield kid here."

"Say what?"

"Are you claiming this land? I don't see the owner."

"He's takin' care of some business, but yeah it's my land."

Zell hadn't looked at it that way. "Just you saying it's your land, don't make it so."

"Chalk's my boy. That say enough?"

Zell stared at him for a minute. "Okay... we'll move on... for now, but how can you be so sure he's your son?" Zell turned and walked to his horse. The Checkered Kid did the same, along with the rest of the Sliding D men.

Speck rode in beside Pap. He could see he was sitting in a silent rage. Zell's last comment drove all the way to Pap's inner being. His eyes cut to Speck. "The apostle Paul wrote he had a thorn in the flesh. I can sure understand that. I've got my own. I'd end Zell's life, but it would be murder. He's no match for me with a gun."

Speck tipped his hat back on his head. "No, he's not, but I understand the want of wanting to kill the reprobate. On another note. There's not a cow, calf, heifer, or steer out there belonging to us."

"I figured. Send a couple of the boys in different directions to look for any sign. These cattle Zell has here tromped out the trail. There's no telling which way they took 'em, but I'm bettin' they're grazing on Zell Davis land. The rest of us will head back to the ranch. I've got some thinkin' to do."

"You mean we're giving up the search?"

"What?" Pap seemed preoccupied.

Speck raised his voice a bit. "The search... we giving it up?"

"For now. Let me think on this."

"Pap, we've never give up on nothing. We can't let this bushwhacker get away with this. He's killed a man and wounded another. I say we..."

"I say! You listen!" Pap turned his head away.

"Yes sir... Boss!" He stared at Pap with stern eyes. Speck had never been called down by Pap. He knew by that tone something was eating at him in a big way. Whatever it was it was more important than cattle.

The doctor left Pooh with his leg elevated and told him to stay off it for a few days. He thought he would be alright but if it were to get infected, he could possibly lose the leg. It was then that Pooh wanted to send for Sitting Dove. He said she was good with Indian medicine. She would take care of him and his leg. Chalk suggested he wait until Pap returned before he sent for her. Pooh wasn't happy about waiting, but he knew enough about Pap that he felt it a good idea.

Chapter 10

Pap and his men rode into the ranch late afternoon and unsaddled. Chalk greeted them and told him of his incident in town. He wanted Pap to see the prisoner he had taken right away. Chalk went to the root cellar, brought him out and presented him with hands tied behind his back.

Pap walked up to the man and hit him hard in the face, causing him to fall backwards onto his back. "Get up, you murderin' bastard! Get up!" Pap moved in on him and kicked him in the ribs, knocking the breath out of him. "Get up!"

Looking wild-eyed, Pap turned to his men. "Pick this back-shootin' murderer up and hang him on the post! Take his clothes off! All of 'em! I'm going to show this back-shootin' murderer what happens to cowards like him. Snub him tight!"

The Dockin boys grabbed the man and snubbed him to the snubbing post. They ripped his shirt off and took his pants off, leaving him standing there in nothing but his birthday suit. Pap had disappeared. In a couple of minutes, he reappeared with the Saint Maker in his hand.

"Now, I want to know who got my cattle, and who murdered my man, and wounded another one! I want to know... and I want to know now! You hear me!" Pap brought the long whip full length behind him. He then put a full chew of tobacco in his mouth. "You're going to tell me everything I want to know before I'm through and some things I don't care to know. You're gonna call for mama. You're goin' to talk! You killed a man, wounded another. Time to square things!"

"Mister, I didn't shoot anyone. I don't know what you're talking about!"

"You're making the call." Pap brought the whip with a mighty lash across his back. The man yelled out. Again, he brought it across him. He yelled again. "Now, where's my cattle?" He brought the whip back across his back again. It made a vicious sound. A streak of blood rose up just under the skin. Some bled through and ran down his back.

"You can go to hell!"

Pap brought the Saint Maker across his legs this time. The man made short quick breathy sounds from the pain of the whip across his tender legs. The stinging leather tore open the flesh on the man's thighs. Pap brought it one more time across his legs. The cowboy tried to hold it, but he yelled out and began to cry. Pap brought it back again.

"Mister, you're going to hang when I'm through here. You can get it over with and hang quick or you can prolong the agony. It's about the last thing you get to decide for yourself. I know you work for Zell Davis. You could have punched cows, but you chose to punch holes in innocent men." He brought the whip across his back and then his legs. He screamed out.

"Where's my cattle?"

"I don't know! I had nothing... to do with it!" He was trying to talk at the same time he was sobbing. Blood was dripping from razor like gashes in the man's legs, back and arms.

"Have it your way!" Pap brought the Saint Maker full length behind him and prepared to bring it hard across his legs.

"I don't know! I don't know where your damn cows are!"

The whip wrapped around the legs of the crying man again. Pap brought the whip across his back two more times as the man sobbed with every breath.

"You are a murdering lying thief! You're going to talk, or you'll die right where you are!"

Pap started to bring the whip across him again when Chalk caught hold of it. The Dockin men were wide eyed stunned, and at the same time somewhat relieved. They had never seen their boss whip a man like that.

"Pap, he's had enough!" Chalk's voice was full of determined conviction.

"What? Who do you think you..." Pap realized it was Chalk. He then looked around the corral at all the faces staring at him.

Slowly he coiled the whip up. "You're right. He's had enough. Let him hang there." His eyes darted from man to man. "Speck, feed and water him. Hang him in the mornin' but give him a chance to talk."

Pap walked to the man he had been whipping. "Mister, by mornin' that back of yours is going to be one sore mess. You can save yourself a lot of pain if you come with the truth. I want my cattle, and your confession to the crime of murder. I'd like to hang a whole man, but I'll hang what's left if you don't cough up the whereabouts of my cattle."

"Boss man, Pap." The man was breathing quick hard breaths, but he could talk.

"Did you say something?"

"Yeah... come closer."

Pap bent down close to him so he could hear what he was about to say.

"Boss man, you go to hell on a black horse!" Then he spat in his face.

Pap took his bandana and wiped his face off while looking at the man tied to the post. "Well, I'll give you this, you're a tough one... and you're loyal. But come mornin' you'll be one hung loyal sonofabitch." He threw the whip down, turned to Speck and looked at him for a long moment. "Have some of the boys put some loose pants on him... leave him tied." He glanced at Chalk, turned and walked to the house.

Speck walked over to Chalk. "Son, you done a wrong thing. I know it's harsh, but law out here can be harsh at times. It is what it is. You make it and live by it. You die by it. Law has to be delivered and maintained. Maybe it seems mean and cruel, but it's what we got, and we know the consequences when we break the law. This man here shot and killed a young cowboy. Even if he didn't pull the trigger, he was with the man who did. He also rides with the bunch that's stealing Dockin cattle. He's a murdering criminal, Chalk. It may seem a little cruel and mean to you, but the man is bad. Now we'll hang him sure in the morning. We'll know where those cattle are, too. This is the West, son. This is our way. If you can't handle it, pack up and go back to Kansas City. Out here you either get tough or you die. Only the strong survive."

That was the moment Speck got through to Chalk. He understood the strong survive and the weak die. That was the way of it in Kansas City. "I understand what you're saying but if he had kept whipping him, he would have died before he could tell us anything."

"That may be, but Pap is mighty good at knowing how much a man can take. He's an old hand at doling out punishment. He's the best at getting information out of a man. Pap has been his own law ever since the Dockin Ranch was recorded as doing business in the United States. Until now, nothing or anyone has interfered with that. If you weren't who you were, you would be hanging on that snubbing post, or on a horse leaving the Dockin spread." Speck stopped and looked at Chalk for a long second. "For what it's worth, Pap was extra hard on the man for some reason, harder than I ever seen him be. You stepping in, well, maybe it was supposed to be. Still though, wasn't your put in." Speck patted him on the shoulder and then walked towards the house.

Chapter 11

Ben Watts was awake when Zell and the Sliding D boys rode back into the ranch. For some reason, he hadn't taken Ted and Huey with him this time. Ben noticed them when he got up to get a drink earlier in the day. He saw them both outside messing with a young colt.

He watched as the Checkered Kid came across the barnyard to the bunkhouse. "Well, what happened?"

The Kid looked around the room making sure they were alone and then spoke. "We made off with three hundred head of the Dockin cows. I could have shot Dockin, but that isn't what Zell wants. Myself, I'd shoot the big feeling bastard and call it a day."

"Kid, I'm wondering what this feud is all about. It sure ain't about grazing rights. It's not about boundary lines. It's not about water rights. What do you reckon?"

The Kid took his gun out and began to practice twirling it. Ben sometimes marveled at how good he was at doing that. "I tell ya what I think, Ben. I think it goes back to when they were partners in some cattle dealings. Some of the things Zell said to me makes me think it goes farther back than either one of these ranches. The conversation between Dockin and Zell today makes me think it, too. I can tell you this much... it goes back to when they were kids."

"Oh?"

"Yeah, Pap Dockin and Zell Davis had words, and Zell said as much."

"Then it's something personal, it ain't cattle or range."

"Yeah, it's personal alright." The kid laughed.

"What are you laughing about?"

"Ole Zell. I got to hand it to him... he's a slippery one. Dockin rode up on us, but we had the cattle hid. Dockin accused Zell of stealing his cows, but old Zell, he was calm and collected... for the most part anyway." The Kid stopped twirling his gun and holstered it. "Ben, I'll tell you something. I'm calling Pap Dockin to a showdown. Sooner or later this job will call for it anyway."

"You're what?"

"You heard me."

"Why?"

"Hell, he took Quint Hobbs. I have to take him. I couldn't ride out of this country not knowing if he was faster than me." He grinned as he cut his eyes around at Ben. "There's another reason I don't like him. Rides around like he owns the whole damn country. He's big feeling and I don't like it."

"Kid, there are more famous gunnies than Pap Dockin to build a reputation on. And I think you're miss figuring Pap Dockin. His cattle were missing, and he went looking for them. I would bet he was a little upset about them being stolen. That's not feeling big, Kid. That's taking care of business."

"Well, he acted mighty big that morning he killed Quint."

"I don't guess you ever have."

The Kid shot a look over at Ben full of irritation. "Well, he's going to have to face me, that's all. He took Quint Hobbs and Quint was no one to shine your boots for you. He might shoot a man in the back, but he was fast and good when he had to be. That over the hill ranch owner Pap Dockin took him easy." A mischievous smile appeared on the Kid's face. "You know how it is, Ben... I just got to know."

Ben knew once the Kid got something in his head, hell nor high water could stop him from going through with it. He wished he could talk him out of the notion of trying Pap, but he knew better. He might as well leave it. "Kid, how about a game of checkers? I'm bored to death."

"Set 'em up."

When Chalk walked into the Dockin house, Pap was sitting in a big chair staring at the fireplace. Sarah and Vivian were preparing the table, but they were very much aware that there was trouble between the two men in the house. Sarah smiled at him for reassurance.

Chalk was disturbed about offending Pap, but he just couldn't watch the man suffer any longer. Another minute or two of that, and the man would have died. "I'd like to... well, I'm really sorry if I stepped over the line today."

Pap's eyes darted back and forth from Chalk to the floor. "Look, you put me in a hard place. I don't want to get off on the wrong foot with you. I mean, I've waited a long time to have my, you, or someone like you in my life."

Chalk frowned at the comment. "What exactly does, 'someone like me', mean?"

"Speak a little louder."

"Someone like me? What are you getting at?"

"Take your boots off."

"Sir?"

Pap looked up at him. "Take your boots off."

He looked around the room at Sarah. "I don't know."

Pap was impatient. "Do it." He stared at Chalk with a determined frown.

Chalk sat down and pulled his boots off slowly. He cut his eyes at Pap sitting in his chair looking at the fireplace. He wasn't looking at a fire. There wasn't one.

"Take your socks off."

"I don't know what you're trying to do here."

"Say again?"

"This is silly."

"Take the socks off." Pap sat stern faced.

Chalk reluctantly pulled his socks off and then sat back in his chair. "Okay, now what, my pants?"

"No... the socks will do." Pap stood up, took three steps over to Chalk and grabbed him by the ankle. He pulled his leg all the way up to his face. Chalk was almost on his back in the chair. Pap took his other hand and spread Chalks' toes apart. He began to smile, and then he started laughing. "I knew it! I knew it! I just figured if you inherited my big hands I got from my dad, you might have inherited my web feet I got from my mother!"

Pap dropped Chalk's foot with a thud. He then shouted for the women to come into the room. Sarah was already standing in the entrance, watching Pap with concern and great curiosity. "Chalk is a Dockin! He's a by God sure enough Dockin!"

Chalk was somewhat bewildered. "I didn't think there was any doubt to start with, Pap."

Vivian came running out of the kitchen.

"Viv, he's a Dockin! Chalk is a Dockin!"

"I knew that. Why are you so excited, or should I ask why you questioned it?"

"Say again?"

"You questioned it?"

Pap suddenly got a sheepish look on his face.

"You hadn't questioned it, but suddenly you are."

"Well, things got a little crossways with me today. It ain't nothin' I want to talk about." He was referring to the comment Zell made about not knowing for sure the boy was his.

Chalk shook his head in disbelief. "Once again I find myself the subject of conversation but am left out of the whole thing." He looked down to his bare feet. "Well, except for being asked to take my boots and socks off." Chalk was confused and was slowly starting to feel oddly uncomfortable. Something was amiss, something wasn't right. "I thought you and I knew we were father and son at camp last night."

"Yeah, well, we did. It don't matter, you're my son. You have the same web feet I have. You have my hands, my feet, and my good looks."

Vivian laughed. "Chalk is good looking, but he got some of his good looks from his mother." She smiled at Chalk. "Web feet?"

Pap looked at Vivian. "Say again? I didn't get all that."

"I said you should have known he was your son, because he was so good looking. No one could deny him being yours. You're the best-looking man in the Texas Panhandle." She laughed again.

Chalk wasn't laughing. "Pap!" Chalk's voice was loud. The room went silent. "I get it now! You started having doubts about me! I don't know why, but you did. You weren't heated up over that cowboy I caught. You were upset because you thought maybe I wasn't yours. That cowboy took an unmerciful whipping because you somehow began to doubt me yours. What started those thoughts? What happened after I left you this morning? Another thing, if you had doubts then, who the hell did you think I was? I have learned enough about you to know you don't have thoughts unless something happened to provoke them. What did you think, my mom was a whore? Did someone say something to that affect? Maybe Fayet Billings, the new puncher? I mean, he's the only new man. Your other riders are old hands. You would have already heard talk from them if there was any. My mom was a good woman."

Pap turned red in the face. "No, it wasn't nothin' like that son. Your mom was a Southern Belle of a lady far as I was concerned. Look, all that matters is we're father and son and we're together."

"That may be, but I feel like you need to mouth me, check my teeth, make sure I fit the age I should be." Chalk never smiled as he looked away from Pap.

"No need to get all sour."

"Is that right? What if I had doubted you being my father? I haven't questioned it, but I could have. Take off your shirt, take off your pants, take off, take off... see what I mean?"

"I'm sorry, you got a right to be sore. I let my good sense go and listened..." He caught himself and stopped talking. He busied getting a chew, and then walked over by the fireplace to spit. "It doesn't matter now, me and you will whip the world. We're family."

"Why is it okay now and it wasn't a minute ago?"

"Cause damn it, I said it was!" There was silence for a long eternal moment as they stared at each other. Slowly a faint smile appeared on Pap's face, and then one appeared on Chalk's. Then almost at the same time they grinned, and from there they broke into loud laughter. They hugged one another and even got down in the floor wrestling around on it like two kids.

After Pap and Chalk came to terms with each other the women began to prepare the supper table. Pap asked Chalk to walk outside with him for some alone time. They sat down on a swing at the end of the porch which faced the corral where the cowboy was tied.

"In the mornin' that cowboy out there will hang, he has to. If we let a man live that done what he did, law would cease to exist out here on the High Plains. The Texas Panhandle is a lonely pretty land, but it's hard too. I know city livin' ain't nothin' like this wild country. It's a tough place with tough ways."

Chalk eyed Pap before speaking. "Pap, we had our city ways, too. I saw a man get two fingers cut off each hand before he coughed up information for me and my boys."

"Say again? I didn't catch it."

"I've seen men lose fingers until they talked. Where I'm from we had ways, too."

Pap was surprised. "You mean you were in a gang?"

"No. I had a gang. I was considered one of the best at getting information out of someone. Pap, my mom wanted me out of the city because I was becoming known by the law and other gangs as the man to go to for whatever you needed. I had money being a gang leader, but I used it all paying doctors and medicine bills for mom. I may not know much about being a cowboy yet, but I do know about tough."

"I see." Pap suddenly had a new view of his long-lost son. He was tough, smart and had sand. "What about Sarah? Was she involved in that world?"

"No. Sarah was working in a hospital where Mom was at. That's where I met her. She was another reason I wanted to get out of Kansas City. My way of life would have put her in danger. I wouldn't have that if I could help it." Chalk paused for a second. "I know you brought me out here to straighten me out on the way things work around here. You're right in doing that. I overstepped a little. This is your land and I hope will be mine, too. I also know I need to earn my way and earn my status, my place. Fact is, I don't want anything given to me."

Chalk stopped, took a breath and pointed towards the corral. "That cowboy out there, he wasn't going to give you anything today. By the time he was ready, he would have been unconscious. They say you can make a man talk and I have no doubt... but he's not one of them."

"You're right." Pap looked out at the man hanging on the snubbing post. "I wronged him. I was upset about somethin' else and took it out on him. That was wrong. It won't keep him from hangin', but I was wrong to come at him so hard. I guess I owe you for stoppin' me, but in front of my men... that was tough to accept. Even if I was wrong, I'd a killed anyone else for steppin' in like that. It's somethin' not done."

"I understand, but if you were to do it again, I'd step in again. I wouldn't want to, but I would." Chalk stared into the eyes of his father. Those eyes were staring back. He saw both love and anger in them.

"You got Dockin blood alright. I may have to rethink how I do things around here. They'll be Dockin law but me and you got to admin... admin..."

"Administer."

"Yeah, we got to administer the punishment and agree on it. There ain't no ranch that can survive or prosper when the bosses can't get along."

Sarah came to the door. "Time to wash up."

Chalk was smiling. He had just been told he was to be a boss on the Dockin spread. He had finally found his father and was about to become a father himself. Life was grand.

Chapter 12

At near four in the morning, Chalk got dressed and walked out to the cowboy snubbed to the post. "Would you like some water?"

"Yeah... sure."

There was a canteen hanging on the corral fence. He uncorked it and gave him a drink.

"Good, that was good. Thanks."

"Welcome. What's your name?"

"Tom Willis."

"Well, Tom, what you say we parlay a little."

"Yeah, sure. I ain't had anyone to talk to all night."

"Look, you're going to hang sometime after daylight. That's just the way of it. It's the law. Your partner admitted to killing Johnny and wounding Pooh. I don't know if you done any shooting, but you were in on it. Either way you're going to hang. So... since you know that, why not do something in your life that the Man Upstairs can look favorably on. Do something that would go in the right column, instead of the wrong. One good deed can wipe away a lot of bad ones. When I leave, maybe think about asking for some forgiveness. It might make dying mean something." He could see Tom was listening. "Now here's what I need. I want to know where those cattle are hidden. I also want to know who it was took them." Chalk sat silent.

Tom finally looked up at him. "Can I have another drink?"

"Sure."

Chalk held the canteen for him. He drank it down slow. Once he drank his fill he began. "The cattle are one-mile due northeast of your place. Ride to the backside of your patch. When you hit the valley floor head north until you get to the mouth of the canyon the cattle are in. There's a big rock at the entrance. There's a bunch of bones lying beside the rock. A cow died there a couple years back. As for who took the cattle, the Comanches did that."

"Yes, but they handed them off to someone."

"Look, I've given you the cattle. You catch your own thieves."

"I guess that's fair enough." He got up to leave, when Tom stopped him.

"Mister."

"Yeah."

"Good luck."

"Thanks." Chalk smiled at the man snubbed to the post. As he walked away Tom raised his voice. "Wish me luck!"

"You don't need luck, Tom. You need God. Since you aren't going anywhere, and you've got a little time. Maybe introduce yourself to Him. He'll know what to do for you."

"Yeah, reckon so." He stared at the ground with his head hung in shame.

At six in the morning Pap walked out to give the prisoner a drink of water. "Son... wake up. I'm sure you could use a drink. I need to make a thing right with you. I was too hard yesterday. I took what was eatin' at me, out on you. For that I'm sorry." Pap retrieved the canteen and uncorked it. "Now... that don't change anything, you're still going to hang, but I won't be tryin' to get you to talk."

He paused and looked at the prisoner. "Son." He leaned down closer. There was a pool of blood around his feet. He caught hold of his hair and pulled his head up. His throat had been sliced from ear to ear. He looked around the corral but didn't see anyone about. It was evident someone didn't want the cowboy talking. He started back to the house when he met Speck coming across the yard.

"Morning, Pap. I see you beat me to him. I was going to water the prisoner myself. I hate for a man to go thirsty."

"I didn't get the first part, Speck, but that cowboy isn't thirsty, he's dead."

"The hell he is."

"Yeah, someone didn't want him around. His throat has been

cut. They near cut his head off."

"Poor devil."

"The devil? The devil didn't cut his throat, a man did."

Speck smiled and said nothing. "You have any idea who killed him?"

"Not right off, but I'm thinkin' on it. Let's put the body in the barn and then go to breakfast. The women folk are gettin' around makin' biscuits and I don't know what all. It's kind of nice havin' women folk around. You do all right as a cook, but."

"You better hope they stay. I'm through cooking. You go to talking down about my cooking." He smiled. He knew Pap said that to change the mood. A man's passing is a sobering thing.

Chalk took Fayet Billings and two of the old hands with him to find the cattle and bring them back to the Dockin Ranch. They left just before daylight. They rode over to his hundred-acre patch and down over the backside. He found where Zell and his men had made camp. He didn't pay any attention to all the cattle tracks. He knew where he was going. They rode quietly for about a mile and stayed to the side of the valley floor with the most shadow. If there was trouble, they could hit the brush quickly and be out of sight.

It was like Tom Willis had told him. The big rock with the cow bones was a little over a mile up the valley floor. It was good daylight when Chalk dismounted. "Boys, I figure they'll have a couple guards posted up this canyon keeping an eye on the cattle. I want two of you to stay here with the horses. Me and Fayet will walk in. If we find anyone, we'll take care of them."

"Chalk, you sure you want me to go?"

"Yeah, I'm sure. Why wouldn't I?"

"Well, these other fellers have been around here a lot longer than me. They know the lay of the land."

"It's a small canyon, Fayet. It's got two sides and they have to come out this way. All we got to do is be quiet and get the drop on them before they do us."

"Yeah, that's what I'm worried about."

"You worry too much." Chalk took off. Fayet had no choice but to follow.

Pap, Speck and Pooh were sitting at the breakfast table waiting for everyone to sit down. When they did, one member was missing. "Where's Chalk? Tell him he's holdin' up a hunger train in here." Pap laughed as he looked at the two women who didn't laugh with him. "You girls cranky of the mornin's are you?" He received a silent smile from both of them. "What's goin' on?"

Pooh spoke up. "Pap, Chalk took three of the men and rode out this morning."

"He did, did he? Where was he goin' to?"

"He said he was going after your cows."

Pap had a grim look on his face that slowly turned pale looking. He wondered if it was Chalk who cut the cowboy's throat. His mind was racing. He thought he had to be the one. How else would he know where the cattle were? He said he was good at making men talk. He even had his own gang. Maybe he couldn't lose his dark ways. Pap was worried. This was pure murder. Cold blooded as it could get. Pap questioned it all. He wondered if Chalk was trying to prove he was worthy of the Dockin name and ranch. He didn't know what to do for the first time in his life. He couldn't just let it go, it was murder, but this was his son, his boy. Pap swallowed hard. He knew what had to be done if it turned out Chalk was guilty.

"Pap, there's thought to be given here." Speck could read him like an open book. He knew what he was thinking, what he had to be thinking. The thought had crossed his mind, too. That maybe Chalk was the one who killed the prisoner.

"I'm given thought already, Speck. Pass the biscuits please."

"Franklin, Chalk is just trying to please you, that's all. If he can find your cows, I think he will feel he has proved himself to you in some way."

Sarah, Vivian and Pooh were not aware of the early morning incident regarding the dead man. Pap and Speck had seen fit to leave it that way for the moment.

"He may have gone a little too far."

Vivian didn't understand. "It won't hurt for him to try and find your cattle... will it?"

"No." Pap got busy with his breakfast plate but was only half eating.

Vivian and Pooh kept looking at him and Speck. She was wise enough to know something was wrong and Pooh also knew there was more to the story than Chalk riding out at four in the morning. Sarah was so innocent she suspected nothing.

Chalk was right. Two guards, one was on each side of the canyon. "Fayet, you move up higher on the side of the hill. If one of these ole boys gets away, shoot him before he gets out of the mouth of the canyon. He'll have to come down this trail before he gets to the mouth of it. You'll be above him here, should be an easy shot."

"I'll be ready."

Chalk noticed he was fidgety. "I know waiting on something to happen can make a man nervous, sit tight and take a deep breath every now and then." He turned and headed off through the brush. He kept the trees between him and the two guards, though it was hard to do. He hoped the guards were tired and sleeping.

It took him thirty minutes to get within forty feet of the first guard. He was about to take another step when a bullet cut a limb over his head. The guard across the hollow had spotted him. The other man dove behind a rock.

Chalk fell behind a small rock and tried to hide behind an oak tree from the one across the way. They had positioned themselves where they could shoot any intruders from both sides of the canyon. They could watch each-others back. Another bullet knocked a piece of bark off the burr oak he was lying beside. He knew he had to move and quick. He jumped straight down the hill. That put him dead even on the side of the hill with the one guard. He fell in behind a rock that concealed him from both shooters and decided to wait them out. He wanted to give Fayet time to see what was going on and come a running.

Chalk waited behind the boulder for what seemed like forever. He listened and heard nothing. He knew he was within thirty to forty feet of the shooter on his side of the canyon wall. One of them would make a move soon. He was beginning to wonder where Fayet was. Suddenly a noise, it was the guard. Chalk smiled. He figured the shooter thought his partner had put a bullet in him. The cowboy took two more steps when Chalk rose up and fired. The bullet knocked the Sliding D cowboy off his feet, and he rolled all the way to the valley floor, about sixty to seventy feet below.

The other cowboy across the hollow fired five times. The bullets hit the boulder Chalk was behind but that was all. Now he only had one to contend with unless others showed up. He rose up and shot three times. One of the bullets must have gotten close. The cowboy broke and ran across to his horse. As he mounted, Chalk aimed and fired. He was on the mark. The cowboy doubled over but kept riding. He was heading for the entrance to the hollow. Chalk listened. There was gunfire but too much. Chalk knew Fayet was missing. He knew the cowboy had to come right by Fayet but he was mighty nervous, and that doesn't spell good shooting. There was silence, then two more rifles farther down the hollow opened up. Chalk knew Fayet had failed. He hoped the other two were better shots than him.

When the three Dockin riders rode up, Fayet wouldn't raise his eyes to look at Chalk. "I'm sorry. Hell, I couldn't hit anything. I shot all around that running cowboy. He was slumped in the saddle and I was all shook up I guess."

"It's your first time to shoot at a man I reckon. What about you two?"

"He's rode his last horse. We both put lead in him. He hit the ground like a sack of feed."

Chalk nodded approval. "Let's get these cattle back to the ranch. We'll take 'em across my place and straight to the Dockin Ranch. Better put on your slickers, a rain is coming in."

One of the cowboys looked back towards the west. "Yeah, may be some wind with it."

Chalk turned to the boys riding with him. "Here I am shooting it out with rustlers and don't even know the names of the men helping me. You boys got names?"

"Bailey Harris. This here is Art Teague." Art was tall and slender and going bald. Bailey was average height with black curly hair.

"Good to ride with you, Art, Bailey."

They both nodded the same.

Pap was supposed to have taken Vivian around to show her the place the day before but got back too late. So, he and Vivian planned a picnic and since there wasn't a hanging to interrupt the event, they left at mid-morning. He wanted to get the murder of the cowboy off his mind. It was eating at him that Chalk might be the one who killed him.

Speck hitched the buggy up and had it waiting for them. Pap helped Vivian up on the buggy seat, and then the two of them drove around looking at the ranch until just before noon. They stopped alongside a small creek. A spring coming out of the bank was feeding the stream.

Vivian took her shoes off, raised her dress and waded out into the cool water. "Take your boots off and join me!" She laughed at Pap standing on the bank.

He looked around to see if he could see anyone on the horizon riding around. When he didn't, he pulled his boots off and rolled up his pants. He gently stuck one toe in and then the foot. Vivian walked over to him. "Let me help you, it's not that hard." He reached out his hand. She took hold of it and gave him a big tug. His foot slipped out from under him and down he went, taking Vivian with him. She was laughing and splashing him at the same time, and he was doing the same to her. When the excitement stopped, Pap had her in his arms. They were both wet from head to toe. He kissed her long and passionately. The water being only a few inches dee, he laid her back over into the water and kissed her. "Vivian, I've fallen in love with you. I knew I was feelin' things at the Prairie Grass Cafe. I didn't want to think it, but I knew. I hope you don't take this the wrong way, but you being Paula's half-sister somehow makes it easier to accept. Can you understand that?"

Vivian was searching his eyes. "I understand. I didn't come here to fall in love, Franklin, but I have. I came here to make sure you and Chalk found each other. Paula made me promise to do that for her. If you warmed up to each other and became father and son, so much the better. Paula left me a letter towards the end and asked me to come here, once Chalk came to claim and settle his land. You were an unexpected surprise. Falling in love was the last thing I expected to happen to me."

"I'm glad you came." They turned over on their sides and let the water run parallel through them.

"I am, too."

"One thing I'm curious about. Did Paula ever talk about how she felt about it all? She was so damn protective and private with everything. You being her sister, did she ever confide in you?"

"Paula was distraught over her situation... being pregnant." She paused and looked into Pap's eyes. "Not knowing for sure whose child she was carrying, it caused her to have mental anguish. She was ashamed. The truth is, I don't think she even wanted to be around me, because I knew what happened to her... and I had done well. She had a child out of wedlock and was dirt poor. Oh, she loved Chalk with all her heart, but she couldn't face anyone who might know the story of it all. We visited, but she would not let me get close. She was quiet mostly. I do know she loved me. She loved her little boy... and Franklin, she loved you. She could talk to me through a letter easier than in person. She wrote me when Chalk turned three years old. She knew and was convinced he belonged to you. She said he had your attributes." Vivian smiled. "The same ones you discovered. When her health was failing, I came by and looked in on her once. Chalk wasn't there. Until we met here in Mason City, he'd never seen me. Paula was the strangest person. She didn't talk much and didn't tell her son anything about me. I don't know why, unless it was, she felt she failed at life and I hadn't. Yet... at the same time, when she could go no further... she reached out for me to see that the two men in her life found one another."

"I'm glad she had you."

"Tell you a secret."

"Ok."

"I've always wondered what you were like because of the way Paula was turned. I knew you had to be a special man with a strong personality of some kind. I never dreamed those virtues would rope me in, too."

Pap stared at her for a moment. "I'm glad you came here."

"Me too."

"Vivian, I need to tell you something. I'm afraid something bad may have happened, and if it did, we have a big problem. Chalk may have my physical traits, but he may not think like me. I believe he has a problem." He looked at Vivian and then began. "I think he killed that poor cowboy last night. The one we had tied up in the corral."

"Franklin! You surely can't think that? If you think Chalk capable of something like that, then you have a long way to go to know and understand your son. I know enough about him through the few letters Paula wrote to know he's not a murderer. He's had to be tough, but murder? I scoff at the idea. After meeting him, I know he is not capable of murder. That's insane."

He looked at her for several seconds while they sat in the water. "Vivian, I want to believe that, but last night Chalk told me how him and his gang used to pull information out of a man. It was mighty damn tough."

"You're mighty tough, too, aren't you?"

"Say again?" Though they were just a few inches apart, the running water interfered with his hearing when she spoke softly.

"Tough, aren't you tough?"

"Yes, but." He looked down the stream and then back to her. "Chalk went after my cattle before daylight this morning. He took three men with him. How did he know where to go? He had to get that information somewhere, and the only place he could have gotten it was from that cowboy."

Vivian stared at him as if she could not believe he had gone there. She was becoming angry. "Pap Dockin." She dispensed with calling him Franklin. "If you don't start having some faith in that young man, your chances of having a lasting relationship won't last as long as cotton balls in a tornado! You'll lose him before you get him. Last night you doubted him even being your son. You beat everything! I think I know why you doubted, and I think I know where that doubt came from. Oh, what faith you have. How easily you can doubt. You had the poor child take his clothes off, so you could be sure your blood ran through his veins. Well, Mister Dockin, why don't you try to have a little faith in your blood? Is it easier to believe an enemy over your own son?"

Pap might be hard of hearing, but he heard every word of that loud and clear. His face was poker jaw stern, then slowly a smile appeared. He pulled her close and kissed her long and hard. "You are good medicine for me, Vivian."

"As long as you take your medicine, you'll be ok."

"Yes dear." The two of them laughed, then waded to the creek bank and retrieved the picnic basket. Pap looked back towards the ranch. "Looks like they're goin' to get a rain back at the house, and that's good. I have corn and hay fields needing the rain." He carried the basket over to a big tall sweet gum tree and sat down with her. She had packed the basket, but he had a surprise for her. He slipped a bottle of wine in while she wasn't looking. Everything was perfect, everything but Chalk. That remained to be seen.

Chapter 13

The rain that was moving in on Chalk and his men became a thunderstorm with small hail in it. The wind was blowing and gusting high from time to time. It was raining so hard Chalk could barely see the cattle, and they refused to move. Bailey rode over to where Chalk could hear him above the rain. “Chalk, these cattle aren’t going to move in this storm. They’re bunching up on us. I say we push ‘em over to that grove of trees yonder and wait this thing out!”

“Okay!”

“I’ll get that lead cow started. They’ll follow her. I don’t want ‘em breaking out here and there hunting cover. We’d never get them all back!”

The lead cow was breaking for some smaller trees to the right when Bailey headed her off. He then pushed her forward. Chalk held back catching anything that tried to peel off. He watched Bailey work the cow. It was something to watch a good cow horse in action. He was astonished that the horse could stand up on the wet grass. He was slipping, but the cow wasn’t fighting it too hard either. She was looking for a place to get away from the horse and blowing rain. He watched as the herd made for the stand of trees.

Bailey motioned for Chalk to ride over in his direction. The wind was getting stronger. “Boss, there’s a bluff hangs out over that bank yonder way, best I remember! We could get a little shelter and watch the cattle from there at the same time!”

“Lead the way! We’ll follow!” The four cowboys rode in a fast lope to the spot he was talking about. They bailed off their horses and got in under the ledge. They had to sit down and bend their heads a little to fit, but it was dry. The horses faced them while each man held his reins.

“Bailey, I’m sure glad you knew about this place.”

“I grew up here. I know every rock and cave in this country. Ole Art, he’s from out Arkansas way, so he’s not as familiar with the land as I am. He don't know a whole lot anyway." Bailey got a jovial jab in at his best friend.

Art chuckled at him. "The less I know, the less I have to do, which makes me smarter than you."

Chalk was liking the two cowboys. "Bailey, you called me Boss a minute ago. I'm not working for the Dockin spread... at least not yet."

Bailey laughed. "You are on this drive."

Chalk smiled. "Guess you're right." He looked at Fayet who was sitting to his left. Bailey and Art were sitting to his right. "How did you come by the name Fayet?"

"My mother's name was Faye."

"I see. I don't guess you ever said where you were from. I'd guess, Texas."

"I was born in Texas but left home at sixteen, drifted up into Kansas... Dodge City. Broke a few horses here and there. After a couple years, got a job working cattle. Been doing that ever since."

"I was born there. Mom left Dodge City when I was a youngster."

Bailey jumped in the conversation. "What outfit?"

"What?" Fayet cut his eyes to Bailey. "Oh yeah... the Double S. I worked the Double S."

That got Art Teague's attention. "Who owns that outfit? I've worked all over Kansas, and I've not heard of the Double S." Art hung his head down even further, looking around Bailey, waiting for an answer from Fayet.

"It's in northwest Kansas, south of Holster."

"I thought you said you came from Dodge City?"

"I... I did. But I worked a spread up in Holster once. I didn't get along with the foreman, so I drifted back down to Dodge."

"I see. I sure thought I knew all the outfits in Western Kansas, must have missed one. I worked a ranch or two down around Hays. Sure thought I knew all the spreads. Oh well."

"Yeah, guess you missed one."

Chalk looked over at Art. "I thought you were from Arkansas?"

"I am. I done some drifting too. Got off down into Texas when I was seventeen, caught a drive to Sedalia, Missouri. Fell in with a couple ole boys working the Double Eight out in Kansas. I ended up working for the same outfit. Before I came back, I worked several ranches. I ran onto ole Bailey on one of my trips back home in Arkansas. We kind of met by circumstance."

Bailey laughed. "Yeah, Chalk, we met in jail."

Art had a proud grin on his face. "You know how cowboys are. We both got a little drunk. After the law turned us loose the next morning, we had breakfast together and I just tagged along with him. I guess that's the way I work. I run onto someone I like, I follow 'em to where they work and get hired on." They all laughed at Art's matter- of - fact attitude about it.

Art looked over at Fayet again. "I sure would have thought I would know the Double S. Maybe I did and forgot it. I'm getting older."

"Yeah, you're all of thirty." Chalk smiled and winked at him.

"Twenty-eight to be exact."

Chalk smiled as he checked the storm. "Boys, the rain is letting up. What do you say... ready to move some cattle?"

"You're the boss." Bailey grinned and stepped to his horse.

The wind had died down and the rain was nothing more than a heavy drizzle.

Chalk and his three drovers brought the cattle into the Dockin place before Pap and Vivian got back from their picnic. Chalk changed out of his wet clothes, had something to eat and was telling everyone about his exciting cattle driving adventure. Speck, Ellison and Sarah sat at the table listening to him tell about the storm and how they got the cattle back. He was halfway through his story when Pap walked in with Vivian.

"I see my lost cattle found their way home." He smiled as he looked at the three of them.

"Yeah, me and three of the boys found them and brought them in."

"I'm not used to my guests taking off with my help chasing after stolen cattle."

"Well, I did think about waiting, but I figured you could rest while I tried to find them. Besides you had other guests." He looked at Vivian and then at Ellison. Then he looked back at Pap. "I didn't think the storm reached south of the ranch, but you and Vivian are soaked as bad as me and the boys."

Pap blushed, and Vivian's eyes went straight to the floor. "I must go get cleaned up." She retreated to her room in a rather big hurry. Pap suddenly turned and headed toward his bedroom. He stopped. "Chalk, soon as I get on some dry clothes, I would like a word with you in private."

Chalk felt like a first grader being asked to stay after school for punishment. He looked at Sarah with concern in his eyes. The texture of Pap's voice was what caused him to feel something was wrong.

Speck was an old hand at knowing when to be hard to find. He motioned to Ellison to follow him outside.

Pap came out of his room with a fresh shirt and pants on. He poured himself a shot of whiskey and drank it down. He then addressed Chalk. "I'd like to speak to you in private." He looked at Sarah.

She started to leave but Chalk spoke up. "Hold on here. You got anything to say to me it can be said in front of her."

"The way of it is better said among men."

"It's alright, honey." Sarah gave Chalk a smile of assurance. "I'll go see if I can help Vivian with something."

Chalk didn't like it, but he let her go. "Alright Pap, you have what you wanted, we're alone, what's on your mind?"

"I want to know how you knew where the cattle were."

"That's it? That's easy. The prisoner you hung told me."

"Didn't hang him. I don't hang dead men."

"Dead men? What's that mean?"

"It means he was too dead to hang this morning."

Chalk stood staring at Pap. "Well, he was alright when I seen him. What happened to him?"

"Someone cut his throat."

"Who?"

The two of them stood in the middle of the room staring at one another.

"I was hoping you could tell me."

"No, I haven't any idea." Chalk paused, for he suddenly understood the question. "Wait a minute, you're not thinking I killed him?"

"The thought crossed my mind. After thinking it over, I didn't figure it that way."

"Well good, because I didn't touch the man. I found out about the cattle by reasoning with him. He would only give me the location of the cattle. He wouldn't give away Zell Davis as the one who rustled them. Even though we found them on the Sliding D, it doesn't prove he stole them. Anyone could have taken the cattle and drove them on Zell's ranch, making it look like him." Chalk walked over to a softly padded chair. "Pap, there's no doubt he done it, but we don't have real proof, not yet."

"That's true. Chalk, what time did you talk to the prisoner this morning?"

"Around four."

"I saw him a couple hours after that. Someone cut his throat between four and six." Pap paused in thought. "Someone working for us killed the man. They didn't want him talking. That means we have a Sliding D man on our ranch. Zell Davis has a man working for me."

"Who?"

"I don't know, but we'll find out sooner or later."

"You got any suspects?"

Pap sat silent for a minute or two. "I might. Speck hired two new cowboys yesterday. One of them was the one killed at the camp last night. Do you think the other one had time to kill the cowboy we had prisoner, before you left?"

"Well... maybe... I don't know. He did act peculiar when asked about where he was from, and his answer didn't suit Art. One other thing... he shot and missed one of Zell's men watching our cattle. He was nearly point blank from him."

"Fetch Art for me, I'd like to talk to him."

"Sure, I'll be right back." Chalk left the house and brought Art back within a few minutes. Pap met them on the front porch with Speck and Ellison present.

"Art."

"Yeah Pap?"

"This Fayet Billings feller... do you like him?"

"No." Art's demeanor changed.

"Why not?"

"He's a liar."

"He is?"

"For damn shore he is. Lied about working for the Double S in Kansas. I know every outfit in Kansas, and there's no ranch running a Double S brand up there. There's the Double 8, Six Gun Six, the Standing Pine, the Slant 8, the Lazy F and the Circle Y. A man lies about what he's done, and maybe where he's from, makes me wonder what he's hiding."

Pap lit a cigar and offered the men one. They smiled and took him up on it. "I think we need to have us a talk with this Fayet. Lyin' about where he worked don't prove him a Davis man yet... but he's standin' in a loop of suspicion."

Pap and his group of men left the porch and walked down to the bunkhouse. To their surprise Fayet wasn't there.

"Pooh, where's the new man?"

"Oh... he went to town." Pooh looked a little worried.

"He did?"

"I told him he better not, but he said he had a powerful thirst. Said he didn't figure you'd miss him for a couple hours. I told him the boss might not like him leaving without first checking that it's okay." Pooh blushed suddenly. "I did ask him to tell Sitting Dove I was laid up, and that maybe she needed to come look in on me."

"You did? Pooh, is she coming to kiss it?" Pap smiled. Then Speck and the boys grinned at him, too.

"I hope so." Pooh took the teasing in stride.

Pap, Speck, and Chalk saddled up to ride into town. Ellison decided to stay at the ranch. His senses told him to stay clear of the trouble between Fayet and Pap. They rode in silence all the way to town. Pap recognized Fayet's horse tied in front of the Dry Rock Saloon and dismounted. They tied their horses to the hitching rail alongside Fayet's and walked in slowly. They spotted Fayett sitting at a corner table by himself. Pap and Speck sat down across from him while Chalk sat to Fayet's left. They ordered a beer each from the bartender and all the while Pap stared at Fayet. "I don't guess you and I have properly been introduced. I'm Pap Dockin the man you use to work for. You're Fayet Billings from up Kansas way, Dodge City I think it is... worked the Double S."

"Yeah... that's right." He looked at each man worriedly. "Ah, worked for..."

Pap reached and slapped him. "No man leaves the ranch durin' a workin' day unless he sees Speck or me."

Fayet dropped his hand to his gun. "No one has ever slapped me."

"Say what?"

"I said no one has ever slapped me!"

Pap slapped him again. "You're slapped twice now; anyone ever do that?"

"You old." Fayet remembered what Speck said about calling

him an old man, and he was there the morning Pap took Quint Hobbs in a gunfight. "No, no one has ever done that... but maybe I had it coming." Fayet was red with anger and embarrassment.

Chalk was surprised when Pap slapped Fayet, but Speck wasn't surprised at all. He knew his friend and he knew what kind of meeting this was and what it was about. He knew exactly what was coming from his friend and boss, Pap Dockin.

"You stopped working for me the minute you left my ranch without giving notice you were leaving. I slapped you for lyin' to me. I slapped you the second time for mouthin' off after lyin' to me. There is no Double S outfit in Kansas. I figure you to be a Davis man. Whatever I owe you... pick it up tomorrow."

"You got me all wrong."

Like a striking rattle snake, he slapped him again. "You seem to be on the slow side of learning anything new. Telling the truth would have to be new to you. Don't lie to me. I can't abide a babblin' liar."

"I ought to kill you."

"What's holdin' you back? A lack of intestinal courage?"

"I don't have to put up with a half-crazy old man like you. I'm not working for you now."

"No, no you're not, but you do have to humor me a little here. Strikes me you're another one of those gun hands Zell has brought in. If you're not, that would make you a plain and simple murderer. Let's see the knife, the one you used on your own man. The one tied to the snubbing post."

"I don't carry a knife." Fayet became nervous.

Pap leaned over the table to within two inches of his face. "I can't prove you cut that cowboy's throat last night, but horseshit smells and you got it all over you."

Fayett's eyes darted back and forth at each man sitting at the table and then settled on Pap. "You keep what you owe me. Good day, Mister Dockin." Fayet got up quickly and walked to the bar. He ordered a drink just as one of Zell's men walked in. The man walked to the bar and stood beside Fayet.

Pap was sure he was meeting the cowboy to give him information. It would be news to Zell the three hundred head of cattle he bought from the Comanches were back on Dockin land.

The two stood at the bar for a few minutes, and then Fayet turned around where he could face Pap. He had a grin on his face. "Old man." Fayet and the other cowboy stepped away from the bar with their hands out and near to their side irons.

Pap didn't hear him call him, 'old man', but he was facing the bar and saw Fayet and the other gunman step away from it. Their hands were readying for a gunfight. Chalk had just enough time to turn around and see what was happening as Fayet and the other cowboy went for their guns.

Pap already had his gun out and under the table. He blew two holes in Fayet before he cleared leather. Chalk fired twice, but not before the other cowboy fired and hit Speck. Fayet and the Sliding D cowboy lay dead on the floor. Speck was sitting up against the wall, bleeding badly. He had fallen backwards over his chair and Pap was already hovering over him. "You're going to be alright, Speck. You just hang on. Someone go get Doc Zimmer!"

The bartender ran out for the doctor while Chalk got a glimpse of worry on Pap's face. He knew then how much he truly loved his friend, Speck. He might be a hard man and run a tough ranch, but underneath that crust was a man with a good heart, and it was showing.

Speck had gone into shock by the time the doctor arrived. Doctor Zimmer had come immediately and went to work on him. He stopped the bleeding and then wrapped the wound. The bullet hit Speck in the right shoulder and caused substantial blood loss. He would need lots of rest to build back the blood. Pap and Chalk carried him to the doctor's office and put him in bed. The doctor let Pap know he would spend at least three days under his care. That was perfectly alright with Pap. He wanted Speck to get everything he needed to get well.

Chapter 14

Ellison Jones got Bailey Harris to take him to Mason City by buggy and left the Dockin Ranch. He and Vivian talked it over and they felt it was best he went back and tend to business in Kansas City. Vivian also confided in him that she and Pap were very serious about one another. He wished her well and they said goodbye.

After Speck was taken care of, Pap and Chalk left Mason City heading for the ranch, at least that's what Chalk thought they were doing. He rode along beside Pap without a word being spoken. He felt there was something different about him. His demeanor. One thing, he was riding his horse harder than normal. It was then Pap turned on the road that led to the Sliding D Ranch.

"Pap!"

He looked over at Chalk and said nothing.

"Where are we going?"

"Say what?"

"Where we heading?"

"The Sliding D Ranch. If you don't want to go... head home!"

"I'll tag along! This is asking for trouble!" Chalk was talking as loud as he could for two reasons. Pap was hard hearing and riding at a gallop a man must talk louder to be heard.

"Trouble?"

"Yeah, this will stir up more trouble!"

"Zell Davis put a spy on my ranch! And now one of his men has shot Speck!" Pap never looked at Chalk again as they rode towards certain confrontation.

They were within a mile of the ranch when they met Zell and five of his men riding on the road towards them. "Whoa!" Pap brought his horse to a sliding stop and Chalk did the same.

Zell and his men stopped in a cloud of dust in front of them. There was only twenty yards between Zell and Pap as they stared at each other.

Pap finally urged his blue roan in beside Zell and then leaned in towards him. "I come to give you final warning. Two of your boys are bone yard dead back in Mason City. Fayet Billings and the man he was supposed to meet. They put a bullet in Speck. A bullet meant for me. A bullet in me is one thing, but Speck… that's another. You mess with me or my business from this day forward, and I'll come gunnin' for you. I'll kill you sure as hell, no matter what is or has been between us."

Zell never looked at him the whole time he was talking in his ear. He could feel Pap breathing on him. "I didn't shoot Speck, and as for a Fayet Billings, I don't know anyone by that name. I suggest you get out of my face, and off my land before I have my boys blow you out of your saddle."

Pap leaned back. "I see I'm wastin' my time. It's too bad about you, Zell. You have the makins of a good cattleman. The problem is, you have a flaw in you that won't allow it. You have a sickness inside you. Back in Alabama when we were youngsters, I didn't think folks treated you right. I always figured you bein' a bastard child was a poor excuse for why they didn't. It's come to me it wasn't that at all. They could just see what I couldn't. Mom couldn't stand the sight of you, and the old man, he said you'd never be any good. I see he's called it right. You and me have never gotten along and never will. We both just keep festering and warring. It's my fault this thing is still going on. I should have killed you years ago. A man has a limit. I'm close to mine. I hope you're smarter than I think you are. If you're not, you'll wake wide eyed one early gray morning wondering what in hell is happening." He sat staring into the eyes of Zell and then reined his horse around without another word.

Zell and his men sat in the middle of the road watching Pap and Chalk ride away. "I cherish the day I kill that high and mighty sonofabitch!" Zell whirled his horse and road back to his ranch.

Pap didn't ride back to the ranch house like Chalk thought they would. Instead he took him for a ride over the ranch. They rode up to a big oak tree setting all alone on a high hill. They turned their horses around under the shade of the tree and sat looking out. The view was beautiful. They could see for miles. The ranch house and barn could be seen, along with cattle in different meadows on all sides of the ranch house. There were large grain fields and a blue stream twisted and turned, threading through the property. The Dockin Ranch was big and beautiful. Some called it an empire.

Pap looked over at Chalk for his reaction to it all. "I wanted you to see what will be yours one day."

Chalk was stunned by his statement. He hadn't thought of inheriting the Dockin Ranch. When he looked out across it, he was at a loss for words. "It's something to see alright. I don't know what to say. It's really beautiful."

"Something to see? I'm sorry... I don't catch everything."

"I said it's beautiful up here."

Pap smiled. He pointed over to one corner of the place. "That's your little patch that joins mine."

Chalk looked at it and laughed. "Yeah, well that puts it in perspective. That is a little patch when I look at it from up here. It's grown up with brush and weeds some, too."

"Weeds can be dealt with when worked at."

"I like it up here, Pap."

He smiled at the idea Chalk liked his spot on the hill. "I ride up here at least once a week. I think clearer up here. It seems to relax me some, too. It's my favorite place on the ranch. I always thought a house would look nice here." He stuck a chew of tobacco in his jaw. "See those trees over there to the right? That's where I take a dip in the summer. It's taken me twenty years or better to build this place up." He paused and tried to look at Chalk without him knowing he was looking. "Want to know a truth?"

"I reckon."

"I used to come up here and imagine watchin' my son work cattle down there. I could see us goin' for a swim after a day's work. I even had a horse picked out for you." Again, he paused. "That's him you're sittin' on. I raised him myself. His name is Night Train, black as the night and big as a train. Rides as good as any horse I ever sat." Pap spit tobacco juice out to the side of his horse. "Chalk, this place is half yours right now if you want it."

"Pap, I don't know what to say... I mean, you don't know what kind of rancher I'll make."

"I've seen enough out of you to know I'm makin' a safe bet. Son, you're just like your old man... and I made a fair rancher. You'll do alright." He leaned up in his saddle. "Follow me." He started down the hill in a careful walk. They rode over to the water hole that he had pointed out and dismounted. There was a log lying by the bank. Chalk could tell it had been sat on a lot because it shined and was slick. "I've sat here a lot of afternoons and nights. Chalk, you're lookin' at one of the best catfish holes anywhere on this little creek. I caught a twenty pounder one night. You like fishin' I guess?"

"I don't know, never have fished."

"Well, we'll fix that. Me and you will fish this hole in a day or two. Course, you'll never be able to beat me fishin' mind you. I hold the record for most and biggest fish. Ask Speck, he'll tell you. What do you say we take us a dip in that cool water?"

"You mean butt naked?"

Pap hadn't waited for an answer. He was already taking his boots off. Before Chalk could get his off Pap jumped into the blue hole of water in nothing but his birthday suit. Chalk laughed and followed in behind him. They splashed around acting like kids for twenty minutes. Pap was in his glory. He was enjoying his son and talking of the future.

Chapter 15

Ben Watts slipped a shirt on his back for the first time in days. It was comfortable, but the bandages kept it from rubbing the cuts or it wouldn't be. He walked down to the corrals where the Davis ranch hands were. Ted and Huey were messing with a three-year-old bay colt. The other boys were watching from outside the corral. The colt was a salty one, but Huey seemed to have a way with horses, be they gentle or full of spirit. Ben watched for a few minutes in admiration.

Ted had the colt snubbed and Huey was on his back. When he turned him loose the colt went into the air. He took three jumps and came down stiff legged. After the three hard licks, he leveled out to a smooth bucking rhythm. Huey brought him under control and dismounted after circling the pen a couple of times. He got off and blew in the colt's nose and whispered in his ear. Ben smiled. He knew the boy made friends with the youngster. Ben thought about Huey and figured him the only one on the ranch worth killing. He wasn't like his dad and big brother. He'd rather raise good horses and run cattle than chase after hate and revenge. Huey smiled when he saw Ben. "Hello Ben, glad to see you up."

"What did you tell the colt?"

"Awh... I told him we'd see a lot of country together. If he treated me right, I'd do the same by him."

Ted laughed. "I never heard of such foolishness. You think a horse understands all that?"

Huey slipped the halter off the young colt. "I know he does."

Ben didn't like Ted's comment. "I do, too."

"You, Ben?" Huey was surprised and liked it.

"Yeah me, Huey."

Zell and five of his men come riding in at a fast lope from their confrontation with Pap. Zell dismounted and hurried into the house. He was inside for about ten minutes and reappeared with the Checkered Kid. The Kid had gotten in good with Zell. He was even given the extra bedroom. Ben shook his head, the Kid was working this job hard, but not with a gun. He was spending his time with the boss and staying shy around his old partner, Ben. That thought made Ben smile. It also made him feel he better be cautious around the Kid regarding what his thoughts were from now on. The Kid might turn on him, he wasn't the same.

Zell smiled when he saw Ben. "Good to see you up and around. I figured you would be laid up for at least a week."

"Getting stiff laying around, needed some fresh air." He looked from Zell to the Kid. "Hello Kid, how you been? Haven't seen much of you."

"Doing fine. I've been kind of busy." The Kid purposely avoided looking at him.

Ben eyed him closely. He was certain the Kid had his own game going, one in which his partner Ben Watts would not be a part of.

"Ben, I want you and the Kid to come up to the house. Ted, you come along."

"What about me, Pa?"

"I need these colts rode and made into using horses."

Huey smiled. He had offered his services but was hoping he wouldn't be asked to leave the corrals. He knew whatever his father was meeting about, it wasn't horses or cattle. It was something to do with Pap Dockin.

Everyone found a chair in the Davis living room while Zell poured them a drink. "Ben, you think you can ride?"

"I think so. Where to?"

"We're going to light a fire tonight, a big one."

The Kid smiled at Ben and then Zell. "Hey Ben, you remember that range war in Tray County, Texas, me and you were in?"

Zell handed everyone a drink.

"I remember. And if you remember I wasn't too keen on the idea of it."

The Kid paid him little mind. "We burned sodbuster houses, barns and sheds. Made for some big fires. That will be nothing compared to this."

"Spell it out, Kid." Ben didn't know if it was his back hurting that made him irritable or the way the Kid was acting.

"Hay and corn fields, Ben. Dockin fields!" The Kid laughed and took a drink of his whiskey.

Zell poured himself another drink. "We leave at midnight. Dockin lost three hundred head of cattle the other day, which is just the beginning. If he loses his fields, he won't be able to get his cattle through the winter. He would have to buy feed and hay, and have it shipped in. There's not any profit in that. If he keeps losing cattle, he won't be able to make payroll. We'll starve him out, to the point all his cowboys ride off. They may like him, but they have to live same as everyone else."

Ben didn't like it. "I don't know about this, Zell. Why not face the man straight on?"

Zell flew mad and threw his glass in the fireplace. "I told you I don't want him dead! I want him broke and out of business! I want him to suffer first, and then we'll kill him!" He looked over from Ben to the Kid and Ted. "Hell, I may end up with the Dockin place. I'll put Ted running it and make the Kid foreman."

Ted took a shot of his whiskey. "We don't want old man Dockin dead, but Cranfield is another story. I'm killing him on sight!" He smiled with a glint in his eyes.

Zell became angry again. "You don't touch a hair on that boy! You hear! He's not part of this!" Zell realized he had lost his composure and then lowered his voice. "You two got off on the wrong foot, that's all."

Ted was surprised at his father calling him off Cranfield, but he wasn't deterred. "I get a bead on him, he's dead!"

Zell reached over and slapped Ted clean out of his chair. "You'll do as you're told is what you'll do! We overstepped with the Cranfield boy! I think we need to make it up to him. Ted, I want you to cut that buckskin filly out of our using horses and give it to him. He has a hundred-acre patch, he'll need a horse to ride over it. It ain't much land, but still a man needs a good horse."

Ted was bewildered. He picked himself up off the floor while rubbing his jaw. "Why are you looking out for him? You've never done nothing like that before."

Zell hesitated with an answer. "We have no quarrel with him. I think we kind of did him wrong in town the other day, that's all. I want to let him know we can be neighborly."

Ted wasn't buying it, but he would do what he was told.

"Rest up boys, we're going to have a long night."

The only one Zell had told about meeting Pap on the road earlier was the Checkered Kid. Having Pap Dockin in his face in front of his men was too much. He would bring him to his knees now.

Ben stood up. "Well, guess I'll see you boys later."

Zell smiled and patted Ben on the arm. "Yeah, get some rest. It's going to be a tough night."

While Ben was walking back to the bunkhouse his mind was going back to what Zell said. So, he would make the Kid foreman if he got his hands on the Dockin spread. Ben knew he would not work for the Kid if that happened. He smiled as he stepped up on the steps to the bunkhouse, and then looked back towards the main house. Ben had firsthand experience with Pap, and to his way of thinking, Zell had his hands full. Getting his hands on the Dockin Ranch would be one hell of a task. He didn't much like what Zell had in mind for later in the night either. In fact, he was fast concluding he didn't like Zell Davis period. He turned, entered the bunkhouse and shut the door on a sour deal.

Zell, Ted, Ben, and the Checkered Kid rode out at midnight ready to light the sky up. The fuel would be Dockin fields. The Kid rode beside Zell, while Ben and Ted rode behind. Ben was thinking about the two ranch bosses as he rode along in the dark. It was one thing to hire your gun out, burning crops and stealing cattle was another. This wasn't something Pap Dockin would be doing. To Ben it was plain coward's work. He had always been a gun for hire, sneaking around in the dark was more like something outlaws do. After the burning out of the sodbusters the Kid spoke of earlier, he swore he would never be guilty of that cowardly act again. It was rubbing Ben wrong the further he rode.

They had loped along for at least twenty minutes, and then the pace slowed. They walked the horses for another thirty minutes and went back to a lope. Ben didn't know how long they rode like that, but his sore back was feeling every jar of the horse. They finally came to a halt. Zell dismounted and built a fire, then went to his mount and brought short stakes wrapped with rags soaked in kerosene. Everyone had dismounted waiting for orders.

"Boys, we light these things and then we light hay and corn fields. We'll light up Dockin's whole western sky." He laughed. "Ben, I don't figure on using you for lighting the fields. Your back being cut up and all, I don't figure you could ride fast and hard enough to spread the fire. I want you to ride to where you can see the Dockin house and shoot three times if you see any riders coming. I don't much think there will be. We should be long gone by the time they see the fire, but I'm not leaving anything to chance."

Ben was relieved at the notion he didn't have to actually light the fields. He mounted up slowly and rode to a spot where he could see the ranch house. The fields looked big. One large hay field and a fair-sized corn field. He sat on his horse feeling something he had never felt before, sick to his stomach. The thoughts of destroying prime property made him feel dirty. To him facing a man was honorable. What they were doing certainly was not. He looked to the other side of the fields and saw a small fire beginning. He watched as it became larger. It wouldn't take long before the sky would be lit up. His mind was racing with thoughts and turmoil building within him. He realized he couldn't do it. He touched his horse with spurs and headed towards Mason City. Ben Watts was through working for Zell Davis. He knew Zell would be guessing as to what happened to him when he didn't show up. Ben knew the Kid would figure it out because he had told him how he was feeling about it all, and how he liked Pap. He also figured Zell would send the Kid gunning for him. He hoped that wouldn't happen. He rode hard for town where he would wait for the Kid or whatever came.

Chapter 16

Pap couldn't sleep for worrying about Speck. It was nearly one o'clock in the morning and he was looking at the stars from his front porch. He had been staring at them for nearly an hour when Vivian slipped quietly in beside him.

"What's wrong, Franklin?"

"Can't sleep. You don't need to be out here."

"Where do I need to be?" She smiled at him with loving eyes.

"I swear. No wonder I'm... in love with you. You're the kind of woman it takes for a man like me, unafraid and... and beautiful." He was standing with both hands on the rail of the porch. He reached over and put his hand over hers.

"Franklin, do you believe in destiny?"

"I believe in a Higher Power... God. I think He brings things together that need to be brought together."

"I like that. He brought us together for His destiny."

"Just like a woman, turned it around on me and the Man Upstairs too." They both laughed.

"I see you and Chalk are really getting along good."

"I'm sorry?"

"You and Chalk... you're getting along well."

"Yeah, the boy is alright. He's not afraid of nothin' and that includes work. He'll do. We took a ride across the place today. We even took us a swim."

"Oh?" She smiled. "I wish I could have been there."

"Well, we wouldn't have gotten... oh... I see. Now are you going to make me believe you would have watched two men in their birthday suits taking a swim?"

She laughed.

"Vivian, you are something." Suddenly, he froze. "Fire!" He jumped over the rail and ran out to the middle of the yard where a dinner bell was hanging. He grabbed the iron rod hanging on the post and rang it as fast and loud as he could. The Dockin cowboys came piling out of the bunkhouse half dressed.

Some were hopping on one foot while trying to get a boot on the other.

Chalk came out of the main house with gun in hand. Sarah was standing on the porch with Vivian. "What's wrong, Vivian?"

"I don't know, honey. Franklin and I were out here talking, when all at once he ran to the bell and sounded an alarm. I thought he said... fire."

Before Pap could tell them why he rang the bell, some of the cowboys were pointing. Pooh yelled out. "Fire! Hell, boys, the world's on fire!"

Pap then started giving orders. "Pooh, you take the best men we have with plows and teams! Get all six pair of our draft horses harnessed and get out there to the fields! Plow enough furls to stop the fire from travelin'! The rest of you, wet down all the burlap sacks we have and get hoes, shovels, rakes, anything that can put out a fire! Let's move!" He searched the men. "Art!"

"Right here!"

"You and Bailey each get a wagon hitched up, load a couple barrels full of water on them, get movin' now!"

"Boss, that won't be enough water to put out a fire that size! The whole sky is lit up!"

"Say again?"

"We can't fight that fire with that little dab of water!"

"It ain't for fightin' fire! It's for drinkin' and soakin' burlap and for puttin' anyone out if they catch on fire! Pray they don't!"

"Yes sir!" Art and Bailey went racing off after the wagons.

Pooh came around the end of the long barn with the Dockin buggy. He stopped in front of the house. "Let's go Pap! The boys have took the teams on already!"

"One minute!" He ran back inside passing Chalk on the way. When he came back out, he was wearing his side iron. Chalk grabbed Pap as he passed back by him. "What do you want me to do?"

He wasn't sure what he said, but he figured he knew what the question was. "Chalk, I figure the fire burning up my hay and grain was set by Zell Davis, pay back for the little conversation we had this afternoon. Saddle your horse and ride like hell to your place. See if you can see or hear anything from there. From the old house place sitting up on that hill you might see the one's that set the fire. Don't try to take 'em alone. I need proof it was him."

Before Pap could say another word, Chalk bailed off the porch and ran to the barn for Night Train.

Pap jumped on the buggy and found Vivian already in it. "Viv, you have to stay... awh, never mind."

Vivian looked back at Sarah as the buggy was lunging forward. "Sarah, you stay inside! I'll be back!"

Chalk came out of the barn in a run on his horse and slid to a stop in front of Sarah, dismounting as he did. "Honey, I've got to go! I'll hurry, I'll hurry back!" He kissed her and leaped aboard Night Train.

"It's okay. You're needed out there! Go!"

He whirled his horse and spurred him lightly, leaving Sarah standing on the porch alone.

Maybe it was the excitement. Maybe it was the fact that she had felt a contraction a couple of days ago. Whatever it was, Sarah was about to deliver a baby... possibly by herself. She had walked back into the house and got as far as the door to her bedroom, when suddenly she felt something wet. Her water broke. She began to talk to herself aloud. "You have to stay calm, Sarah." She made her way to the kitchen and put water on the stove. She knew the linens were in the closet and was going for them when contractions hit... she was in trouble. The contractions were less than five minutes apart. She cried out. "Oh Chalk, I need you! My wonderful man, I need you!"

She wanted to go back to her bedroom, but she needed to build a fire in the cook stove to heat the water. The wood was in the wood box next to the stove. She bent down to get a stick and suddenly felt faint. She spoke aloud. "God help me. Help my baby. He deserves a chance. You brought him through the fire at our place. You've got to bring him through this. Please do that for me, Lord." When she tried to straighten up from the wood box, she became dizzy and didn't feel it when she hit the floor.

Pap jumped from the buggy before it had come to a stop. The Dockin ranch hands were already fighting the fire. They had raced out on barebacked, bridled, and haltered horses. They didn't bother to saddle them, saving time was everything. What did take some time was unloading the turning plows from the wagons. Within minutes four teams were turning soil in front of the oncoming flames. The grass to make hay was going fast, and the corn was burning too. But all wasn't lost yet. If Pap had been sleeping instead of standing on the front porch, the fields would have gone up in smoke without a fight. He at least had a chance to save something.

Pooh took one of the teams and cut a furl as close to the advancing fire as he could while the other teams cut over and behind him.

Pap took fifteen of his men with wet burlap sacks and fought the flames back ahead of Pooh and his team, hoping to give him a clear straight row to turn.

Art Teague came running with a fresh bucket of water in each hand to wet the burlap. That was when Pap saw Vivian. "What are you doing?"

Her face and arms were black, and she was soaking wet from perspiring. "You need everyone you can get to fight this fire... I'm helping!"

"Stay close to me!"

He turned and ran on ahead of Pooh and his team. The big draft horses were pulling hard and fast. Pap had bought a pair of big black drafts, a pair of sorrels, and a gray pair six months ago. He planned to produce more grain and hay this year, so he added the three pair to the other three pair of bays he already owned. He had doubled his corn crop with the extra horses. The black team Pooh was driving was pressing hard into the collars and pulling the plow at a slow trot.

There wasn't a big wind, but the breeze was enough to make the fire reach at least fifteen feet high as it consumed the tender grass and corn. The soaring flames made the low hanging clouds gleam like burnished brass.

Bailey Harris raced out into the field with his wagon loaded with barrels of water and the men immediately ganged around it. One barrel was used for drinking water and the other was for soaking the burlap. They had already used up the water from Art's wagon.

Bailey yelled at Pap. "Looks like we've stopped it in some places, Pap!"

"What!"

"Stopped it, I say!" He pointed back behind them.

"Yeah!"

Pap soaked his burlap and headed back out. He ran as hard and fast as his legs would carry him. They felt like lead, heavy and slow. He could see Pooh and the team out ahead. He knew he could not catch up. He stopped and yelled for Bailey to bring the wagon to where he was standing.

Suddenly, he was missing Vivian. He looked through the smoke and saw her lying crumpled on the ground about twenty yards back. He ran and picked her up immediately. The exhaustion and heat had obviously overtaken her. He stumbled once as he carried her towards the wagon.

Bailey saw him and realized he was carrying Vivian. He let out a yell to the team loud enough to be heard in Mason City. "Yehaw! Get up in there, Buck, Molly!" The team hit the pulling collars together jerking the wagon forward and then raced across the field to Pap.

"Whoa! Whoa up!" Bailey set the brake and jumped from the wagon to help with Vivian. Together they laid her on the bed of the wagon very gently. Pap took his bandana off and soaked it in water. He bathed her until she finally made a sound. "You're going to be alright, honey. You tried to do too much... it's my fault."

She looked at him and smiled. "It was my choice to try and stay up with you. I couldn't, that's all." Her face was black with ash and smoke and she was perspiring. But her smile was beautiful, making Pap feel much better about her.

Pooh came back with the team and stopped at the wagon for a drink. He saw Vivian lying in the wagon bed with Pap and several of the men looking on. "What happened?"

Art looked around at him. "She found a chunk of gold in one of them furls you cut, and Bailey tried to take it away from her."

"I'll be damned." Pooh stood there for a minute and then grinned. "Art Teague, I ought to give you a whoopin' but the fire is all but out, and I'm too happy and too exhausted to take you on. Besides, I figure you didn't do a thing while we was all fightin' the fire." Everyone laughed, even Vivian.After Pap saw she was going to be alright, he stood up in the wagon. All the men gathered around him amid blackened earth and smoke. It became deathly quiet except for the popping of an ember every now and then. "Men... you done good... damn good. A thing like this is a little more than a man signs on for. You'll all get extra pay at the end of the month."

They all gave an approving yell. They were laughing and slapping each other on the backs.

Pap looked back towards the Davis Ranch. "It's not a secret me and Zell Davis are at odds. This thing just got mean, damn mean. Looks like we've lost half of the field of hay or better, could have lost it all. The corn didn't fare much better. It's hurt us. Things could get difficult." He paused and took a breath. "Where there's a will there's a way. I'll figure through on this."

He stopped again, took his hat off and wiped the sweat from his forehead. “Any of you wants to collect your pay and ride on... they’ll be no hard feelin’ towards you. A war has started. I aim to see that Zell Davis pays, pays for the whole hog of it. It’s my fight, but anyone that rides for the Dockin brand... well, there’s bound to be trouble... bound to be some lead flyin’. A man could get killed. If come morning you’re saddled, I’ll understand.”

Pooh stepped up on the front of the wagon. “Pap, you’ve done right by us boys. Hell, they ain’t another outfit on the High Plains what would treat us the way you have. We’re family here. We’d like to die here. We’d like to be old men doing it, but we’ll die young if that’s the way of it. For me... I’m here for the damn drawin’.”

“Yes sir, me too!” Bailey stepped up beside Pooh and looked at Pap. “Pap, we all plan to live as long as you and you can watch us while we do it!” The field that was full of fire was now full of laughter. The Dockin ranch hands were staying.

Chapter 17

Sarah woke up on the floor. She was bleeding from her head and blood was also on the floor at her feet. The baby was coming. She crawled around to where she could put her back against the wall. There was enough room for her to put her legs up against the big heavy cook stove. Her legs were bent back towards her at the knees as she pushed against the stove. The pains were now coming seconds apart. "God, You've got to help me here! You can take me, but You can't take my baby. I asked, and You gave, but You haven't given until he is breathing." A terrible pain hit at that second. "God, please!"

Sarah half yelled, and half cried out with the next push. "You're going to be a stubborn little boy, aren't you?" Again, she pushed. She was breathing fast and taking big breaths. Every inch of her was wet. Again, she pushed. She was giving it all she had. Sarah knew she had to give it all or the baby would die inside her. There was no one there to help them. She had to do this by herself and knowing that made her even more determined to deliver the baby. Again, she pushed.

Chalk rode hard and fast to his hundred-acre patch. He thought he heard a rider on the road to Mason City but wasn't sure. He sat there on his horse looking towards the Dockin ranch. It was sure some fire. It seemed to light up the whole sky. It made it easy to see out across the rolling hills. He looked to the east and saw nothing, then the northeast. That was where he saw movement. He talked to Night Train about it. "Wait a minute ole boy. I see a rider, maybe two." He touched him with his spurs and eased in the direction of the movement. "Funny, whoever that is, they seem to want to watch the fire as well. Could it be these boys started the fire and now they want to see how good of a job they did?" By the time he got to the hill the riders had been sitting on, they were gone. "Well boy, where do you suppose they went? I got a notion they went straight over this hill and caught the road that takes a man to the Sliding D. Let's me and you see if we can catch up with them. Pap wants some proof. If we happen to be able to see those riders riding to the Sliding D, I think we will have proof."

Chalk rode another two miles and suddenly realized he was in trouble. Night Train blew his nostrils like he heard or knew something was wrong. Something didn't belong on the road with them. He was right. The riders were waiting in ambush. They came out on both sides, all three shooting. The first bullet missed. Chalk drew and fired. His bullet knocked the rider directly in front of him from his horse. He fired two more times before two bullets jolted him from Night Train. He rolled, trying to get to the brush beside the trail. Another bullet caught him high in the leg. He tried to get to his feet but fell forward beside the Sliding D rider he had shot. He was surprised when he saw it was Ted Davis. Another bullet hit close to Chalk's head. He shot back until his gun was empty. He knew his shots were close. One of the riders turned and ran. Then another bullet whizzed by his head from the rider who stayed to fight. Chalk lay still, he was out of bullets and hurt badly.

Night Train had turned and ran back the way he came. Chalk knew he was heading for home. He felt that was a good thing, for he was in bad shape. He was either going to be finished off by the gunman or he would bleed to death. He hoped Night Train showing up with an empty saddle would send help in a hurry. He would be a father soon and he planned on being around to see him. He slowly, and with his last bit of strength, reloaded his gun.

Chalk had no way of knowing how true his thoughts were. He would be a father any minute. He rolled quietly into an old hollow tree, cocked his gun and waited.

When Pap and Vivian walked through the front door, she immediately knew something was wrong. Call it woman's instinct but she knew. "Franklin."

"What... what is it?" He tried to reach for her when she ran towards Sarah's bedroom. She came back out and stopped. "Sarah!" Not a sound. She ran into the kitchen while Pap stood in the living room. A chill ran down his back when he heard Vivian cry out.

Pooh, Bailey and Art were standing outside near the bunkhouse washing off, congratulating each other, when they heard a horse coming. Bailey recognized the horse first. "Boys, look yonder, that's Night Train! Whoa! Whoa! Whoa up ole son." Night Train shied away, but Bailey managed to catch hold of the bridle. The reins had been snapped and were only a foot or two long. He had stepped on them while running and snapped them off clean. "Pooh, you better get Pap. This isn't good. There's blood on the saddle. There's blood all over it."

Pooh ran to the house and knocked on the door. No one answered. He stepped inside. "Hello! Pap, you're needed out here!" He didn't see or hear anyone. Then Pap appeared from the kitchen walking very slowly with a look of shock on his face. "Ah... Pap, we got trouble out here."

He looked at Pooh like he didn't comprehend what was being said, like he wasn't even standing there.

"I say, we have trouble."

"I heard you. What kind of trouble?"

"Night Train came in without Chalk. There's blood all over the saddle."

Pap looked back towards the kitchen and then back at Pooh. "Well, I don't know... I... Pooh, go get Bailey and Art. They'll have to..." Pap paused again looking towards the kitchen. It was then, Speck walked through the door.

"I want to know what's been going on here since I've been gone. I'm not away a full day and all hell breaks loose."

Pap's eyes regained some of their light when he saw his ole friend. "Speck, I'm, I'm glad to see you... but didn't the doc want to keep you in bed?"

"Yeah, well I ain't. I would have been, but I saw a glow in the sky all the way from Mason City. I knew it was our spread. I figured what it was... I guess we lost the fields?"

"Lost the what?"

"The hay. The corn."

Pap nodded. "The crops. Yeah."

"Well, we can't cry over the cream we lost, we'll just drink the milk." Speck half turned and looked back out the door. "Pap, I saw Night Train outside. It doesn't look good. The boy is in trouble, bad trouble."

Pap sat down in his big easy chair. "Speck, get some of the boys and..." He looked back at the kitchen. "I can't fix this, Speck. Sarah, she's... she's." He stopped and put his face in his hands.

Speck realized what Pap was trying to tell him. Tragedy had struck the young Cranfield family, and Speck became visibly uncomfortable. His friend, his best friend, was sitting before him crying silently. In all the years they had known one another he had never seen Pap Dockin shed a visible tear. Speck reached and quickly rubbed his eyes before the tear forming rolled down his cheek.

"Pap, this one arm is in a sling, but I can ride. Me and the boys will go find Chalk. Will you be alright?"

When Pap was sure he could speak, he looked up from the chair. "I need you to do that, Speck. I need you to do that. I'll make do. Viv, she's got her hands full, and I'm going to need to help her. Take Bailey Harris with you and a couple of the boys. Luke Tanner would be good. He's not just a puncher, he's a damn killer when he has to be. Leave Art, I'll need him here. Tell him to gather three or four of the boys and wait outside on the porch. You bring my boy back. Can you do that for me, Speck?"

"You know I can." Speck's voice cracked with emotion for his friend and for Sarah, the lovely girl he had come to know and like.

Chapter 18

It was breaking daylight when Speck, Bailey, Tanner, and three of the ranch hands rode across Chalk's hundred acres. It was there they picked up Chalk's trail. Bailey was known to be a fair tracker and he needed to be now.

"Speck, this trail is heading towards the Sliding D spread. Darn near straight at it."

"Yeah. Mount up. I got a bad feeling."

They rode for an hour real slow. Bailey was getting off and on, making sure he was on the right trail. "Speck."

"Yeah."

"Chalk picked up three more horses with riders here. Looks like three of them are in a hurry, and Chalk is easing along." Bailey stared off in the direction the trail was going. "Maybe not easing along slow enough though."

"Yeah, he's crowded 'em... ain't he?"

"I'm betting." Bailey mounted up. "Speck, we can pick it up a little. I could follow these tracks blindfolded."

The trail led to the road that went to the Sliding D Ranch. That was when they kicked their horses into a faster lope. They rode for about five minutes like that until they rounded a bend and slid to a halt. There were six men in the road and seemed to be searching for something. Two of them drew guns and started shooting.

Speck and his men dismounted behind some rocks. "Looks like these ole boys want a fight. They sure as hell aren't sociable."

"Not at all... and that's too bad." Bailey grinned. He liked a good fight.

Bullets peppered the rocks they stood behind while Speck and his men returned pistol fire. "Bailey, Tanner, you boys get your rifles. I can't shoot anything but this pistol myself, but I'll give 'em hell if they get by our rifles."

They pulled their rifles from the scabbards and returned the next round of fire with the long guns. Tanner's first bullet was dead on. One of the Sliding D men fell out onto the road critically wounded.

The Sliding D boys had dug in on a bank to the upper side of the road. That might have been a strong hold but for one thing. They were in front of the hull of the sycamore tree Chalk was lying in. He had crawled out about six inches. He didn't have enough strength to really raise his gun and aim, but he shot in the general direction. That caused the Sliding D men to panic. They mounted their horses to make a run for it.

Bailey raised his rifle, fired and hit one of the riders trying to make his getaway. He fell from his horse and rolled out of the road. The rest of the Sliding D men kept riding not daring to look back.

Speck went to where Chalk was laying in the old tree trunk. The boys gently pulled him out. After he saw the bullet wounds, he looked at the rest of the boys with determined eyes. "We've got to get him out of here and to a doc or he's done. Bailey, you and the boys cut us some poles to drag him on. One of you other boys needs to ride to Mason City and in a damn hurry... whoever has the best and faster horse. Get Doc Zimmer and have him meet us at the Dockin Ranch. Hurry! Time's a wasting!"

They were in luck, where creeks and hollow trees are laying there is always pieces of wood lying around from flash floods. Bailey and his men gathered driftwood poles and tied them together with rope to make a travois. They lifted Chalk on it as gently as possible and secured him as best they could.

Speck walked over to where the dead Sliding D boys were laying. He hoped Zell or the Checkered Kid was one of them but no such luck. "Boys, we done two of them in... but look here. I believe old Chalk done some damage, too. Someone bled out here, and over there's a few drops. Looks like someone rode away from here in a damn hurry. I'd say he rode off with a bullet belonging to Chalk Dockin."

Bailey and Tanner along with the boys looked at Speck with surprise. He'd called him Chalk Dockin, not Cranfield.

Speck's eyes were glassy as he noticed the surprised look on the men. "Well, the boy is a Dockin. He fought like his old man. He's a Dockin and I'm damn proud to know him."

Bailey spoke up. "The rest of us are, too. There's just something you can't explain about Chalk Dockin." They mounted up and headed for home.

What should have been an easy thing to do after midnight turned disastrous for Zell. His son, Ted, lay dead in the parlor. The Checkered Kid took a bullet to one of his left ribs, and Ben Watts never showed up. He wondered if Pap had shot him or did the shooter that killed Ted get Ben, too. He never heard any shots in Ben's direction.

Zell got up and poured a shot of whiskey, drank it down and threw the glass hard into the fireplace. "The sonofabitch has killed my eldest son! He'll pay with his life! I'd planned to ruin Pap Dockin... but he'll answer for this with his life." Zell turned from the fireplace and faced the Checkered Kid sitting in a big plush cowhide chair.

"Mister Davis, whoever it was that followed us, he was a shooter."

Huey was sitting in the room listening and becoming angry. Finally, he could not take anymore. "Dad, why can't you think of someone else just once? Ted, your son, is dead! Can you not take one minute out of your angry life to mourn him? What is wrong with you? I understand the Kid. He's a natural born killer. Nothing affects him. He hasn't any feelings. But you, that is your own flesh and blood lying in there on the table. Give him some respect." Huey stared into his father's eyes. "Maybe you just don't know what the word means." Huey kicked a hole in the screen door as he left the house. Zell sat his whiskey glass down and never said a word.

The Kid smiled. "Well, I guess we got that."

"Yeah, we got that. He's right. Ted deserves more. We'll bury him tomorrow. It'll be a proper funeral. We'll bury the other two boys killed this morning, too. I think maybe we'll pull in our horns until proper time of mourning has been had, and then... and then hell will thunder over Pap Dockin. I don't figure him to sit still for what happened to his fields. He'll come. I'd bet on it. But I know him, he'll take care of preservation first. So, we'll hit him hard before he's ready."

The Kid poured a drink and sat down. "What do you mean, preservation?"

"He's lost his winter hay and feed. He'll either sell off livestock or figure out a way to keep them. I don't see any way he can do that. He'll have to make a cattle drive first. He'll look to the long of things, not the short. You see, he won't gamble on the showdown being quick and easy, so he'll take care of things for the future first. He's a patient man. He won a many a battle in the war by being patient. It takes a quite a bit of time to drive a herd to Dodge City, Kansas. When he does get back, he'll come huntin' me."

"Let him come. I'll put a bullet right between his eyes."

"No, if he takes cattle north, we'll burn his place to the ground, and pick him off along the drive somewhere. He'll be an easy shot out in the open pushing cattle along. First, he crawls in the dirt. Then kill him."

"You sure got yourself one big ole hate for Dockin, but a respectful hate."

"Kid, they don't make men like him anymore... but me and him called it quits in business, as friends, as anything, a long time ago."

"I don't know what your quarrel is about but pulling in our horns a few days suits me. I've got to let this rib heal up. I don't face anyone hurting this bad. I'll lay-up awhile. See you in the morning."

"Damn right you will. I've got a son to bury. Ted might have been a little slow in the head and with his hands, but he always tried to please me, unlike Huey. See to it all the ranch hands are present." He paused for a second. "I've never been the father I should have been to my boys. I figured the rougher on them I was, the tougher men it would make them. Ted... he tried. Huey doesn't seem to give a damn what happens, long as he can fool with horses. He's nothing like me or his brother."

"I'll make sure the boys are all there. See you."

"Wait a minute. What do you think happened to Ben?"

The Kid smiled. "I think he quit."

"Why?" Zell's eyes widened.

"Ben has something I don't have."

"What's that?"

"A heart."

Huey Davis saddled his bay paint and rode to Mason City. In his eighteen years of life he had never ridden to town for a drink alone. This seemed like the time to do it. He hated his life. He loved the ranch, loved the horses, but detested the turmoil. His father was consumed with hate for Pap Dockin. Huey himself didn't know what it was that made his father carry such a torch for revenge. Whatever happened between the two of them was well before he and his brother Ted came along.

Huey rode to the hitching rail in front of the Dry Rock Saloon and dismounted. He walked in and glanced around the room. The light was dim, but he saw Ben Watts sitting at the back of the saloon. He ordered a drink at the bar and then walked to Ben's table.

"Can I sit?"

"Sure, Huey. You're not who I thought would come walking through those swinging doors from the Sliding D."

"I bet." He smiled. "Things went bad for the Sliding D last night and early today. Ted was killed. The Checkered Kid took a bullet to a rib. It's not bad but he'll be sore. Two of the ranch hands were killed this morning in a gun battle. It seems they winged the cowboy that killed Ted."

"I'm sorry about your brother."

"Yeah." Huey cut his eyes at Ben. "I think I always knew Ted would die from someone's bullet." He paused and glanced at Ben. "My father and the Kid are sure curious about you. Their kind of speculating on what happened to you. What did happen?"

"Huey, I've had a belly full. I'm a gun hand. This thing between Zell and Pap I didn't sign up for... hiding in the dark and burning crops. Next, they'll want me to shoot cattle and horses. I'll face a man, face his guns, but to steal his cattle and burn his crops... not in for that"

Huey took a sip of his beer. "I see." He shut his eyes and breathed deep. The smell of whiskey and fresh sawdust on the floor filled the air with an odd fresh kind of scent. He needed the change. He wished he could open his eyes and things would be alright, but he knew that would not be. "Ben, you got to know when they find out you ran out on them, they'll be gunning for you? They're going to blame you for Ted's death."

"Yeah, I know. I paid for a room here in town. I figure to wait on them here."

Huey drank his beer down. "Why not ride on?"

"Not my style."

"I wish you luck, Ben." Huey studied him a moment. "You know, you're not like the Kid."

Ben smiled at that. "I've begun to look at life differently these days, Huey. I liked watching you work those colts." His smile left. "I'd like to try my hand with the ponies but this gun hanging on my side keeps me from it."

"Well, I'd tell you to come try one, but I doubt you'd be welcome at the ranch now."

"I know what you mean. I probably wouldn't make a wrangler anyway."

"Depends."

"On what?"

"If you have the heart."

"Heart?"

"A man that has an understanding heart... a horse will take to."

"That lets me out. I don't have a heart."

"I wonder about that, Ben."

"Huey, I've done too many dark deeds to have a heart."

"Something made you quit my dad." Huey got up to leave and paused for a second. He leaned over the table and shook Ben's hand. He looked him in the eyes and smiled, then he walked out the swinging doors of the saloon.

Ben smiled as he sat there alone. He wondered and questioned what Huey said about his making a horse trainer. He didn't want to let his mind dream things impossible. He was a hired gun... few ever become more.

Chapter 19

Chalk was placed carefully in a bed with the help of Art, Bailey, Tanner, and Pooh. The rest of the ranch hands stood in the entry of the house while others gathered out on the front porch. They had all come to like and respect Chalk. He showed courage and made himself one of them quickly. There was talk among the men to saddle up and take the Sliding D Ranch apart one board, one man at a time. Speck put a stop to that kind of thing. He called everyone in and gave them a talk.

"Boys, I understand how you feel, 'cause I feel the same way. But we're not riding anywhere until Pap tells us we are. When he gives the word, we'll ride over the Sliding D like locust over prairie grass. Right now, it's wait and see. Chalk... he's bad... real bad. Little Sarah." Speck had to grab his breath and hold it a minute. "Well, it's a sad time here on the ranch." Speck turned his head and looked out into the yard. "Tomorrow will be a sad day. Somehow, we'll get through it, we'll manage it. You boys be dressed in your best, hear? In your best." Speck couldn't say anything else, he just couldn't, so he nodded his head and walked out into the middle of the yard. The ranch hands stood and sat around the rail with their heads bowed in respect and sorrow, occasionally stealing a look at Speck.

At ten o'clock the next morning some of the ranch hands picked Chalk up, bed and all, and carried him through the French doors on the east side of the house. He was unconscious but that didn't matter. They took him out to a shade tree where a cemetery had been fenced off. Sarah Lea Cranfield Dockin would be the first one laid to rest in it. Six of the Dockin men carried her pine box and set it down beside the fresh dug grave. Chalk had not regained consciousness for even a moment, but Pap wanted him there anyway. He stood on one side of Vivian while Speck stood on the other. She wore a black dress with a black veil and hat. She was silently crying while holding Sarah's little baby boy. Pooh was standing behind them with Sitting Dove who had been sent for to help with the baby and Sarah.

Pap had not uttered a word since he had asked Speck to go find Chalk, other than to ask Speck to carry Chalk out to the grave site. Pap gathered himself and stepped forward. There was not one sound except for a small bird in a tree and a cow bawling in the distance.

"Boys, men, good people. I'm like a tree with bark knocked off it. In any direction from this ranch I'm known as a tough hard man. You know me for what I am and who I am." He stopped, looked around at all of them and then continued. "Even a tough man can hurt." A faint crack came in his voice. "I've seen the toughest of cowboys shed tears when faced with more than they could bear."

He stopped to catch his breath and stared at the pine box before him. Slowly his eyes raised. "I didn't get to know Sarah like I thought I would. She was taken too soon for that. Here's what I know about her. She was kind... a sweet girl. She was tough and determined. She brought a life into this world while givin' hers for it. She had a beautiful smile and married a good man, a Dockin, Chalk Dockin. There's not a doubt about her bein' in heaven, for that's where angels go. She went to a beautiful place and left a beautiful gift... to be loved and taken care of." He stopped. Silence seemed forever and made the moment feel unbearable.

Speck cut his eyes to Pap and waited for what he was about to say.

"I'll put the fire out in hell before any harm comes to my grandchild." He looked up at the sky. "Lord, this young wonderful girl didn't have to die. A sickness caused it. It's my fault, for not stompin' it out long ago. I've not faced up to what I knew needed faced up to. I don't know if sin caused this. I'm not the one to say, and I'm sure as hell not good at understandin' the Good Book. Does sin cause evil or was evil already? You hold those answers. I've weighed in anguish over what I knew one day would have to be attended to. If that which causes pain can be done away with, then it shall be. The only thing I know to do is kill it out." He paused and looked around at his men. "I guess that's about it. That's all I have to say." He stepped back beside Vivian.

The ranch hands picked up the ropes to the pine box and slowly lowered Sarah into the ground. Vivian tried to be silent but cried out just for a moment and then gathered herself.

Sitting Dove began to sing in Comanche a beautiful death song. Once Sarah was lowered, Vivian gave the baby to Pap. His rough hands were awkward at taking hold of him, but he managed. Vivian bent down and threw a hand full of dirt on the box.

"Goodbye, sweetheart. I promise you... we will take good care of your baby." She turned, and they walked back to the ranch house as the boys picked up Chalk and carried him back to the front room.

Zell Davis stood over his son, Ted, at straight up noon. All the Sliding D ranch hands were present. A grave had been dug beside his mother who had died from the flu ten years past.

"My eldest son Ted has gone to be with his mother. It's a sad day for the Sliding D, for me and Huey, but I'm sure Ted and his mom are dancing around the Throne together. Ted was more like me than his ma, stubborn and tough. He was a good son, I'll miss him." Zell looked over at Huey, turned and walked to the house without saying another word.

It was an awkward moment. The ranch hands stood not knowing quite what to do. Finally, Huey spoke up.

"My brother had his faults. All in all, I'd say he was alright, not perfect, but none of us are. He's in the hands of the Maker now. I loved him, and... and I leave it at that." Huey was the only one with a tear in his eye. He picked up a shovel and began burying his brother. There were several more shovels and the men began picking them up, and soberly began shoveling dirt over the wooden box.

Chapter 20

Pap sat beside Chalk's bed for three days and seldom ate or drank anything. He just sat there with his head in his hands.

The doctor worried Chalk was bleeding inside. He just couldn't be sure. If not, he had a chance if he didn't get an infection or take pneumonia.

That afternoon Speck asked to have a word with Pap. He reluctantly left Chalk alone following Speck out to the kitchen where Vivian was at. Speck picked up a cup of coffee and handed it to Pap.

"Drink this. You haven't had anything in days. If you don't start eating or drinking, you'll be in a bed with Chalk."

"What kind of bed would that be?" Defiance covered his face.

"A sick bed." Speck knew Pap was alluding to, 'a death bed'.

"My son ain't dyin'... but I should be. This fight between me and Zell has gotten Sarah killed, and my son is in there barely holdin' on. None of this would have happened had I done the right thing years ago. I should have killed Zell Davis then. My son and his wife were innocent of all this. Her death was uncalled for and I'm the blame."

Speck rubbed his chin and sat down at the table. "You can't blame yourself for what's happened here. Zell Davis is to blame. He's crazy, plain crazy. You've tried to call him off more than once."

"Yes, and I'm smarter than that. You don't call a mad dog off... you kill it."

Speck looked at Vivian and then back at Pap. "We need to talk. Pap, we've got troubles the size of large herds around this ranch. Vivian and I need to have a word with you."

Pap sipped his coffee and then sat it down. "Talk."

"Well Pap, we keep losing cattle every now and then, and we got to figure out how we're going to winter our livestock. The fire burned over half of the corn and nearly half of the hay field. Winter ain't all that far away. We haven't bothered you with it knowing how things are with Chalk, but we need to know what you want to do."

Pap eyed the both of them. "You think I'm worried about cattle? I finally have my son and I'm about to lose him at the same time. Speck, the two of you take care of the ranch. I'll take care of what really matters, my son." He had a certain amount of defiance and sarcasm in his voice.

"Franklin, Speck and I love you. We love Chalk and this ranch. We know the pain you're in, we're..."

Pap unexpectedly sat down at the kitchen table and held his hand up. "Look, I'm wrong here. I'm easy riled since Chalk got shot to pieces. That doesn't make it right." He looked around at Vivian. "You two, 'deal makers', got a plan?"

She took the floor from there. "Yes, we do. Since I own half of a freight company, I propose we haul not only corn in from Dodge City and possibly Kansas City, but haul loads of wire tied hay. Ellison sent word that the railroad has now made it to Amarillo. If that is the case, we can also ship grain and hay to Amarillo by rail. We would already have our freight wagons down here and could haul the grain and hay from Amarillo to the ranch."

"I see why you own a freight company. Not a bad idea." Then Pap shook his head in disagreement. "Good ideas sometimes can cost a fortune. That would. No, we can't be shippin' grain in here. It would take two, three good years to get back to plum."

"Why would it? I can forgo the shipping fee, and we can buy grain cheap in Dodge City. In fact, Ellison can bid corn and hay on the market and get us bottom dollar prices. Ellison is a shrewd marketing man. Why not use his expertise? Franklin... at least think about it." She poured a cup of coffee for Speck. "I've got to check on the baby, I'll be right back." She left and came back within a few minutes.

"Pooh has a fine woman. She knows how to care for an infant. I think we should hire her permanently."

Pap was about to speak when he stopped. “You think what?”

Vivian smiled. “I think we should hire Sitting Dove permanently.”

“I was hopin’ my hard hearin’ got it wrong, but I see it didn’t. When did this happen?”

“What?”

“You doin’ the thinkin’ on who gets hired around here?”

“The moment you told me you loved me.” She smiled at him and batted her eyes purposely.

Speck burst into laughter.

Pap looked at Speck with wide eyes. “What’s wrong with you?”

“I think there’s going to be a joining up celebration.” He took a big gulp of his coffee. “Yes sir, a joining up!”

“Well, a man has to ask a woman before there’s a joinin’ up’ and that hasn’t happened yet. Too much trouble laid at my door to think about gettin’ tied up.”

Vivian laughed. “Truth is, Speck, he doesn’t have the nerve or the backbone to ask a woman to marry him. It’s more convenient to live quietly with a woman.” Vivian was getting her first shot at teasing the man she loved.

“Now look here, I don’t have to take out of order talk.”

“I know how you can prove me wrong.” She smiled and then Speck threw in.

“Yeah, I know how you can prove her wrong.” He sat there grinning, waiting for a retort or something to happen. It did.

Pap looked at Vivian, then at Speck, then back at her. “Well, I... don’t need to be forced into anything here.” He became quiet and refused to look at either one of them.

“I’m not getting any younger, Franklin Dockin. I thought you were the kind of man that went after what he wanted?”

“I am.” He looked away from her and Speck. He felt Vivian was the brashest, loveliest, most wonderful woman he had ever met. She was the kind of woman he needed. “Alright then, alright, if that's the way of it." He stood up and walked over beside her. His left shoulder was touching her left shoulder. She was facing Speck, and Pap was facing the door leading out of the kitchen into the big living area of the house. He was going back to sit with Chalk. He turned his head slightly towards her. "Vivian, it would pleasure me mightily if you would join... if you would accept my hand... in matrimony."

"I'll think about it."

"You'll what?" His voice became louder.

"I'll think about it."

"I heard you. What the hell does that mean? The two of you goad me into askin' you."

Vivian kissed him on the cheek. "I would love and adore being your wife, Franklin."

Speck stood and shook hands with Pap and danced a little gig in the middle of the floor. He gently took Vivian by the hand, bent down and kissed it. "Hot damn, a join' up!"

"Yeah, a wedding and my son, Chalk, will be the best man."

Pap turned and left the room without another word. Vivian and Speck suddenly felt subdued and alone. They were jubilant one second and restrained the next. For a moment, just for a moment, they had gotten Pap to forget his troubles, his worry. There wouldn't be any wedding or true happiness on the Dockin ranch until the outcome of Chalk was known. Doctor Zimmer was worried about the persistent fever, low grade to high at times. Chalk was getting weaker by not eating. A miracle was needed.

The next day in the early morning, Chalk awoke. He asked for Sarah but then fell unconscious. At noon he awoke again. He could see Pap sitting in a chair beside his bed. "Sarah. Where's Sarah?"

Pap had dosed off. He jumped when Chalk spoke. "Son." He grabbed hold of Chalk's hand.

"Sarah?" His voice was just above a whisper.

"I've got something to show you, Chalk." He ran to the kitchen and found Vivian and Sitting Dove. "Bring the boy! Now!"

Vivian carried the baby to Chalk and laid it beside him. "Say hello to your son."

He tried to smile. "My son?" He looked at him through weak hollow eyes. "Sarah, where's Sarah?"

Vivian's smile retreated. "She's resting, Chalk."

He swallowed. "His name? Sarah named him?"

"Not yet." Vivian looked away.

Chalk slowly turned his tired eyes from the baby boy back to her as a tear slowly formed and ran down his cheek. "Vivian... Sarah and I had the name for a girl and a... boy." His voice was fading. "His name... is Crandall. Crandall Wayne Cranfield Dockin... Cran, for short." He looked Vivian in the eyes. "Sarah is gone, isn't she?"

Vivian bowed her head. "Yes, she is, Chalk."

"When you didn't know his name, I knew." He looked over at Pap. "Please leave me alone with my boy a few minutes."

Pap put his arm around the two women in a gesture to usher them out of the room. He stopped and looked back at Chalk. "Son, Sarah was... she was a fine woman. My little grandson... he's going to make the Dockin name even more than it is. The three of us... we'll raise some hell." He smiled and left the room feeling unsure as to what to say for the first time in his whole life.

Chalk stared at his little boy for a minute or two and then spoke to him.

"Cran, your mother... she's... this isn't what she and I had planned. There's a reason for all things. God knows the why. Your mother loved you, son." Chalk felt tears streaming down his face. "I love you, Cran. You're going to grow up and be a fine man." He looked back towards the kitchen. He was too weak to call out, so he tipped over the pitcher of water sitting on the edge of the little table by his bed. That brought them running in a hurry.

Pap was the first one to him. “Chalk, are you all right?”

“Dad.”

At first Pap didn’t know he meant him. “Yeah. Yeah, Son.”

“You have a boy to raise.” He swallowed hard.

“Son, don’t talk like that. You’ll be alright. You’re a fighter like your old man.” Somehow calling himself old man sounded good at that moment.

“Cran is going to take my place. You wanted to raise me but that wasn’t meant to be. Raise my son. Raise your grandson.”

“Chalk, you’ll be up and around in no time. Me and you, we’ll raise Cran together.”

Very faintly Chalk smiled. “I’m already gone... Dad.”

Vivian could not help but cry silently.

Pap tried to speak but his voice wouldn’t come. He waited and then spoke. “What do you mean?”

“I’m already with Sarah. God means for you to raise Cran. Raise him, Dad.”

“I know you’re missin’ Sarah... but you got to stay here and help me. Hell, I don’t know nothin’ about kids. I need you.”

“You’ll manage... you’re Pap Dockin, my dad. There’s nothing he can’t do. I’m proud to know I’m a Dockin.” He stopped. “Let me... rest.”

“What, son?”

“Rest.”

“Sure, yeah, well sure, rest. We got cattle to see after and horses to break. You need a lot of rest for that. Get all you need.” Pap was talking fast, he felt weak like his legs weren’t going to hold him up as he turned to leave. His heart was pounding as he tried to look through blurry eyes.

Vivian gave the baby to Sitting Dove and squeezed Pap’s hand as she searched his pain filled eyes. “Franklin, we have to accept what comes, what Chalk wants.”

“You think he wants to die?”

"No, but I think he knows he's not going to pull through."

"No! I won't hear of it!"

Vivian touched Pap on the cheek. "I think he wants to stay here with his son, but he knows he is about to join Sarah. Franklin, God works in mysterious ways. You didn't get to raise Chalk, so God may be giving you Cran to rear."

Pap looked at her for a long moment and then left the room abruptly. He walked out on the porch where he sat on the swing and began rubbing Duke's long hound dog ears. He didn't want to hear talk of Chalk not pulling through.

Chapter 21

The Checkered Kid rode into Mason City looking for Ben. He was told, by a barefooted boy crossing the dusty street, that he would find him at the Dry Rock Saloon. Ben was there just as he'd been told. The Kid walked in and stood at the bar beside him.

"Hello, Ben."

"Hello Kid, been expecting you."

"That so." The Kid ordered a shot of whiskey and drank it down. "You and me, we've been partners awhile now. So... I owe you this much."

"This much?"

"I'm not going to gun you, least not now."

"Well Kid, that's decent of you."

He smiled. "Fact is... I've got a sore rib. A lucky bullet got a little close. Where did you get off to the other night? Things got real interesting after the fire started. Ted was shot dead and we lost a couple of the ranch hands. Never figured you to run out on me."

"I didn't. You rode out on me. What I rode out on, was a job that stunk to high heaven."

"What do you mean, I rode out on you?"

"Kid, you partnered up with Zell and left me high and dry."

"Purely looking to the future. I would have brought you in."

"That's just it. You were doing things without me suddenly. You changed, Kid."

"I don't see it."

"Well, it doesn't much matter, now does it? Kid, I don't sneak around in the dark. I'm a hired gun not a chicken thief."

"The Kid laughed. "Chicken thief?"

"They steal chickens at night while they're on the roost. It's pretty much the same thing when slipping around in the dark burning crops while folks are in bed. Might as well be a chicken thief."

"Ben, you always did have guts. Calling me a chicken thief makes me think you ain't got good sense to boot. Like I say, I owe you. I warn you though, don't get in the way or I'll kill you next time. We're even, clean slate."

"Kid, what happened? You and me, we were pards."

"Simple, Ben. Zell Davis has money. You don't. I see an opportunity. I'm taking it." He looked over at the bartender. "How much?"

"Four bits."

The Kid laid four bits down. "I guess this frees you up to ride on out of here."

Ben smiled and looked the Kid dead in the eyes. "Did I say I was leaving?"

The Kid faced Ben; hand low to his gun. "Well, you've always known when to ride in the past. I figure you do this time."

"Kid, I like it here. I don't have any pressing job up the line. I think I'll stick around."

"As long as you don't start working for the other side, no harm."

"Kid, I don't guess it's ever crossed your mind that I might take you?"

"No Ben, it surely never has." He turned and strolled out of the saloon.

The following day Pap walked out to the barn where Speck and Vivian were. She was brushing one of the stud colts. Pap cleared his throat. "I've thought on it. I've got money to buy grain and hay. I'll not hear of bringin' it in without pay."

Vivian looked at Speck with surprise. "I will send a letter to Ellison right away. I'll have him negotiate the grain and hay deals."

"Speck, what about the cattle? What's the count?"

"Well, near as I can tell." He stopped talking mid-sentence. They all heard something and slowly looked towards the house. Speck cut his eyes at Pap. "No."

Pap knew instantly what had happened when he heard Sitting Dove singing a death song from the ranch house. They raced inside as the ranch hands gathered out in the front yard certain of what it meant.

One day later, Ben Watts rode up in front of the Dockin house as Chalk Wayne Cranfield Dockin was being laid to rest beside his wife. Pap was on one knee beside the pine box while Vivian stood beside him.

Speck, Pooh, and the rest of the ranch hands, along with Ben, listened as he spoke.

"God, I've come through droughts and blizzards. I've fought renegade Indians, outlaws, and rustlers. I beat the cholera and chicken pox." He began to lightly shake. "But tell me, how do I get through this?"

Speck stepped over and knelt beside him in an effort to help him maintain his balance. "Speck, I've made my own way with what the Lord gave me. And now He takes my son. Why? Tell me that. I can deal with anything once I know the why. I've never asked the Lord His business, but He's sure as hell messed in mine. I've had enough. I've had enough of Zell Davis and his evil ways. For some twenty years I've had a hole in my heart. Then Chalk shows up. I knew he was my son. I knew. I thought I would die and leave it all to him."

Pap gazed from one end of the pine box to the other. "Why would God bring him here just to take him away?" He became quiet and looked towards the sky. "Alright, You've taken him from me. I can't do anything about that... but I can damn sure do somethin' about the man who has caused all this. I've let things go, been rode hard. Well it's over. Hear me? I'm through! You can bless or condemn me for what I'm about to do, but I'll do it. I'll spit at hell and do it. I'm goin' to wipe Zell Davis from the earth. He raped the one I loved. He's murdered my people and stole from me. He's a Judas. We broke bread together, rode and branded cattle but he turned on me. He couldn't be satisfied with what he had. He wanted what I had, too... even the one I loved."

It had finally come out. It took the strongest most unbearable thing that could happen for Pap to reveal the mystery between him and Zell Davis.

Ben Watts was standing back of the crowd with his head bowed until he heard Pap say what he did about Zell raping the one he loved. He now knew the secret to the feud between Pap Dockin and Zell Davis. Zell had raped his woman. Even so, there must be more. Ben thought he knew a man like Pap well enough to know, he didn't let that kind of thing go unpunished. He had taken a bull whip to him for killing a steer, and he was betting Pap gave Zell a hell of a whipping for raping his lady friend. It had to be something like that for Zell to hate Pap so much. It was all making sense to Ben now. He now understood why Zell stuck up for Chalk the night Ted told everyone he was going to put a bullet in Chalk. Zell wouldn't have it and even told Ted to cut him out a filly as a gift. Ben mumbled to himself. "Either Zell isn't sure whose son Chalk is, Pap's or his, or he has that much respect for Chalk's mother."

Ben faintly smiled. It came to him Zell was in love with Chalk's mother too. It had to be that. Ben thought he had it figured out. It wasn't like Zell to be giving horses away... especially to a stranger. It had to be because he had fallen in love with Chalk's mother same as Pap.

Ben put his hat on and walked towards his horse. He felt like he needed to take a ride over to the Sliding D. This was the kind of news that needed to get around. Ben wanted to personally deliver his new-found revelation, so he could see Zell's reaction. He knew his very first expression would tell it all, be it true or false. Ben smiled as he neared his horse.

Unbeknownst to Ben, Pooh and Bailey were following him to his horse.

"Dinky, whoa up." Pooh had his gun out.

"The name is Watts, Ben Watts." He looked at the gun Pooh was holding. "No need for that."

"Last time you was here I heard Pap call you, Dinky. You got a taste of the whip Pap uses on thieves. What are you doing back here?"

"Truth is I'm looking for a job."

"Here? Huh." Pooh holstered his gun. "We don't hire gunnies." He eyed Ben over like he didn't believe him. "You quit the Sliding D, did ya?"

"Been quit awhile." He looked back over to the small cemetery where Pap and everyone was gathered. "I didn't know about this. I can see it's not the time to ask about hiring on. Maybe I'll ride back this way later."

"Pap won't hire a gunny."

"He might hire a saint." Ben mounted his horse and rode off, leaving Pooh scratching his head and Bailey amused.

When Ben rode into the Sliding D, Zell and the Kid were standing on the front porch. The porch was high off the ground and the landscape sloped somewhat away from the house. Ben stayed on his horse with his hand low to his gun.

Zell had hate burning in his eyes. "Well, Ben, you saved me the trouble of having to look you up."

Ben pulled his gun unexpectedly. "I learned this from Pap Dockin. When you ride into a place that looks like trouble, you pull your gun and have it ready, keeps everyone calm."

The Kid smiled. "I'm beginning to see why you like him."

"Zell, I don't figure you know it, but you and Pap traded out on sons the other night. That was Chalk that killed Ted, and one of you killed Chalk. They buried him today. I figured to tell you, so you could pack up and leave, or barricade up in here and wait for Pap Dockin to arrive."

Zell had a gray look about his face. The news that he killed Paula's boy was a shock, maybe even more so than losing his own son, Ted. He gathered his composure. "Now, why would I run or build a fort for the likes of Pap Dockin?"

"Well, I don't know. It was you that raped his woman and now has killed their son. You knew Chalk Cranfield was Chalk Dockin, didn't you? He looks too much like Pap. You need to run or hide one. Because you aren't any match for Pap Dockin."

Zell was jolted by the knowledge Ben had of his past. "I ought to have the Kid kill you! Where the hell did you hear such a thing?"

"Pap Dockin." Ben now knew it was true. Zell couldn't hide the alarmed look on his face.

Huey was standing inside the screen door of the house and heard what Ben said to his father. He was stunned. He walked out on the porch as Zell turned and walked to the other end. He wasn't facing any of them. He was staring out across a field where cattle were grazing. In his mind, he went back to the day he knocked on Paula Cranfield's door.

She had come to the door and cracked it slightly. "Hello, can I help you?"

"Ah... I'm Zell Davis. Franklin Dockin and me are partners in the cattle business."

"Oh, why yes, Franklin has spoken of you. He's not here right now." She paused. "He has gone to sign some papers on the sale of cattle and get the money for them. I thought he said you were to meet him there?"

"Yes, well, I was but he really don't need me to sign off on the cattle. I had something else in mind. Can I come in?"

"Of course, forgive me for being so rude."

Zell came in and sat down at a small table. "I've been wondering what it was that was occupying Franklin's time. Now I see. You are beautiful. Fact is, you may be the most beautiful woman I've ever seen."

Paula blushed. "Thank you."

"Yeah, well, no need to thank me. Damn looker you are." He looked around and pointed to the adjacent room. "Is in there where everything happens?"

Paula suddenly became uncomfortable. "I'm sorry?"

"Don't play innocent with me. I know you and Franklin have been laid up here for two days. That's okay."

"Sir, I think it's time you leave." She stood up to show him the door.

"No Miss, me and you are just getting started. Ya see, me and Franklin, we're partners, and we share in everything. Now you get your little whoring self in there and get naked. Zell, he's gonna have a little sugar, too." He grinned at her.

Paula ran for the door, but he stopped her. He took her right arm and bent it back behind her until she could not take the pain. He then dragged her to the bedroom and stripped her of her clothes. She tried to fight him off, but he was too strong. He had his way with her twice. It was after the second time that he realized she wasn't a common whore. She had pictures of her mother and father along with another young girl about her age on the wall. He found work payments lying on her dresser for sewing and washing she had done. Zell kept looking at her as she lay across the bed on her stomach, her face buried in the pillow crying. She was magnificently beautiful. She was soft with cream colored skin and eyes the color of turquoise. It was then that something happened to him. She was a good woman, and he suddenly realized it. She was the kind of woman that could put a man in a spellbound trance, the kind of woman a man would want to keep. She wasn't a whore at all. She was just a girl trying to get by. From what he discovered laying around her room, she was a hard-working lady. He suddenly knew he had wronged her. Her putting up a fight wasn't for show. He stared at her as she lay across the bed. When he realized she was not only beautiful but a woman to be respected, he began to feel something he had never felt before. He asked himself who wouldn't feel something for her. She was beautiful, clothed or naked. He was helplessly falling for her. Maybe if he let her know it was a mistake. Maybe he could make it up. Maybe she could forgive him in time. He had no idea when he went to her place, he would be leaving with feelings of love and passion. He wished he could have a do over, but what was done was done. He left very unsettled and remembered going back to try and make things right somehow, but she was gone. He wished many times things had been different, that he hadn't put upon her, and that Pap Dockin had never been with her. Pap always got first choice on everything. He was the one with all the luck.

Zell took a deep breath. Paula was in love with Pap, and she had his kid, Chalk Cranfield Dockin. Now I've killed him. He cut his eyes around at Ben sitting on his horse. "We didn't know who was trailing us... the boy was an accident. I mean, he followed us after we set the fields on fire. Damn you, had you not run out on us, you could have stopped him from following!"

"Yeah, the boy was an accident, raping his mother wasn't. Zell, don't try to lay your deed on me."

"It don't change things! Pap Dockin's days are numbered! He killed my boy and he'll damn sure pay for it with his blood!"

"You raped a woman? Pap Dockin's woman?" Huey had walked up behind his father.

Startled, Zell turned to face him. "Huey, it ain't like it sounds."

"How does rape sound, Dad?" Huey was looking at him like he was seeing his father for the first time.

Zell started to backhand him but managed to restrain himself.

Huey stood facing him unafraid. The new revelation of what his dad had done made him sick of heart. He was determined to stand up to him. Any respect he might have had for his father was now gone.

"Son, I can explain." He reached to him, but Huey pulled away.

"No! Stay back! I'm leaving here." Huey turned to Ben. "Wait on me, Ben, I'm riding out with you."

He disappeared into the house, packed a few things and

saddled a horse. He rode in beside Ben and looked up at his father and the Kid standing on the porch. "I'm sorry for you, Dad." He cut his eyes over to the Kid and then back to his dad. "You two deserve each other."

"Listen to me. Huey it ain't like you think."

They turned and rode away leaving Zell and the Checkered Kid standing on the porch watching them ride out.

The Kid called after them. "Ben, stay out of it! I don't want to kill you! I will! You hear me? I will!"

Zell looked over at him. "I've lost two sons now, all over a damn woman." He turned and went inside slamming the screen door.

Chapter 22

Nine days went by without a sound from Zell or Pap. Maybe the both of them were trying to heal or waiting on the other one to blink first. Whatever the reason, every cowboy on both sides could feel the tension in the air, the dead quiet before a storm.

The roundup went off like clockwork. Pap had put Speck in charge and Pooh was taking orders direct from him. They rounded the cattle up and put them in holding meadows. The Dockin ranch was missing three hundred and thirty-four head according to Speck's count. Twenty-five hundred steers would be sold, and the grown cows would be turned into winter pasture. But, before that could take place, other things were to be tended.

Pap was hard to figure. The Dockin ranch hands thought for sure they would be riding against the Sliding D by now, but Pap hadn't shown a sign of making a move. The one thing they all agreed on as they became anxious, was that Zell Davis must be starting to worry. He had killed Pap's son, and he had to know hell would demand payment.

Speck saddled a horse and rode out to find Pap. He had been gone for several hours which caused him to be concerned. He found him sitting on the old log down by the creek where he liked to fish and swim occasionally. He rode up and sat down beside him. Pap didn't say a word and neither did he. They sat there for a minute or two before Pap finally spoke.

"Speck, me and you have pulled some nice catfish out of here, haven't we?"

"Sure have."

"Me and Chalk went swimmin' here. I told him I would teach him how to fish. You know the boy never went fishin' his whole life. I had lots of plans." Pap had a rock in his hand and threw it in the water. "What the hell happened, Speck?"

"Oh, I don't know. Life, I guess. Life is a mystery anyway you cut it. I wondered that same thing when I lost Rue... what the hell happened? It took some time, but the pain finally eased. I'll always love her and miss her. That will never change. It will be the same for you. The pain will dull some but the love you had for Chalk, that will always be."

"Speck, the boy wasn't here long, yet it felt like we'd been together forever. I can't rightly explain it. I had plans for me and him... I'll not be makin' any plans from here on."

"Is that right?" Speck quickly cut his eyes at Pap, and then away. "From what Vivian told me, Chalk asked you to raise his son, your grandson. That'll take some effort, and some planning along the way. Cran is going to be a fine boy. He's got good blood running through his veins."

"Yeah... Chalk said that." Pap's eyes darted here and there as he took in Speck's last comment.

Speck detected reluctance in his voice. "Pap, that little boy didn't ask for this. He didn't ask to be raised by you. He wasn't given a choice. You can't hold resentment against the little feller. Fact is, you have a duty and you should honor the wishes of his daddy, your son. That boy needs a daddy, like it or not you've been chosen. Are you telling me you're going to fail both your son and your grandson because things didn't work out Pap Dockin's way?"

He looked up from the hole of water he was staring into and cut his eyes to him. "Speck, you don't leave much room to wiggle in do you?" He paused as he stared at the water. "Guess I'm out here feeling sorry for myself. You always could make me think about what I was doin' even when I didn't want to. What do you say we get out of here?"

"Been waiting on you."

They got up and mounted their horses. They smiled at each other and turned towards the ranch house. "Speck, let's kick 'em up a little, we have lots to do."

They rode back to the ranch house side by side in a pretty slow lope.

Ten days after burying Chalk, Pap watched wagon after wagon come rolling in with winter feed for the cattle and horses. Ellison Jones had done as Vivian instructed. The grain and hay problem were solved.

The Dockin ranch hands watched Pap with careful eyes. He wasn't the same as before Chalk died. He was reserved, every move was with purpose. Even when he fed his gelding of a morning he would get up at the crack of dawn, walk out to the barn carrying Cran in one arm, and a can of feed in the other. As soon as the horse was fed, he went back to the house without speaking to one soul. It was like he was there in body but somewhere else in mind. Some of the boys were beginning to wonder if he had lost his nerve.

Pap sent for a lawyer on the eleventh day and made out a will. He divided up his world and left it to Vivian, Cran, Speck, and Pooh, with Cran getting the most. He made provisions for all who worked for him and who had been loyal. They would always have a job and be cared for until, as he put it in the will, when it was time to put one of them down.

The twelfth day was a moment of interest to all. Pap walked out in the yard and rung the dinner bell at one o'clock in the afternoon. Everyone gathered around including the old hound Duke, who never left the shade if he could help it. When all the hands were present, he made an announcement.

"I've called this little meetin' to inform you tit suckin' babies that there's goin' to be a, 'joinin' up' here tomorrow night, and a party to follow. Enjoy it, 'cause I'm goin' to ring this bell one more time." He took his hat off and ran his hand through his hair. "When I do, we're goin' to have another kind of party. The host will be Zell Davis." Pap turned and walked inside the house as the men shouted their approval of the latter party and yelled out congratulations to him and his coming marriage. They were surprised by the wedding announcement, but they had been waiting on the Zell Davis party. They wanted some pay back for Chalk and the attacks on the Dockin Ranch.

At three o'clock that same afternoon, Huey and Ben Watts rode up in front of the Dockin home. Pap met them at the wooden gate in the front yard. "Dinky, what brings you out here? Huey, you've kind of strayed off your range, haven't you?"

"I guess maybe you could say that."

"I did say that."

"Pap, me and Huey here are looking for a job." Ben was looking him square in the eyes.

"I don't hire gunslingers. This is a cattle and horse ranch."

"I know you don't hire guns." He stepped off his horse. "Would you hire a saint?"

"Would I what?" Pap stared at him and then began to grin. "Yeah, Ben, I would."

"What happened to calling me, Dinky?"

"You're not him. Man I knew by that name was a hired gun, not a saint." Pap stuck his hand out and they shook hands.

"Pap, what about Huey?"

Speck walked up about then.

"I just hired Ben Watts here, Speck, and Huey wants to ride with us, too. What do you think?"

Speck was stumped. "You sure about this?" He looked at Ben and then over at Huey. "These boys are... well hell, I don't have to tell you who they are. Have you thought this out?"

"Say again?"

"You thought about what you're doing?"

"What do you mean?"

"Have you thought about what you're asking young Huey to do in a few days?" Speck looked at Ben. "And this'en here is nothing but a gunny."

Ben wasn't surprised by the resistance to hire him. He felt Pap would be the one to win over, but Speck would also have to be convinced. "Was... not now. I just want to work cattle." He looked over at Huey and smiled. "If Huey is right, I might make a hand with young colts, too. I'd like to put these guns away one day."

"Why the change?" Speck was skeptical.

"Oh, I think it started when I took a ride with a man who introduced me to the Saint Maker. It wasn't the whipping... it was something more. Something I don't really know how to explain."

Speck smiled. He knew what Ben was talking about. He had felt the same thing when he met Pap Dockin for the first time. It isn't something a man can explain, but some men command respect, and that was Pap Dockin. "I've got no objections to you riding for the Dockin spread... but Huey, I don't know." Speck looked up at him and then at Pap. "Before you hire him you better tell him what he may be facing."

Pap stuck a chew in his mouth. "Son, we're ridin' against the Slidin' D in a few days. That's your pa we're goin' against. I'll hire you and I won't ask you to ride against him, but I'll not be lookin' at trouble from you either. I've heard you're one good hand with young stock. I knew a man once just like you. He had the feel for it. I could use you in that way. How's that sit?"

"Mister Dockin, I'd be lying if I didn't tell you I was saddened by all this, terrible sad about it."

"Speak up."

"Sir, I know what this is all about. I just found out a few days ago. I left home the same day I learned what the bad blood was between you and dad. I couldn't be a part of what he is doing. I'm sorry for what has happened, both now and before my time."

Pap looked over at Speck quickly. He felt a stab of heart felt emotion at Huey's words. They came from his heart and were true to his soul. "Speck, the boy wants a job, hire him." He turned and walked into the house.

Huey felt he said something wrong. "I was just trying to let him know I understood how he felt."

Duke came up and licked Speck on the hand, causing him to pat his head. "Look, Huey, Pap's been through a hell of a lot the last little while. He's getting married tomorrow and he's not giving much thought to much else. That's about the size of it far as Pap goes. He's hired you, both of you, so we'll let it go at that. Bunkhouse is over yonder. Put your horses in the corral. Welcome to the Dockin spread."

Huey turned and rode towards the corral. Ben was turning to lead his horse when Speck stopped him.

"Ben, you good with that shooter?"

"Made my way... why?"

Speck looked back towards the house. He didn't want anyone to hear him. "Well, Pap would never hire a gunny. He's as fast as any gunny I've ever seen anyway. But the Checkered Kid rides for Zell. I guess I'm wondering if push comes to shove, could you take him, if... if say it come to it?"

"You know I've wondered that myself." He led his horse away, leaving Speck exasperated by the lack of an answer.

The next day Pap had the ranch hands fixing up the house while the lady, who did the weekly cooking along with Sitting Dove, helped Vivian make the big spacious living room look like a place for a wedding and a party. Several folks from town were invited, and Ellison Jones arrived midmorning from Kansas City.

Pap sent Pooh and Ben to town to pick up more provisions for the party, one being a barrel of Dry Rock whiskey. They stopped by the hardware store and picked up a box of cigars, two cans of snuff, and one box of chewing tobacco. Not one thing they were sent to town for was edible food. They had climbed back on the wagon to leave when the Checkered Kid and three of the Sliding D men rode in.

The Checkered Kid spotted Ben sitting on the wagon and rode over beside them. “Ben, what are you doing?”

“Getting ready for a wedding.”

“Oh? Whose?”

“Pap Dockin.”

The warm smile on the Kid’s face slowly faded. “Ben, you‘re a fool. I warned you. You’ve crossed over.” He looked up the street shaking his head and smiling.

Pooh sat still and quiet. He was half scared. He didn’t know what to expect. He did know he wasn’t a match for the Kid if Ben got plugged.

“I’m going to have to kill you, Ben. I’ve never killed anyone I didn’t mind killing. You’ll be my first.”

“Kid.”

“Yeah?”

“Why don’t you shut up and draw.” The first thing that ran through the Kid’s mind was anger. By the time he was ready to draw, Ben had his gun out and on him. “Now, I’m going to ride out of here. You can leave that gun holstered or drop it on the ground. If I’ve got your word we can ride out peaceable, I’ll holster mine and we’ll save this for another time.”

The Kid smiled. “Another time.” He turned and rode towards the saloon.

Pooh let out the longest breath Ben had ever heard. “I thought shore we was dead. I thought that crazy son of a you know what was going to end my meager, worthless little life.”

Ben laughed. “I did, too.”

“Yeah, but you beat him bad to the draw.”

“No... I didn’t. The Kid was mad. He always did have a temper. He was too busy getting mad to draw. I took advantage of that.”

“You’re a cool customer, Ben Watts, a cool customer.” They rode the rattling wagon out of town heading for the Dockin Ranch.

Chapter 23

"I do."

"And do you, Pap Dockin, take this woman to be your lawfully wedded wife?"

"I do."

"I now pronounce you man and wife. You may kiss the bride." The preacher smiled as Pap kissed Vivian softly. The guests and cowboys erupted with congratulations.

Speck, Bailey, Art and Pooh were the first to shake Pap's hand. Pooh was the first to mention his attire. "Boss, I never seen you in a get-up before."

"What?"

"A get-up... never seen you in one."

"Pooh, I don't get married enough for you to see me in one."

Speck walked around behind Pooh. "Why don't you just shut up?" He pointed across the room at Vivian. The other women had gathered around her and were going at it like chickens pecking crushed corn on the ground. "She's mighty pretty, Pap."

"Say again?" The noise from the folks talking in the crowded room made it harder for him to hear.

"Pretty! I say she's pretty."

Pooh seconded the motion.

"Yeah, oh yeah! Pretty as a vase full of poises."

Speck chuckled at his old friend and thought about that. "I guess posies is good enough to compare to if posies are what comes to mind." He looked at Pap without him knowing he was and spoke in a whisper. "You sure are something Franklin 'Pap' Dockin."

Musicians had been hired to play for the party, and the first dance was reserved for the bride and groom. They were beautiful as they glided around the room. The Dockin ranch hands were proud, proud of the man they had come to not only like, but to love. There wasn't one of them that wouldn't walk through hell for him. They had never seen him dance and didn't know he could. Watching him and Vivian made them proud, proud to be part of a life so grand. Working for Pap Dockin wasn't easy, but none of them knew it. They were happy and were treated more like family. Once the dance was finished, the entire floor filled with couples. Pap was shrewd in his invitation to his wedding. He invited all the women he could, so his men would have dancing partners. He even invited the only two saloon girls in town.

The room was filled with music, laughter and chatter. But then suddenly, things went from celebration to hostility. Pap and Vivian were standing by the refreshment bar when the front door to the house burst open from a thunderous kick. It was Zell Davis with the Checkered Kid and two other men. They had guns drawn and cocked. He knew none of the Dockin men would be heeled because of the wedding. He searched the room until he found Pap.

"I've come for my son. Where is he?"

"I didn't hear you, Zell, but it doesn't matter, you're intruding. You and me have differences, and they'll be settled, but not today. I'm tellin you to leave. There have been enough innocent folks hurt over something that happened between us years ago."

"Shut your babbling, Pap! I want my son and I mean to have him... now!"

The room was deathly quiet. All the women had retired to the far wall, while the men stood in front of them. It was the best they could do without guns.

"Here I am, Pa. I'm not leaving with you though. I work for Pap Dockin now."

"The hell you do! I've got a horse saddled and waiting outside. Now you get mounted or I'll shoot the damn bride of this shin dig right where she stands."

Vivian stepped out into the middle of the room and took Pap

by the hand. "Then you will have killed both Paula's son, and her sister."

Zell was stunned. His eyes were like black darts looking for a target. "You're Paula's sister?"

"I am."

"Then you need to leave the room. I'm not leaving here." He was cut short when he felt a gun barrel press against his back.

"Mister Davis, these good people are having some kind of a party. You don't seem to be invited, for sure not wanted. Now you and the three with you drop your guns, and ride on out of here."

Zell and his men dropped their guns to the floor and turned around. Zell was stunned. "Troy Howell! You're a dead man. You work for me."

"I did work for you. I've been laid up at Doc Zimmer's office for a while. I almost died. Did you know that, Zell? The boy that owns the hundred-acre patch saved my life after he found me under his floor. I was hiding under the floor of his house. He fetched me out and took care of me. He told me on the way to the doctor that when I got well, he'd like to hire me to work for him. I liked the boy. Chalk was his name. Zell, I worked for you, rode for you, and you never even come to check on me. You knew I was hurt bad... but you didn't bother to look in on me." Troy looked over at Pap. "Sir, I showed up here to ask for a job." He smiled because of the situation. He came seeking a job and ended up holding Zell Davis, his old boss at gunpoint. He turned from Pap and smiled at his former boss. "So long, Zell."

"Troy, I'll kill you."

Troy cocked his pistol. "Ride!"

"Hold on a minute!" Pap gently gave Vivian's hand to Speck and then took a step towards Zell. "I've turned the other cheek. I've tried to avoid the inevitable, but you've treated me with hate and scorn to the point I would damn near make a, 'Job', from the Bible. Any other man I would have already planted.

Your reckoning hour is nearly upon you. Enjoy this night, Zell, you have but few left."

He looked at Pap searching his eyes. "What's the matter? You feelin' the hate for me you know I feel for you?" He laughed. "You can't come for me. You've got no grain and you've got cattle to take north."

"I've got grain... and hay. We shipped it in. The only thing I have to do before the cattle are sold is rid the Texas Panhandle of you. Chalk took care of two of your bunch when he found my cattle you had hid away. I'll take care of the rest of you."

"Cattle?"

"That's ok, Zell. Time is in short supply for you."

Huey watched his father closely and for the first time, he thought he saw him become unsure of himself.

Zell looked around the room at Huey, and then at Pap. "Go to hell."

Pap slapped him hard across the left side of his face, causing his lip to bleed. Before Zell could react, he slapped him on the right side. He stared at Pap with fire in his eyes, yet he turned and walked out into the night.

Zell had no gun, and no edge to carry it further. Troy Howell was a surprise. If he hadn't been there, Zell would have gotten Huey on a horse and then hit Pap in the mouth in front of his bride and men. He would have humiliated him, but instead, it was Zell who was humiliated. The hour of reckoning between the two men was coming and coming soon.

The Checkered Kid reached down for his gun. "Mind if I pick this up?"

Pap walked to where the gun lay, picked it up and unloaded it. He noticed all the notches as he handed it to the Kid. "Fancy yourself a real hand, don't you?"

"I'll do."

"You what?"

"I said I'll do... you old bastard!"

The Kid didn't see it coming when Pap slapped him to the floor. Blood began to trickle out his nose. Pap spoke softly. "A little respect here in front of the women folk. Pick yourself up and get out."

The Kid nodded to the ladies and cut his eyes back at Pap. "Old man, no one lays a hand on me and lives. You show up at the Sliding D, and you won't see anything but fire coming from this gun of mine. It'll be hotter than your hay and corn fields."

He turned to leave when suddenly he felt himself being lifted off the floor by the seat of his pants and shirt. Pap rushed him through the door and heaved him out into the front yard, causing him to roll all the way to the gate. "Get on your horse and ride."

The ranch hands and other guests clapped their hands and laughed at Pap's disposing of the Checkered Kid. Once the Kid was gone the music started and the party resumed. Pap, Speck, and Troy made their way to the kitchen.

Pap was looking Troy over, boot to hat. "I'd like to thank you for what you did in there."

"I owed Chalk. I was near dead when he got me to Doc Zimmer."

"I wasn't gettin' all that was said in the other room, but I heard the word, job. You here for a job?"

"I'd like one. I'll give you fair work. I figure I owe Chalk my life. Sir, I'm a cowboy, not a gun hand. I didn't want anything to do with attacking your place that night. That's why I peeled off from Zell and the rest when we left out. I was hit, and I wanted to get away from them." He looked down at the floor. "I heard through the Doc..."

"Talk up, son, I don't hear good."

"Sir, you aren't that old. I don't understand why you can't hear me better... some kind of accident?"

First a smile appeared on Pap's face, then it changed to a grin and then he laughed. "Son, Troy, you're goin' to do well here at the Dockin Ranch. I see why Chalk liked you. I like the hell out of you already. Some of my hands could learn a thing or two from you." It was doing Pap's heart good that Troy thought him young like.

Speck silently rolled his eyes.

Troy didn't know what to make of Pap's reaction. "Ah, yes sir. Ah, sir, I wouldn't be here right now if it wasn't for your son and I'd sure like a shot at making you a first-rate ranch hand."

Pap laughed when he looked at Speck. "You hire this boy or wish you had. He's got a good eye. Said I was too young to be having hearin' problems."

It tickled Speck to see Pap carry on. His old friend was happy. He had a new bride and was nearly called a youngster. "Yeah, I think we hire him despite his eyesight. If it hadn't been for him, I wouldn't be getting to drink all the whiskey I want tonight." They laughed, and the Dockin Ranch had a new hand.

Once all the guests were gone except for Ellison, who was given a bedroom to stay over in, Pap took Vivian to his room. He had the lady who did the weekly cooking prepare the bed and had ordered roses to be laid across the pillows. A bottle of wine was sitting on a silver tray with two long stemmed crystal glasses.

Vivian felt like a princess. All she could do was smile for the first five minutes.

Pap poured the glasses not quite half full which Vivian noticed. She was surprised that a rough, tough man like Franklin Dockin would know to pour a glass of wine to half full.

They sat and talked for a few minutes until he reached over and kissed her. "I feel like a giddy kid. For a while I thought the Man Upstairs was playin' a joke on me. That a woman like you could love a man like me."

"Franklin, you're a good-looking man in a rugged sort of way... and I love you."

He leaned over towards the oil lamp and blew it out. For the next little while, the both of them would need no light.

The next morning after all the horses and the hound Duke had been fed, Pap walked out to the dinner bell. He picked up the iron rod and began to ring it. The men gathered around with anticipation on their faces. He looked out across them and counted twenty-three men.

"We ride today. We ride on Zell Davis. If any of you wants to rethink goin' with me, this is the time to speak up." None did. "Huey, Bailey and Art. You boys stay here and watch after things. It might be that Zell could have a man watchin' the place. If he does, hide the women and defend them... one of you ride after me if it happens."

It wasn't sitting well with Bailey and Art to stay behind. They wanted a piece of the action. "Boss, maybe you could let me go along, hell... I..."

"Speak up, Bailey!"

"Awh, never mind."

"We ride in thirty minutes. Load your rifles and side irons. Speck has an extra box of shells for your rifle and your six guns. If you ain't wearin' a forty-five, Speck can dig one up for you."

Bailey walked over to Speck and picked up a box of shells.

"What are you doin'? I thought Pap told you to watch the place."

"Speck, I've never disobeyed the first order given me, but either fire me or let me ride with you. Me... and ole Art here, we got to knowing Chalk while waiting out a storm. He was a man, a friend, and a by God cowboy. I know he was a little green, but he had the makin's of being one of the best damn cowboys to hit the Panhandle. He was our boss for a few hours. He put me in the mind of Pap dead out. I figure to set some things right. Now, you can let me go along as working for the Dockin Ranch or I'm going along on my own."

"Yeah, I guess that goes for me, too, Speck." Art walked over and picked up a box of shells.

Pap smiled when he saw what was happening and intervened. He cut his eyes at Troy Howell. "Troy, you said you were a cowboy, not a gunny. I'm asking you to stay here with Huey. I guess Art and Bailey are going with or without my blessing."

"I'll do it, Boss."

Pap's eyes were a bit sad when he spoke to Huey. "Son, it's a hell of a thing. I'm going to attack your place while you're here watchin' mine."

"Yes sir… it is. But these aren't normal circumstances. I love my pa but he's most crazy, like a mad dog. If you don't ride against him, he's going to kill, and keep killing."

Ben Watts knew Huey spoke from a sad heart. He had really gotten to know him over the last little while. The two of them had shared a room at the Lazy Day for a while and had become partners. "Huey, you still think I could make a wrangler?"

He grinned. "Sure you could. The rest of this bunch may not know it but you're a push-over, got a heart bigger than Texas." He stared at Ben for a second or two. "Just don't get yourself killed before you get the chance to try."

Ben succeeded. He had a purpose in asking a question that had nothing to do with the event at hand. He wanted to change the mood and get Huey thinking about horses, his love.

Pap turned to the men. "Saddle up! We ride!"

Any thoughts from the Dockin hands about Pap maybe losing his nerve had been erased.

Chapter 24

Pap kissed Vivian goodbye and led his men from the ranch at a slow lope. She went back inside and was greeted by Ellison.

"I realize Pap doesn't think of me as someone to depend on with a gun, however, I took his shotgun off the wall and have loaded it with buckshot."

There was a big leather chair close to the far wall. He dragged it out to the middle of the room and sat down. "If anyone comes through that door other than Huey, Troy Howell or the law, he's going back out loaded with two barrels of this stuff."

"I'm seeing another side of you, Ellison."

"I have you know I was quite the bird hunter in Pennsylvania as a young man."

"Would you like some coffee?"

"I think I would."

She left and was only gone a few minutes. She had a white ceramic pot and two cups sitting on a tray. "Sugar?"

"No... you know I don't take sugar." He looked at her while she poured. "Viv."

"Yes, I know... we need to talk."

"I swear, you always could read my mind."

She smiled as she handed him a cup of coffee. "I'm ready to sell if you are ready to buy me out. I'm through with the business. I'm happy here. I've never been happier. Oh, I guess I'm worried some with this ordeal involving Zell Davis, it's enough to make anyone worry. I know Franklin can take care of himself, he has for years. I'm happy here, and I'm in love."

"I know you are. A blind man could see your happiness by the feeling in the air around you."

"Thank you, Ellison, but flattery isn't going to buy my half any cheaper. I tell you what we will do. Bud Spencer at the Kansas State Bank can put a value on my half, I trust him. I assume you do?"

"Yes, of course."

"Alright then, it's settled. How is the coffee?"

"It is splendid."

There was a knock at the front door. She got up and opened it and stared in disbelief at who was standing there.

Pap Dockin and his men rode to within a half mile of the Sliding D Ranch and stopped. "Boys, we get off and lead our horses from here. I don't want any dust stirred up or loud hooves hittin' the ground. If we ain't settin' a horse when the shootin' starts, our aim will be a lot better. Shoot to kill. When I give the signal, open up with those rifles and keep shootin'. I've got it figured Zell will have a couple of guards watchin' the road, and that will be about it. I've not come after him after all he's done, so he's relaxed some. He'll think I'm celebrating my wedding today. I know him. He's lazy, not one to strategize and put a battle plan together. It's near ten o'clock. I know what he's thinking. If I didn't come at daylight, I'm not comin'. Me and him fought in the war together. You could count on me to attack at sunrise before the enemy had time to wake up good. I'm countin' on him remembering that. Fact is, not too long ago, just to throw him off, I told him I would wake him some gray early morning."

It was just like Pap said. Two guards posted and they weren't paying attention. Bailey and Art slipped up on them and knocked them out with rifle butts. Then Pap signaled to open fire and rifles began throwing lead at the Sliding D Ranch. Bailey picked off the first man who was standing by a corral holding a rifle in his right hand. Art was busy taking out a man on the front porch of the house. He must have been a guard because he had a rifle cradled in his arms. Two men ran for the barn, but rifle slugs spun them around leaving them bleeding in the dirt. Pap and his men walked towards the house firing their rifles at will. Three more Sliding D men fell from Dockin bullets. The windows in the house were shattered, and holes were appearing in the front door and walls. It must have been too much for one of the cowboys in the house, because he came out blazing. Pap dropped him with one bullet. He toppled from the high porch to the ground with a thud. The battle was raging in other parts of the ranch as volleys of rifle and pistol shots could be heard in any direction.

One cowboy came charging out of a corral on a barebacked horse. He fired his pistol dry and hit one of the Dockin riders in the right leg. Ben Watts took the man from the saddle with one quick pistol shot. He fell dead with a bullet to the head.

Suddenly bullets rained down from the loft of the barn, dropping one of the Dockin men to his knees. He was the youngest cowboy on the payroll. He had fallen face down. Pooh ran to him, checked the wound and found the bullet had passed through his right side. He had a chance if he didn't bleed to death. Pooh took his own bandana off and stuck it in the hole to slow the bleeding down some.

Speck was shooting as he came across the opening to where Pooh was. "Is he alive?"

"Yeah, barely!"

Speck grabbed the boy by one hand and Pooh grabbed the other. They drug him to the side of the barn and assessed the situation. "Pooh, I'd take him inside, but I have a feeling the barn is full of angry Sliding D men. Another thing… I'm going to have to lose some weight. This here excitement is tuckering me out!"

"Yeah, you need to lay off the cornbread and buttermilk." He grinned as Speck gave him a hard look.

The Checkered Kid was the one that dropped the young cowboy and was drawing down on another one when a bullet knocked glass from the window into his face. He was inside the house with Zell and one other cowboy.

Zell looked out at the mayhem. "Kid, we're going to have to make a run for it!"

The Kid laughed. “Not yet we aint!” He drew down and fired. Another Dockin rider fell behind the watering trough by the barn. The Kid laughed as he searched for another.

Pap saw the man fall and ran to him. He got down in behind the trough and examined the wounded man. “You alright?”

Bailey turned around to face him. “Hell no I ain’t alright, I’ve got a bullet in my left shoulder! Bleeding pretty good.”

Pap looked above his head and saw a saddle draped over the corral rail. He reached up and took the cinch loose just as a bullet ripped a path across the seat. He took the cinch and laid Bailey’s arm in the middle of it. Then he used his belt, ran it over his shoulder and through the ends of the cinch and drew it up. That would hold the shoulder tight until he could see a doctor. “This will have to do. Can you shoot that pistol?”

“I’m just waiting for you to get out of the way.”

Pap grinned at that. He liked Bailey a lot. He then looked up and saw the barn was on fire. It was then, seven men piled out the front doors where Speck and Pooh were at. The Sliding D hands didn’t know the two Dockin men were beside the barn. It was a fatal mistake. Pooh and Speck opened up on them at the same time Pap, Ben and Bailey did. Ben was across from Pap, hidden behind a wagon. Three of the men went down quickly, but the other four were firing at will. Pap fired three times, killing two of them. Ben took out one and would have taken the last one, but the man threw his gun away, and held his hands in the air. The shooting had died down some, when a bullet hit a fence post in front of Pap, not three inches in front of his face. He whirled and fired towards the house, causing several more Dockin men to open up on it.

Zell grabbed the Checkered Kid’s arm. “Kid, we got to get the hell out of here! They’ve damn near killed us all!”

“You run! I’m not through yet.”

“You crazy bastard! You can stay, I’m leaving! Pap will kill us all if we stay here! We’ve got to go!”

"I've got to get a shot at Ben. Go on, I'll be along."

A lamp exploded within a foot of Zell. The bullet came from Pap's gun. He looked at the Kid who was smiling while he was shooting out the window. The other Sliding D cowboy was looking around as if asking Zell what they should do.

"Let's get the hell out of here. If the Kid wants to die in here, let him." They ran for the back door and stopped beside it. Zell looked out and motioned for the cowboy to go first.

Art Teague had made his way around to the back of the house and was waiting for anyone who might have the idea to make a run for it. The first man came out shooting. He had a gun in each hand and was firing wildly. Art was standing behind a pear tree and fired twice, knocking the cowboy back against the house. Zell fired three times while running for cover. One of his shots creased Art on the side of the head. He fell to the ground as things momentarily turned dark. He got halfway up and realized too late; Zell had walked back towards him. He felt two bullets from Zell's gun hit him in the chest area.

Bailey had just walked around the corner of the house where Art lay. He shot at Zell but missed. He wasn't seeing very well and was feeling dizzy. He felt something else after that. The Checkered Kid had come out of the house behind him, and Bailey was unaware. "Cowboy!"

Bailey whirled just in time to catch a bullet just above the collarbone. The Kid smiled as he watched him spin around and fall. He stood over him and laughed as he unloaded his spent cartridges on Bailey's chest. He reloaded and trotted away, thinking he had hit Bailey in a more vital area. There was so much blood on his shirt from the previous gunshot wound it ended up saving his life.

Pap and Ben came around the end of the house and found Bailey lying next to Art in a pool of blood. Bailey was beginning to come to himself when Speck showed up with a canteen of water. He knelt beside him and offered the canteen. He took a large drink and then suddenly stopped. “Art!” He suddenly recognized Art lying next to him. “Art. Wake up, Art.” He pulled at his bloody shirt trying to get him to respond. “Art, damn you. Don’t you check out on me.”

Pap laid his hand on Bailey’s shoulder and patted him. “He’s gone son.”

Bailey slipped his hand under his best friend’s head and lifted him up. “Partner, hell, what have you gone and done? What the hell am I going to do? I got you this job and you run out on me. I don’t want to have to do my job and yours, too.” Bailey looked from Art to Pap with pleading eyes, knowing all was in vain.

“Bailey, Art wouldn’t have it any other way. You or him either one. You know that.”

He searched for something to say. “Art hasn’t any family I know of. I’d be obliged… if you put him somewhere close to Chalk. The two of us really liked him. Art always wanted to ask him what Kansas City was like. Maybe he can now.”

Pap smiled. “I think Chalk would like a good partner.”

Chapter 25

"Mrs. Dockin, I'm sorry but this man wouldn't let me come and tell you he was here. He just walked up on the porch like he owned the place and knocked."

"That's quite alright, Huey." She turned her eyes to the stranger wearing a badge. "May I help you?"

"Maybe. I'm Deputy Marshal Cooper... Baldy Cooper from Tonto, Texas. I sure could use a drink of water if you have one."

"Yes, of course." She turned, and he started to step inside. "Sir... wait outside. You haven't been invited in. Had you respected the wishes of Huey and let him announce you, then you would be welcome. However, you have acted unbecoming an officer of the law. Therefore, you can wait outside with Duke."

"Duke?"

"Yes. He's the hound you see lying under the porch swing. Even he waits to be given permission." Duke raised his head up when he heard his name. Vivian disappeared and came back momentarily with a glass of water.

He drank the glass down without taking a breath. "That was mighty fine. I thank you. Now, to why I am here."

Vivian interrupted him before he could get started well. "First, where is Tonto, Texas?"

"Ah... it's a little town just north of Amarillo. I come up here on orders from Marshal Thorp in Amarillo. He got word there was trouble up here in Mason City. Since Tonto is twenty miles closer than Amarillo, he asked me to ride up and look about the trouble. Story is, there's bad blood between two ranches."

"Well, you have seen. Now you are free to leave."

"I'm afraid it's not that easy. You see if there's trouble here, I'm charged with putting an end to it. I'm to bring in anyone that breaks the law or hinders me in my duty."

Huey spoke up. "We've been our own law out here all my life, and way before I was born. Tonto is several counties south of here. We don't need any law meddling around here."

"Times, they are a changing." Baldy Cooper had an arrogant smile about his face.

Vivian looked at Huey. "I'm trying to think of who could be having trouble out this way."

The deputy smiled. "Ma'am, you are Pap Dockin's wife... correct?"

"I am."

"There's no use in trying to fool me. The storekeeper in Mason City told me all about the trouble between Zell Davis and Pap Dockin."

"I know nothing of any trouble between Zell and Franklin."

"Have it your way." He turned to leave but stopped. "I'm going to look into this. You should have treated me a little better. I may have to make an example of Zell and... and Franklin." He smiled and turned for his horse.

They say an animal can tell a good-hearted person from a not so good-hearted one. Duke bailed from the porch and grabbed the deputy by the seat of the pants as he tried to mount his horse. He ripped the seat of his britches completely out before he turned loose. The deputy pulled his gun to shoot him and found that Huey, along with Troy, had him covered.

Huey smiled. "I wouldn't if I were you. Tonto, Texas will be minus one marshal if you do."

"I could arrest you for threatening a peace officer."

"Yes, but you don't seem to be trying to keep the peace."

"What's your name?"

"Huey Davis. Zell Davis is my father. This here is Troy Howell. He did work for Zell, but he went to work for us last night."

"I thought... well, now this is the Dockin Ranch?"

"It is. Me being here should tell you there's no trouble between the two ranches. Rumors can spread like prairie fire, can't they? I'd say you're a victim of nothing more than a rumor or a silly joke."

"I plan to get a room in Mason City. I'll be staying there until I get to the bottom of this."

"Good day then." Vivian shut the door. Huey let the hammer down on his gun, smiling at Troy as he did. Baldy rode off with his pants torn and his pride bruised.

Vivian was standing inside the door after she had shut it on the deputy, wondering who could have alerted authorities in Amarillo about trouble between the two ranches. She suddenly looked up and as her eyes moved to Ellison she spoke aloud.

"The law. Ellison, a little bit ago you said if it wasn't the boys or the law coming through the door you were going to unload that gun on them. Why did you say... law?"

Ellison turned the color of a red tomato. "I took the liberty of contacting what I thought to be the nearest marshal's office while I was looking into the routes and transporting of the grain shipments. I spoke to a marshal there and asked him to send a deputy out here to put a bridle on Zell Davis."

"Oh no. Ellison, do you not know what you have done?"

"Why... I thought some law and order would be looked on favorably."

"Ellison... this isn't Kansas City. You may have just gotten my husband hanged."

"Vivian, I think you're over-reacting."

"Ellison... if you thought we had trouble before, you've seen nothing now. It won't matter to Frankin if that man calls himself the law. You don't understand. Franklin has been his own law all his natural life. This thing with Zell and him started way before law was heard of where he came from. It will finish without the law. If this Baldy Cooper was to put Franklin's back up against the wall he will kill him. Then more men with stars on their chest looking to make a name for themselves will show up."

Ellison began to see what she meant. "Vivian, I'm sorry. If I've made matters worse, I'm truly sorry."

"I know you are. It's not your fault. You've never been around men like these. They were the men that tamed this land. Not the city boys wearing their little top hats and bow ties. It's the ones wearing six guns strapped to their sides that conquered the West and made it where people like you and I could live in it."

"Maybe I should go." He leaned the shotgun up against the wall, put his hands on his sides and stared at her. He didn't know what to do and felt terribly bad about what he had done.

"No, stay. We must tell Franklin what's happened, that's without question. Once you have talked to him, then you should go ahead and see the banker about buying my half of the business."

Ellison had a sick feeling in the pit of his stomach, and it wasn't about seeing the banker.

Zell had several horses in a makeshift corral just over the hill from the ranch house. He planned to use them to get away on, if things were to go bad with Pap. The Checkered Kid caught up with him just as they got there. Two other Sliding D men were there waiting. Zell looked at them with disbelief. "You two the only ones that made it?"

"Afraid so. I saw Kenny Matthews and seven others being taken prisoner. The rest was shot to hell."

Zell looked back towards the ranch. "Damn Pap Dockin! Damn him!" He looked to the Kid. "Let's ride, Kid!"

"Where to?"

Zell looked at him with fire in his eyes. "We'll ride out to the line shack. I need time to think."

"Not much to think about. We lost. You lost. The ranch is under Dockin control, and I guess everything else you have. I really don't see any reason to ride out to the line shack with you. Hell, you ain't got nothing I want." The Kid cut his eyes around at the other two Sliding D men. "What about it? You want to ride with this out of business old man? Or maybe ride with me, someone that's going somewhere?"

They looked at one another and stepped over by the Kid. "Deal us in."

"Alright, McCurry, you're in. You and Jordan saddle us up some ponies. We'll ride to Mason City."

McCurry was a tough looking black headed cowboy but was uneasy with riding to town. "Wait a minute, Kid. The Dockin bunch may come looking for what's left of us. That would be the first place they would look."

"How can they prove we were at the ranch during the showdown?"

"It won't matter, Kid, we're Sliding D."

"You three aren't taking my horses." Zell went for his gun.

The Kid drew and cocked his gun before Zell could clear leather. "Who's stopping us?"

Zell let his gun settle back into place. "I knew not to bring in outside guns. No loyalty."

"The only thing I'm loyal to is money. You're broke now."

"I still got it in the bank."

The Kid laughed. "How the hell do you plan to get to it? I figure you're done. There's better on up the road, but first I've got to settle with Ben. He went against me… and there's another thing. He don't seem to think I can take him. I can't ride out of Mason City and him not knowing that I can." The Kid grinned and mounted the horse Jordan saddled for him. He tipped his hat to Zell as the three of them rode out.

Zell hollered at them as they rode away. "I'll see you in hell!" He caught a horse out of the corral and saddled it as fast as he could. There were five more mounts and saddles left. He turned them out and rode for the line shack.

Chapter 26

Five of the Dockin men came back with bullet wounds. Two came back strapped across their saddles. Art Teague and the young cowboy, Henry Ode, were dead. There were seven prisoners taken and made to ride back to the Dockin place. Twelve Sliding D men were killed. Zell and the Kid were unaccounted for.

Pap had a look on his face unlike anything Speck or anyone else had seen. They dismounted in front of the barn and corral and no one said a word.

Vivian, Huey, Troy, and Ellison came out to meet them. "You're alright!" She put her arms around him.

"I'm okay. Art and the Ode boy didn't make it. He was too young. I should have made him stay here. Art, well, he just had a run of bad luck." Pap put his hand on Vivian's shoulders. "Give me a minute, can you?"

"Of course."

He looked at the seven Sliding D men still mounted on their horses. "Speck, you know any of these boys?"

"Yeah, I know ole Watkins there, the thin faced wiry looking cowboy. He's worked for Zell a couple of years. He worked for J.T. Barnes down on the Red before that. Good hand, but a little on the tough side when he gets to drinking. Kenny Matthews is another, nothing mean about him, just a prankster of sorts. A fair hand and good natured. He's the easy-going type. Matthews is a foreman, but Watkins is the one to get everyone's attention with, if that's what you're after."

"Watkins gets mean, when?"

"When he's had a few snorts."

"Then he's the one I would like to talk to. Bring him."

Speck and Ben took Watkins off his horse with his hands tied behind him and brought him to Pap standing on the front porch.

"They tell me your name is Watkins." Pap took a big chew of tobacco and stuck it in his mouth while staring at the man.

"Yeah, I'm Watkins. I'm from down south a ways." He was eyeing Pap's tobacco. Pap took his knife, cut him off a chunk and stepped down from the porch.

"I'm going to need my hands untied to stick it in my mouth."

He cut the ropes freeing his hands. "Ben, if he tries anything, kill him."

"It'd be a pleasure."

Watkins stuck the chew in his mouth, eyeing Ben Watts as he did. "Good tobacco."

Pap looked towards the cemetery where Chalk lay. "Watkins, up until a few days ago I'd either be hangin' you and your friends about now, or you'd be tied to a whipping post. I've already brought in a guilty verdict on the lot of you."

"Guilty of what?"

"Ridin' for Zell Davis."

"Wait just a..."

Pap grabbed him by the throat. "Shut up! I can't hear you all that good anyway. I'm talking, you listen. Zell has attacked me, killed my son, my men and burned my place. You ride for him and that makes you guilty by, by association." He turned him loose and looked over at Vivian. "Did I get that right?"

"Yes, it would be association."

Watkins rubbed his throat while eyeing Pap. "You crazy bastard, they ain't no law..."

Before Watkins could finish what he was saying, Pap hit him in the left eye. "Now, pick yourself up and listen." Pap stared at him long and hard. "I'm thinking you need to see what this old man can do with a bullwhip."

Speck was standing by Pap with the whip in hand. He took it and backed away from Watkins. Then like a rattler he let loose, cutting the tip of Watkins left ear off. He grabbed it in pain, and blood ran through his fingers immediately.

"You ready to listen?"

"You've cut my ear off!"

"Just the tip. I'll cut something else off a lot more important if you try me any further. Now here's the way I'm goin' to handle things. You and those other six are ridin' out of Mason City. You ride until you're clear of Texas. Ride all the way to Arkansas or head west to Colorado or Nebraska. I don't care where you go just as long as you go. I see you back in Texas again, I'll shoot you dead. I won't hesitate. You understand?"

Watkins spit his tobacco out on the ground. "You say I leave this area, or you'll try to shoot me down."

"No, I will shoot you sudden dead. No try about it."

"I never did like not being able to go where I please."

"Boys, string this sonofabitch up!"

"Hold on! Hold on here! I said I didn't like it. Didn't say I wasn't going along. I'm thinking I might ride up into Kansas. Hire on to one of them spreads up that way."

"No, no you won't ride up Kansas way. I don't have any luck with cowboys up Kansas way. You can ride south, east or west but not Kansas."

"You're a hard man, Pap Dockin."

Ben put in on that. "Watkins, you're getting off light. I'd take him up on his offer and ride like hell out of here."

Watkins wiped his mouth with his shirt sleeve while he held his hand over his ear. "I believe I'll do that. I'm tired of Texas anyway."

Pap walked over to the rest of the Sliding D men. "How about it, does he speak for you boys or do I hang you?"

They all agreed to leave Texas and never look back. Ben and the boys untied the Sliding D prisoners, and gave them back their guns, minus shells.

Once they were gone, Vivian asked Pap to let someone take care of his horse, she needed to talk with him rather urgently. He followed her inside the house and sat down. She poured him a glass of whiskey and sat down beside him in the big open entry room. Ellison was sitting across from them. "Franklin,

Ellison has something to tell you."

Pap had a frown on his face. "Well... alright." By Vivian setting it up for Ellison to speak, he knew it was important.

"Sir, I'm afraid I've made a terrible blunder."

"Oh?"

"You see, I thought... well I thought."

Vivian became annoyed. "Oh, let me tell it. Franklin, Ellison tried to help us out." She looked at Ellison and faintly smiled to reassure him he wasn't going to be burned at the stake or snubbed to a post while waiting on the Saint Maker.

Pap was frowning. "Help us out, in what way?"

"Listen to me, Franklin. Ellison sent word to a marshal in Amarillo about the trouble between you and Zell."

The expression on Pap's face changed so sudden it caused Ellison's eyes to widen with fear.

"Seems like you folks up Kansas way just can't keep from messin' in my business. Can you tell me what in damnation caused you to do such a stupid thing? I thought city dudes prized themselves on bein' smart."

"Pap, I've apologized to Vivian already, and I offer my apologies to you as well. I've made a terrible error. I was only trying to help."

Vivian put her hand on Pap's arm. "A deputy marshal from a town called Tonto showed up here today looking for you. I tried to convince him things were alright, as did Huey. I'm afraid he didn't believe any of us. He rode back to Mason City. I think he is staying at the Lazy Day." She smiled and squeezed his arm. "The seat of his pants was gone when he left here."

"Oh?"

"Duke didn't like the man."

"I don't like him either then."

Pap got up and walked to the door and yelled for Speck.

He came in and poured himself a drink. "What's on your mind?"

"You and Ben stay saddled. We're takin' a little ride."

Speck went to the door and hollered at Ben to keep his saddle on. He nodded in acknowledgment.

He turned to Pap. "Where are we going?"

"We're goin' to see a man about a dog." He looked over at Vivian and smiled.

"First, I have to see the man of the house." Pap left the room and went in where Cran was sleeping. "Hey, son." He was sound asleep. Pap touched him on the cheek. "I can't give you back what you came into this world losin', but I'm trying to make some things right that have been wrong for a long time. You sleep. Me and you are goin'to raise some hell one day." He glanced behind him, making sure Vivian didn't hear him using foul language around Cran. "Your daddy gave me charge to raise you. I'm goin'to do my best. I sure hope you take to a worn-out cowboy like me. I'm goin' to do my darndest to get you to like me. Heck, I'll even let you call me 'old man'." Cran smiled and Pap's eyes became big when he did. Vivian had walked up behind him and touched his back. "Did you see that, Viv? He smiled when I said that."

"I sure did. I think you have a partner coming on." She wasn't going to tell him the baby had gas and it made him smile.

"Yeah, me and him... we're goin' to ride, rope, and brand-um."

Chapter 27

Pap had sent Troy Howell for Doctor Zimmer and waited until he arrived before he rode for Mason City. Once the doctor was looking after his men, he mounted up to go.

"Where you boys headed?" Troy had walked out on the porch of the bunkhouse as they were mounting up.

"Mason City."

"Mind if I go along?"

Pap nodded his approval.

"Pap, I need to tell you something. When I was in getting the doctor, I saw the Kid and two Sliding D men go in the Dry Rock Saloon. One other thing, it seems there's some trouble with the Comanche."

"Trouble with mange? I'm not havin' trouble with mange. Is mange botherin' you?" Pap had a serious look on his face.

"No... I said there's trouble with the Comanche Indians."

He chuckled and looked over at Speck. "I need to give these ears of mine to somebody for trinkets. They damn sure ain't doin' me any good."

Speck laughed and then became serious. "I bet it's the same bunch that burned Chalk's cabin and stole our cattle for Zell Davis."

"May be."

They turned to ride when Luke Tanner rode up beside them. "I'd like to join this little parlay if I can."

"I reckon so."

Bailey limped out on the porch with his shirt off and bandaged from belt to chest. He sat his hat down over his head real easy like. "You boys aren't thinking of riding off without me are you?"

Pap found that both amusing and admirable. "I appreciate your spunk and toughness, Bailey. This time you've got to sit one out."

"Pap, I can ride."

"You done your part already. You stay here and take it easy. I'm sure they'll be another time." He looked past Bailey and raised his voice. "Vivian, take care of this hard-headed cowboy here. Bring him a glass of water and a six-gun. He can sit out here on the porch with Duke and shoot the next law man that shows up." He smiled at Speck and Ben. They laughed and then rode out.

They had only gone about a mile when Huey caught up with them. "Pap, I sat the last ride out. I can't do that again." They stopped momentarily and then walked their horses along as they talked. Pap looked Huey dead in the eyes. "What if your pa shows up?"

"I'm guessing by that pa is still alive. Well, I guess if he shows, we deal with it." They rode along a little further.Huey wanted to talk to Pap. "Mister Dockin."

"Yeah."

"Pa, he ain't been much of a pa to us boys, especially after Ma died. She kind of kept him in check. I don't know if he loved us or not. He seemed to begrudge us, and I've never known why."

"Huey... Zell." Pap paused and looked away.

"Yeah?"

"He has some problems. They started as a child and grew as he did. I guess he just never figured out how to deal with them."

"You think it was because he didn't have a pa himself?"

"He had a... well, maybe."

"Mister Dockin, you've known him longer than anyone. Is there something you're not telling me about him?"

Pap sat silent for a moment. "Huey, I've not told what I know about most things all my life." Pap clicked to his horse and they all moved into a soft lope, leaving Huey wondering what was just said to him.

Pap and his men rode into town and dismounted in front of the Lazy Day. "Ben, you boys keep an eye on the Dry Rock. The Kid may still be in there. Watch the streets. He could be waitin' to ambush us, though I doubt it. Slingers like him need an audience." He turned and went inside the hotel, as a curious crowd was beginning to congregate in small groups up and down the street.

Pap turned the register around and read the guests list. Baldy Cooper, room eight.

"You looking for me? I'm sure looking for you." Baldy was standing near the bottom of the stairs watching as Pap let his finger stroll down the list.

"Are you Cooper?"

"At your service."

"Well now, Cooper, I understand you were out to my place this morning. Thought I would save you the trouble of comin' back. It seems my dog don't like you, and I sure don't want your pants torn up again."

The smile that was on the deputy's face disappeared. "Oh, I wouldn't let that happen again."

"Well, it ain't just that. You see I figure if ole Duke don't like you... neither do I. The wife tells me you were a little on the rude side. I'd like an apology for that before we discuss your wastin' your time here in Mason City."

Baldy Cooper had never been so insulted and talked down to in his life. "Don't mess with me old man. I'll take you to Amarillo in chains. I'd rather take you back to Tonto, but the marshal of Amarillo said to bring anyone needing jailed... to him."

"I've been a little hard hearing, so be sure and speak up or come down here closer."

Baldy walked down the last two stairsteps. Pap walked over to him and without warning, hit him flush in the mouth. Baldy went flying backwards and fell against the wall. Pap walked over to him while he was trying to shake the cobwebs out of his head. When he could focus, Pap was sitting in a lobby chair holding Baldy's own gun on him. Pap's pistol was still in its holster.

"Now, would you like to start over?"

Baldy stared at Pap and slowly answered. "Yes sir. Please accept my most humble apology for the way I acted out at your ranch. Now hand my gun over."

"Not yet. Apologize for calling me... 'old man'. You can call me Pap or Mister Dockin, but not an old man. I may be forty- five and that ain't twenty, but old man I'm not."

"I'm sorry." Baldy held out his hand for the gun. Pap laid it in his palm with a slap.

"Viv tells me you came out here to check on some trouble. Long ways from home, aren't you? I guess you boys take in quite a swath of territory?"

Baldy had a handkerchief out wiping blood from his lips. "We do. I could arrest you for assaulting an officer of the law."

"No... no, you couldn't do that, and I'd rather talk about Marshal Thorp. That I think you can do."

"I can. Marshal Thorp sent me out here to see what the squabble was about. You've just hit an officer of the law. Though you gave my gun back, I've got to take you in."

"So far all you've gotten was a lesson in manners. You mess with me further, and you won't see Tonto, Amarillo, or any other town in Texas again. There are places out here you can disappear, and no one would care. If I was you, I'd let the schoolin' I've given you in manners be the end of it. I can be one hard sonofabitch if pushed to it." Pap smiled. "I can call myself names, you can't."

Baldy Cooper just stood there. He thought things over for a second or two, and then smiled. "Alright, I'll let it go this time. Now, back to what we were talking about. Marshal Thorp sent me out here to look into this little squabble between the two ranches, the Dockin Ranch and the Sliding D Ranch."

"Well, Baldy, the little squabble as you called it is settled. It took care of itself. Most of it was taken care of this morning. It ain't none of your business anyway to be honest. If Ty Thorp had been very serious about doing anything about what was happening between me and Zell Davis, he wouldn't have sent you. And on top of that, Ty is trying to fence in way more territory than he ought. We take care of any problems that might arise in this part of the panhandle."

"What does that mean?" Baldy didn't like the tone or insinuation. At the same time, he wondered how Pap Dockin knew Marshal Thorp. He must have, he called him by first name.

"Which part?"

"All of it."

"Well, It means he would have sent a man instead of a wet nosed kid, and we do our own lawin' here."

Baldy turned red with anger but held his tongue.

"I've got two items of pert... pertinent information for you, Baldy. The first one is that I've been my own law out here on this panhandle ever since I've been here. I took barren land and turned it into a place to raise and graze good beef cattle on bluestem. I've had to be marshal, judge and jury. It has worked pretty good all these years, and It will continue."

"Yeah, but things..."

"Button up. The second thing is that me and Ty... United States Marshal Thorp, kind of know one another. I spent some time with him in Dodge City, Kansas, once, and we played cards and had a few drinks in Horsehide, Texas, several times. Funny how things work out. He married Bet Hightower. I happened to know her, and... well, one thing led to another and over the years we became distant friends."

"Marshal Thorp didn't say anything about that to me."

"No, no, I suspect he wouldn't. He knew if he sent you out here, I'd give you an education. Baldy, you're green as one can come. You may act like you're tough, but I've pissed tougher than you." Pap took his tobacco out to cut a chew.

Baldy pulled out two cigars. "How about one of these?" Though he didn't like being talked down to, he decided to make an effort to be civil.

"Think I will." Pap took one and the deputy lit it for him.

"You need to head on back to Tonto tomorrow. Maybe catch an outlaw on the way back. There's nothin' for you to do here."

"No, no, I'll be staying."

Pap coughed and became half choked when Baldy said that. "Did I hear you right?"

"I'll show you and Marshal Thorp what I'm made of, Mister Dockin, you'll see."

"I knew you were green, but I didn't know you were ignorant. Well, suit yourself. You get in my way or try something foolish, like gettin' it in your head I need to go back with you for handlin' my own affairs... you'll end up in a pine box."

Pap turned to the door and motioned for Baldy. "Come with me." Baldy followed him outside where the rest of the Dockin men were. "Boys, this here is Baldy Cooper, deputy marshal in a place called Tonto, south of here a quite a ways." He cut his eyes to Baldy. "Just north of Amarillo... ain't that right?"

"That's correct."

"Alright boys, you've seen him. You know what he looks like. If he gives you any trouble, shoot him."

Baldy was smiling until he heard him tell his boys to shoot him.

Pap mounted his horse and turned up the street. He never even looked at Baldy. His men followed him, rode up in front of the saloon and tied their horses. Baldy was walking up the street at a fast pace towards them. Pap smiled when he saw him coming. "Boys, right there is a man on a mission."

Speck was curious. "What mission?"

"To die. I know God made him... but it beats me how He plans to keep him alive." Pap looked towards the saloon doors. "Check your guns. If the Checkered Kid is in there... hell will be, too."

Zell rode hard for the line shack and was almost there when he saw two horses tied in the small corral out back. He dismounted and snuck in closer. The horses wore the Sliding D brand. Zell holstered his gun and walked in.

"Boss! You made it. We didn't know what to do, so we hit it hard for this old shack."

"Raff, good to see ya, you too, Pepper. How did you boys get away?"

"We had just saddled up to check the stock in the big meadow. We shot it out for a while, but we were being overrun. So, me and ole Pepper rode for it."

"Yeah, well, we're it. The Kid and a couple of the boys rode out together. Kenny Matthews and several more were taken prisoner. I don't know what happened to them."

"What do we do, Boss?"

"We kill Pap Dockin. I'm not going to be able to go back there and live until he's dead. Let me think on it." Zell reached high up over a board that ran along a rafter and pulled down a bottle of whiskey. "I guess until then we might as well have a drink."

Raff and Pepper both felt they could use a good shot of whiskey.

Chapter 28

Before the Dockin bunch entered the Dry Rock Saloon, Ben caught Pap by the shirt sleeve. “Pap, I know you’re the boss, but the Kid, he’s kind of my problem much as he is yours. I’m asking you to let me go in first.”

“Well, we’re standing out here in front of this saloon like we’re wondering if we’re old enough to go in. I figure we are... after you, cowboy.”

Ben liked being called cowboy. It beat Dinky anytime. He smiled and swung the bat doors open. Pap and the rest of the men followed him in. The Checkered Kid and his two partners were sitting at a table near the end of the bar.

“Hello, Kid.”

“Hello Ben. I see you brought the whole Dockin bunch with you. Afraid to ride alone?”

“You know me Kid... I like someone to talk to.”

“Ben, I heard about the trouble at the Sliding D today. If you’ve come here to try and saddle me and these boys with any of it, I’m afraid we’re going to be a little cold backed to it. We quit Zell yesterday afternoon. We left the ranch before dark.”

“I’m not concerning myself with Zell. Me and you have our own settling to take care of. I’ve come to do just that.”

A big smile came across the Kid’s face as he stood up from the table. “What about your newfound friends standing behind you?”

Pap wasn’t sure, but he thought he knew what the Kid asked Ben. He turned his back to the Kid and ordered a drink from the bartender. Speck walked in beside him, and the rest of the boys bellied along the bar, too. They all ordered drinks with their backs to the Kid. That was Pap’s way of letting him know that the first round of shooting would be between the two of them. Pap was letting Ben have his time with the Kid. What happened after that would be decided then.

“I guess it’s me and you, Ben.”

"Kid, why don't you ride away from here?"

He laughed at him. "Ben, I'm the Checkered Kid. I don't ride away from anything... you know that."

"Kid, I've always been faster than you. I've just never needed the glory for it like you have."

The Kid laughed again. "We've drawn together lots of times. I always beat you, Ben. You never broke a damn bottle before me. I've got nine notches on this gun of mine. How many you got?"

"None. I told you. I don't need the fame. And I don't need to keep notches on my gun to remember the ones I killed. I'd like to forget them."

"Well know this, Ben... the tenth notch on my handle will be you. I'll make it extra deep."

Baldy Cooper came walking in the saloon taking long steps just like he was doing while coming down the street.

"Shoot! Shoot me!" He was repeating what Pap had told his boys to do to him. The problem was that when he hollered shoot, it caused the Kid to go for his gun. It also caused the other two men with the Kid to dive away from the table while drawing their guns. Pap and the Dockin boys spun around and rolled across the floor shooting as they went.

Ben drew as the Kid went for his gun. A bullet went by his head from the Kid's gun, but Ben had already fired and hit the Kid. He had beaten him to the draw. The bullet slammed into the Kid, leaving him standing there in total surprise once he got his balance back. He was stunned, bewildered, and not caring a gun battle was going on around him.

Baldy Cooper was totally surprised by the sudden gunfight and jumped every time a shot was fired. He stood in the middle of the saloon trying to make his self as small as he could, flinching with every shot.

Pap fired three times while lying on his stomach. Two of his bullets found their mark. McCurry, one of the Kid's new partners, took the two bullets in the chest but not until after he had fired twice at Baldy, missing with both shots.

Huey and Tanner emptied their guns at the other shooter, who had dropped behind the far end of the bar. Speck had moved to the end of the bar and was sipping on a whiskey. He had pulled his gun and fired one time. Then he laid it down on the bar and took another drink. The shooting had stopped, and it became eerily quiet.

Pap stood up from the floor. "Anyone hit?"

"Everyone looks to be alright, Boss." Speck then took another sip of his beer.

"What was you doin' while all the shooting was going on?"

"Having a drink. I stepped around to the end of the bar here out of the line of fire. I didn't figure they would hit me since they were firing at you boys on the floor. Oh, but I did hit the one at the other end of the bar. I shot him as he ran down that little hallway that leads out back. I think I hit him in the leg."

Pap cut his eyes at Ben who was standing over the Checkered Kid.

Ben took a deep breath and stared down at his once upon a time partner. "I tried to tell you, Kid."

"Had me thinking all this time I was quicker... smart, Ben."

"Kid." Ben was sick over having to shoot his longtime friend.

"Awh, Ben, I'm glad it was someone I respect."

"You have a sister. You want me to write her?"

"Reckon I've got... the bigger part of five thousand dollars. Plant me and send the rest... to..." He never said another word.

Baldy Cooper was still standing in the middle of the room shaking. He had not drawn his gun, nor moved from the spot where he was when the gunfight started. His eyes were like big white marbles with a little green spot on each of them. Pap walked over to him, grabbed him by the ear and slammed him in a chair. "You greenhorn idiot! I was wondering how God was goin' to keep you alive. Now I'm wondering how He's goin' to keep the rest of us alive when you're around."

Baldy tried to speak but his voice wouldn't come.

"Don't talk. Just don't talk." He turned back to the boys. "Speck, you might have told someone the other shooter escaped."

"Would have, did in fact. I had to wait until the shooting stopped. I could see you boys had the Sliding D boy penned down. If he stuck his head up, I was going to shoot it off. Truth is, I didn't feel like getting down in the floor. I'm getting too old, too heavy, and this bullet wound I got is sore as hell."

"Where did the barkeep go?"

"He's behind the bar."

Pap walked over and peered over the backside of the bar. "If you're not shot to death, get up and pour us a drink. Gunfightin' makes a man thirsty."

The barkeep got up and with shaky hands poured everyone a shot in a glass.

Baldy got up from his chair and slowly walked over to the bar. The Dockin men turned to watch him, including Pap.

"Barkeep, pour me a shot of whiskey." He drank it down. "Another." He drank it down. "Again." He drank the third one slower. When it was empty, he slowly turned to face Pap and the boys.

"Whether Marshal Thorp really wanted me to put a stop to the fight between you and Zell Davis, and whether you really know him or not... I think I'm going to get in another line of work. I'm just not cut out for this." He reached in his shirt pocket and paid for all the drinks. "I'll be leaving in the morning, but I'm not going back to Tonto. I think I'll head up to Bear Creek, Kansas. I got a cousin there... James Hall. He's in the newspaper business. I figure he'll have something I can do." He looked Pap in the eyes. "I personally don't care what it is. Two bullets went by my head during that fracas. I don't know how they missed me."

Pap looked Baldy over from head to toe. “Grace of God I’d say. I think you’re makin’ a wise decision. It takes a certain breed to be a lawman. You’re not it. I wish you luck. Have a safe trip.”

“I appreciate that. You know, I first didn’t cotton to...”

“Baldy.”

“Yeah.”

“Go, ski-daddle... now! Have a safe trip but be on it.”

Baldy stood there with his mouth open. He realized he was being told to vacate the room. He left without another word.

Speck walked in beside Pap. “Why were you so rough on Baldy?”

“The man is bad luck. Gets the seat of his pants ripped out, and then starts a damn gunfight he has nothing to do with, that might have been avoided. It could have come down to just Ben and the Kid. The other two might have thrown their guns on the floor.”

Pap turned to Ben. “You’re fast, no doubt about it. How come you let the Kid beat you when you were shootin’ at bottles?”

“Couple of reasons.”

“Couple of seasons?”

“No, couple of reasons. The Kid needed to feel like he was the best. So, I helped him along.”

“I see... what was the other?”

“Well.”

“Talk a little louder. The little gunfight we had has my ears ringin’ louder than they were.”

“It came to me one day to have an ace in the hole with the Kid, to not give away what I could really do. The Kid had a bad temper at times. If he ever flew mad, well, I better be ready.”

“Seems to me, if you had let him know you could beat him, he wouldn’t have tried you.”

“No, the Kid would have looked for an edge someway. He wouldn’t have shot me in the back, but he would have sure turned the odds in his direction."

Pap took a silent breath and turned to the rest of the Dockin boys. "Well, we got cattle to take to market. We best be gettin' to it."

"Wait a minute!" The barkeep seemed upset all at once. "Who's going to remove these two dead bodies?"

Pap looked at him and smiled. "I'd get a hold of Zell Davis. They belonged to him." The Dockin bunch turned and walked out on the boardwalk in front of the saloon.

Speck had a visible question on his face and Pap saw it. "Alright, let's have it?"

"Zell Davis, that's what. I want to know what we're going to do about him?"

"Well, I don't rightly know at the moment. It's for sure he ran like a jackrabbit. He's hid out somewhere. He may rest up tonight and leave the country."

"I just don't understand it, Pap. Me and you have run down outlaws, Indians, hiders, hell, everything. It didn't matter, we went after them and didn't come back until we hung 'em. Zell has done more to you, to the Dockin ranch than any man alive or dead. Why aren't we riding him down? The cattle have grass. I say we finish what we started. He's all that's left. The Kid is out of the way. There's nothing keeping us from killing him."

"Boys, I know how you feel, I feel the same, but have you given one thought the man is still Huey's pa?"

The whole lot of them showed their embarrassment, for they had forgotten about Huey being his son. He had become one of them and was so quiet they let it slip their minds.

Speck apologized. "We're sure sorry, Huey. We're not all that bright."

"I understand. It's just the way it is, that's all." Huey had many emotions and thoughts running through his own head. He knew his father, and nothing would stop him... but a bullet.

Speck was looking at Pap. "I'd still like an answer."

"Say again?"

"An answer, you hard hearing polecat, I'd like an answer."

"Speck, I have Vivian to think about, have you forgotten that?" He stepped off the boardwalk and onto his horse. "You comin' or not?"

"I guess so, you hard hearing jackass."

"Awh, quit your mumbling."

"I can mumble if I want to. Don't it bother you that Zell is still out there?"

Pap pulled his horse up. "Bothers me more that I can't hear a damn thing you're saying. On the other hand, maybe it's a blessin'. I don't have to listen to you runnin' off at the mouth all the time."

"Oh, so that's the way of it. Well, I'll not have you talking to me like I was a Baldy Cooper."

"Did you say Baldy Cooper is behind us?" Pap let his horse out into a long lope, laughing as he went. He knew he had shut Speck up by hitting a faster pace.

Chapter 29

Jordan Bennett, of the Sliding D, rode out to the line shack after the gunfight in the Dry Rock Saloon. He figured it was the only safe place to be and have a roof over his head at the same time. He had taken a bullet from Speck's gun during the gunfight and was still bleeding some. It had hit him on the side of the hip, cutting a gash all the way across. It bled quite a lot, but it wasn't life threatening. When he rode in, he was met by Zell and the other two Sliding D riders. He was glad to see them and dismounted slowly. The wound was already getting sore. "Boss, the Kid is dead. Ben Watts beat him straight up. Fastest thing I ever saw. The Kid got a shot off, but not in time."

Zell's eyes were wide. "Boss, is it? You quit me just a few hours ago. You sided with that faster than hell dead Kid. You're either crazy or one big damn fool to come back here calling me boss."

"Well... I was wrong. I admit it. A man can make a mistake."

"Not around me he can't." Zell drew his gun and shot Jordan in the stomach. He went crashing back against his horse and drawing as he fell. He fired twice, hitting a window to the left of Zell's head. The other two riders drew and jumped back inside the cabin. Zell fired two more times at Jordan while he was moving back towards the shack's door. Jordan was still holding the long-split reins to his gelding, but the horse was frantically trying to pull loose and finally broke the reins. He whirled and galloped away, leaving a trail of dust behind him.

Bullets were hitting within inches of Jordan's body as he desperately tried to escape the onslaught. He fired again, hitting the door. He managed to get around the end of the little building, and the gunfire stopped. He thought he was safe for a few moments and frantically tried to think of what to do. His eyes widened when he saw his whole mid-section was a bloody mess.

Then suddenly, Zell and one of the other Sliding D boys came around each side of the shack at the same time. Jordan didn't have a chance. They shot him three times in the back and twice in the chest. Zell kicked him to see if there was any life left in him. He never moved.

"See what happens to double crossers, you bastard." Zell holstered his gun, and the three of them drug him off out of sight. Raff and Pepper took his boots, gun, and money. "Boys, we ain't going to be here long enough for him to start stinking up the place. They ain't no use in burying him. The buzzards and coyotes need feeding, too."

They walked back to the shack and opened a can of beans. It was a big can, enough to feed all three of them. Zell smiled. "I guess that big feeling Checkered Kid got his." He took a big spoon full of beans and shoved them in his mouth. "Boys, I've given some careful thought to the situation. Here's what we're gonna do."

The next morning Huey and Ben were saddled and sitting in front of the Dockin ranch house, waiting for Pap to come out to feed his horse.

Pap opened the door and stopped abruptly on the porch, as his right hand fell to the handle of his pistol. It was pure instinct. "Where you two going so early?"

Ben smiled when he noticed him dropping his hand to his gun. "Pap, you may be a rancher, but you took time to learn how to use that shooter."

"Say what?"

"The iron... you handle it well."

"Fair."

Huey smiled at Ben and then looked at Pap. "We're headed home. I figure with the Checkered Kid out of the way and my pa probably out of the country, well, I need to get back and take care of the place. I know you have three or four boys over there watching for him, but I'd sure like to run the ranch. I could make a go of it, I think. I've got livestock depending on me to take care of them."

Pap smiled. "Huey, I was waiting on you to make that decision. I want you to do something for me."

He couldn't imagine what Pap could want. "Sure, what is it?"

"I want you to take the bay stud colt and start his groundwork. Get him thinking about a saddle. Leave the sorrel for now. Come get him later. The two of them need to be apart for a while. It'll do 'em good."

Huey lit up brighter than the fire that burned the Dockin crops. "I'll do it, no charge, just to say I broke a horse of his caliber."

"If you take him, I pay. No argument. You know, Huey, you put me in mind of someone I thought a lot of. You have his same disposition. You'll make a fine rancher." The smile faded. "Son, it's not over with me and your pa, you know that?"

"I know." Huey normally would have ducked his eyes down, but he looked Pap in the eyes instead. He wanted him to know he was a man now and had what it took to face things.

"I'll not be chasin' him across the country. I've got a ranch to run, but he'll be comin' back."

"Pap, we all have to confront what is laid before us. I don't know why pa hates you so much, but it has eaten him alive. He's past talk. The only thing that will stop him... is..." He couldn't say it, but he knew the only thing that would stop his father was death.

"Huey, you've become a man. I don't know when, but you've become a man. I remember the first time I saw you. Your mother carried you in the store in Mason City. You favored, awh, enough. You growed up into what looks like a rancher."

Huey smiled. "Thanks."

Pap looked at Ben sitting with his arms crossed on the saddle horn. "What about you?"

"Well, ole Huey here says I got the makings of a wrangler."

"A what?"

"A wrangler. You know, one of them cowboys that makes a living breaking and training horses. I might have a hand for something besides this gun."

"Huey sees the same thing in you I do."

"I wish you could have seen it a little sooner than you did." Ben smiled as he was relating back to the Saint Maker.

"Yeah, well, maybe the Saint Maker caused you to look at things different."

"No, Pap, it wasn't that. A man has to meet someone he can respect before he'll listen or think about what he's doing. I met him. I do think ten lashes would have gotten the same results." The both of them smiled. "Pap, I can't thank you enough."

"Oh... I don't know. I think a man would feel pretty damn proud to know he had something to do with a man turning his life around, tryin' to make somethin' of his self. That would be thanks enough." He paused as he looked at the two cowboys sitting on their horses in front of him. "Well, if you've got your minds made up, have ole Speck pay you off and put a halter on that bay stud."

"Speck already paid us. Huey tried to get mine, too, said he was carrying me while working here." Ben chuckled and so did Huey.

Pap stood on the porch and watched as they led the colt out of the barn. "You boys won't be the same once you've trained a good horse!" He watched until they were nearly out of sight.

Vivian walked out and stood by him. She noticed his eyes looked bloodshot. "You okay?"

"A pair of real men rides yonder, a pair of real men."

Chapter 30

Four days passed before Pap gave the word to Speck and Pooh to get the boys and start the herd. He had been waiting on word as to where he would be driving them. Turned out they would be taking them to Amarillo, Marshal Thorp country, to be loaded on rail cars. Instead of driving them north to Dodge City or Abilene, Kansas, they would take them south. The buyer was willing to pay five dollars a head more to get Pap to bring them there. The railroad had made it to Amarillo and cattle buyers were working hard to make Amarillo a cattle boomtown. It was a sweet deal for Pap... a deal he planned to keep as long as it lasted. Ellison was the one who put it together for him. It was his way of making up for his earlier blunder. He wired confirmation of guaranteed purchase of the whole herd at a premium price. Pap finally was having some good luck.

While Speck and Pooh gathered the herd, he spent all the time he could with Cran. Every time he held him it took a lot of coaxing from Vivian to let Sitting Dove put him to bed. Pap watched as he fell asleep. He wanted to be with him every minute. He knew he would be gone several days, so he was trying to spend as much time with Cran and Vivian as he could. He, nor anyone else on the ranch, had seen or heard anything out of Zell Davis. It was like he disappeared from the earth. Pap hoped he had left the country. Maybe seeing so many of his men being killed, it put the fear of God in him. He hoped that was the case.

"Viv, would you like to ride out and watch the boys gather cattle from the meadows?"

"Give me a second, I've got to change."

He hitched up the buggy while she took her second, which turned into twenty minutes. She came out of the house in riding pants and a dark blue blouse. She looked beautiful. He helped her into the buggy and they drove out to where the cattle were. They watched for a little while and then Pap drove the buggy to the small creek where they splashed in the water before. It seemed like a lifetime ago. Chalk and Sarah were alive; Cran hadn't come along yet. At first, he felt sadness, but then he saw the spot he held Vivian in the water, the spot where he kissed her. He smiled at the memory.

"What are you smiling about?"

"Us."

"Us? What about us?"

"I'm sorry but the running water makes a sound that sure interferes with my hearin'."

"What about us?"

"This is the spot I kissed you. We came back to the ranch lookin' like drowned rats. Chalk made mention that he didn't know it rained where we were at. You dismissed yourself and I didn't waste any time either." They both laughed. Then he took her in his arms and kissed her long and softly. He was feeling a great deal of emotion all at once, the loss and gain of loved ones. "I love you, Vivian."

"I love you, my darling."

They got out of the buggy and walked along the creek bank for a short distance.

"Franklin, Ellison took care of things nicely this time, did he not?"

"Well he did, but I still feel like I owe him."

"No. He did that to make up for his bringing the law in on us."

"Still... I pay my own way. Overcome my own hardships. It's hard for me to go along with such, but it was you and Ellison, so I'll not fight it."

"He also took care of something else. He is sending the money for my part of the company this week. I should have it before you get back."

"Well, now wait a minute. There's a sure enough hardship, you gettin' that money while I'm gone." He had a mischievous look on his face. "Don't spend it all before I get back."

"I'll see what I can do. We are going shopping for some new fashions this fall."

"We're what?"

"I sometimes wonder if you hear better than you let on. You seem to be hearing right along and then when something comes up that is a little bit contrary to what you might want, then you can't hear at all."

"Okay, we'll go shoppin' this fall." He laughed at her with a sparkle in his eyes. "I didn't hear you good, but good enough."

She put her arms around him, and they kissed until he lost his balance and fell in the grass with her. They stayed there for quite some time. They would try to look more presentable when they returned to the ranch this time.

Zell, Raff, and Pepper rode into the Sliding D, being watchful as they did so. Huey and Ben were working a pair of colts out at the corral. Ben saw them coming and strapped his gun on.

They rode up easy and leaned forward on their saddle horns. "Morning, son." Zell didn't acknowledge Ben.

"Pa." Huey's facial expression wasn't one of jubilation. He turned the colt he was holding loose in the corral.

"I see you have those colts well on their way. Keep 'em rode for me. Once you get the buck out of 'em, you may want to go to town and hire some more men. We need to get the cattle rounded up, pull the calves off some."

"Pa. I ain't working for you."

Zell looked confused. "Who the hell do you think you're working for?"

"Myself."

Zell laughed. "Huey, I've never known you to try to be funny with me."

"I'm not."

The smile left his face. "Why... you little bastard, I'll kill you dead as hell, you try taking my ranch!" He went for his gun.

"I wouldn't do that, Zell." Ben had drawn his gun before Zell even got his hand around the handle. "Raff, you and Pepper stay calm."

"Huey." Zell was looking straight at him. "You ain't taking my ranch. You'll be in hell with your brother before that happens. Mark my words."

Huey looked to the ground and then back at his pa. "I've always wondered if you thought anything of either one of us. Now I know you didn't and don't. Ted always tried to please you. What good did it do him? You didn't give a damn about him, did you, Pa?"

"Ted was a fool and you're nothing but a coward! I've seen the way you acted when you thought I was about to ask you to ride into a gunfight. I raised a yeller son."

Ben smiled. "Oh, I don't know... looks like he's doing a fair job of standing up to you right now." Ben was still holding his six-gun on the three men.

"You put that gun down and watch him tuck tail."

Ben stopped smiling. "Your son is not afraid of you. You've mistaken respect for cowardliness."

Zell took his hand away from his gun and laid it on the saddle horn. "I've got things to do. When I'm finished I'll come back for my ranch."

"Zell."

He turned towards Ben.

"If any of the things you have to do is with Pap Dockin, you won't be coming back. You should be here tending your ranch. Since you're not... since you've abandoned it... Huey has taken over. He might hire you if Pap doesn't kill you and you're still young enough to work after you get out of prison."

"Prison?"

"People go to jail for rape, murder, stealing, things like that."

Zell sneered at him. "We're our own law here."

"Marshal Thorp in Amarillo might get wind of you. Wouldn't

that be the worm in the apple?"
Zell spurred his horse hard and left in a full stride gallop.

Chapter 31

"Head 'em up and move 'em out!" Pooh gave the command to start the drive, while Pap, Speck, and Vivian watched from a short distance away.

"Well, Viv, I guess this is it. I've got to move out." He looked into her brown eyes as they sat side by side on their horses. He leaned over and kissed her.

"Be careful, Franklin. I'll miss you."

He picked up the reins. "Tell Cran I won't be long."

"I will." She waved to him as he and Speck joined the herd.

"You know, Boss, you got a fine woman back there, too fine to be leaving her alone." Speck lowered his voice. "You being an old coot not having a lot of time, you might think about spending as much as you have left with her and Cran." Speck raised his voice again. "I could take these beeves to Amarillo and you could stay here with your family."

"That's a right nice thing to say."

"Well, what about it?"

Pap pulled up. "Speck, me and you are going to make these drives long as the good Lord is willing. I figure Cran will take over when we're done. This being the first trip, I best take them down if I can."

"He'll be an old coot."

"Who will be an old coot?"

"Cran. We're going to live to be a hundred." He slapped his right leg and laughed. "We'll tag along in a wagon sucking our thumbs when he takes over." He burst into laughing again.

Pap grinned. "You're doin' that already once in a while."

"The hell I am!" He jerked his head around and looked at Pap with squinted eyes.

Pap sat there and stared into the eyes of his friend. "Speck, I don't guess I ever said... I've never been one to talk much about the way I feel about someone or anything. Me and you, we've rode the Panhandle together for a lot of good years. I'd like to say... I wouldn't trade one of 'em for anything else I could think of. I couldn't have picked a better partner. Thanks for backin' my play all these years. It's hard to find a true friend. I found one in you."

Speck turned his head away from Pap and mumbled to himself. "I'll be. Here I sit puckering up out here on my horse, and about to ram rod a cattle drive. Last thing I ever expected out of Pap Dockin, was to let me have a glimpse of his heart." He glanced over at him. "Pap, I appreciate what you said. I feel the same. I wouldn't have wanted to ride the high plains with anyone else." Speck looked at him, and then smiled. "Hell, everything you turned out to be you owe to me anyway."

"Say again?"

"You heard me you hard-hearing ole crow bait."

Pap grinned. "Let's move some cattle, what do you say?"

Speck laughed. "Like old times." They set an easy spur to their horses and rode to the head of the herd.

Raff had climbed a tree on a hillside to get a better view of what was going on down at the Dockin ranch. When he was sure they were gathering cattle to make a drive, he climbed down and rode to the line shack. He should have waited longer, for he didn't see them leave with the herd. Zell anxiously met him at the door.

"Boss, their bunching right now."

Zell smiled big. The gap between his front teeth gleamed even more prominently than usual. "Pap is fixin' to drive two thousand head of prime steers north. We'll cut across and be ahead of him by ten miles. We can pick him off with a rifle. We shoot to kill. One of us will get him." Zell smiled. "I've waited a long time for this. I wanted to put him to his knees. I guess killing him will just have to do." He had practically forgotten about Raff and Pepper standing there. "Boys let's have a drink! Tomorrow will be a good day."

Later that evening Pooh rode up in kind of a hurry and dismounted at the campfire where Pap and Speck were sitting.

"You're in a big hurry, aren't you, Pooh?"

"Pap!" Pooh was excited.

"What's wrong?"

"I think some of Sitting Dove's kin is waiting to ambush us."

"What makes you think so?"

"I saw three of them. They joined up with about eight or ten more. I recognized one of them. Sitting Dove called him a lone lobo. His name is Crazy Wolf. I heard he had some braves riding with him. I bet he's the one that stole the cattle that night for Zell. He plum damn spooks me."

"He what?"

"Spooks me!"

"Why does he spook you, Pooh?"

"Meaner than hell looking, that's why!" What Pooh was telling them was serious, still, everyone in the camp laughed.

"I'm meaner than hell lookin', you spooked at me?"

"I've gotten used to you."

"Am I mean looking, Pooh?"

"I need a cup. I'd like to have some coffee." Pooh was being teased by Pap and didn't know quite how to answer. "Depends on who you're asking. Vivian, I guess she thinks you're pretty. Me, I think you're edging right up to ugly, like the rest of us."

"You plum hurt me, Pooh." Pap begin to laugh but was cut short when he saw a band of Indians riding towards camp. Pooh saw them, dropped his cup of coffee and pulled his gun.

"Put it away, Pooh. Hell, you have an Indian woman. You're the last man that should fear a friendly Indian."

"Sitting Dove says he's anything but friendly."

Pap got up from the fire and walked out to meet the small band of Comanches. Speck and Tanner went with him. Bailey and Pooh stood back. The rest of the boys watched and were ready if anything went wrong. Pap raised his hand in show of friendliness.

A stout looking, handsome, square jawed brave, with two blue and white feathers in his hair, rode in on a bay colored paint. "I, Crazy Wolf, you Dockin?"

"I'm Dockin."

"Cut hundred head out of herd, Dockin."

"Say again?"

"Cut hundred head out of herd."

"I heard you. I'd need to know the why of that."

Crazy Wolf stared at him for what seemed like an eternity. "Cut hundred head out of herd, Dockin."

"I give your people, the Comanche, prime beef every winter. I have for near twenty years. I give it to them to eat so they can make it through the snow and winds. I don't give my beef to a damn renegade, so he can get drunk."

Crazy Wolf realized this man knew he was the one that stole his cattle and traded them to the Sliding D for whiskey. "Dockin, you hard man."

"Not hard enough. I should kill you."

Crazy Wolf smiled. "You brave man, not foolish man. You too long in tooth to kill me. Cut hundred head out, Dockin. Your time has passed. I young brave, much brave."

Speck looked straight ahead but tried to look at Pap out of the corner of his eye at the same time. "Easy Pap. He didn't mean anything by the, 'long in the tooth', comment. Even if he did, he doesn't know any better."

"Well, by God, he's fixin' to."

Pap walked up beside Crazy Wolf as he sat on his horse. Six more braves sat on horses behind him, all ranging in ages from thirteen to twenty.

"I've got a great respect for your people. Chief White Hair is a friend. You wouldn't make a decent enemy and sure as hell you wouldn't make a good friend. You're a bugger-eatin' disgrace to your tribe."

None of the Dockin hands expected that from Pap and burst into laughter. Crazy Wolf's eyes darted over to them at the same time Pap reached and pulled him from his horse. It was such a surprise; Crazy Wolf couldn't react in time to do anything about it. He hit the ground on his head. Pap let him get up and then hit him square on the jaw. He plummeted backwards and fell hard. He kicked him in the side and then the head.

"White Hair would have never let this happen! You ain't a warrior, you're a drunk lookin' for a drink! You could never be a proud Comanche warrior. They're a proud people, a good people. You're a low crawlin,' snake! You get up and get out of here. If you come back... I'll kill you."

Speck and the rest of the men had drawn their guns and held them on the other braves who watched the white man knock their leader nearly out. Suddenly one of the other braves turned his horse and rode off. He threw his spear down as he went. The rest slowly did the same. They were embarrassed by the one they had chosen to follow.

Pap picked Crazy Wolf up and sat him on his horse. "Remember, you come back or give me any trouble, you won't see the comin' winter."

Crazy Wolf rode off bent over and was almost out of sight when he slowly came to a stop. He sat for a few seconds and straightened up. He turned his horse and slowly began riding back towards them. Pooh was the first one to notice. "Pap, that Indian is coming back."

Tanner walked out where he could see better. "I'll be. He sure is."

Pap pulled his gun and checked the cylinder.

Speck eye-balled Pap. "I guess they don't call him Crazy Wolf for nothing, do they?"

"He figures he has nothin' left to live for. I disgraced him in front of his braves. He'd rather die than live in disgrace. At least he's got some pride."

When Crazy Wolf was within fifty yards of the camp, he kicked his horse and charged in at a full gallop. He had a rifle raised and was aiming. He fired one round, kicking up dirt out in front of Pap. Slowly and deliberately Pap drew down with his pistol, aimed and fired, knocking Crazy Wolf from his horse's back.

Tanner, Bailey, and Pooh, along with some of the other Dockin hands, ran out to check the fallen Indian. Bailey rolled him over and looked up at the other boys. "He shot this sonofabitch in the forehead while running full out. That may be the best shooting I've ever seen." Tanner and the others agreed whole heartedly.

Speck eased in close to Pap. "They called him Crazy Wolf. Guess they named him right. He was crazy enough to get himself killed."

Pap had a sad look on his face. "Yeah... Speck, have Pooh cut fifty head out of the herd. Run 'em back to the meadow we passed a ways back. Build a good smoking fire. One of the Comanches will find them. They'll take them to their people... now that Crazy Wolf is gone."

Pap Dockin
By Royal Wade Kimes

Chapter 32

Zell realized something was wrong. The Dockin drive should have come by them and be gone already. "Raff, Pepper, mount up. We're riding down the trail a ways... see if we can hear or see anything."

They rode for an hour and found no sign of Pap and his herd. Zell pulled up. "What the hell happened to them? They didn't just disappear into thin air."

Raff rode up on the edge of a rise, and then rode back to Zell and Pepper. "Boss, what if they didn't make the drive? Maybe something or someone stopped them."

"Let's ride down to where we can see the ranch house." They rode in a lope until the Dockin spread was in view. "Raff, ride up on a hill and check it out, me and Pepper will wait here."

Raff was gone for twenty minutes before returning. The evening shadows were beginning to get long in length, and a cool breeze blew gently from the north. "Boss, they ain't a steer on the place that I could see, quiet as a Monday morning church house down there."

"Beats hell out of me, cattle drives don't go south." He sat there for a minute or two thinking it over. "Boys, let's ride down past the house." They spurred their horses into a slow lope. When they had passed the Dockin ranch house they discovered the trail in which Pap had taken the cattle.

Zell was off his horse looking in the direction they went. "Well, he sure as hell ain't taking his cattle to Dodge City. I don't know where he's headed, but he's got a good head start on us... wherever he's going." Gradually a smile appeared on his face. "It's coming dark. I don't know about you boys, but I'd like a nice soft mattress to sleep on tonight." He grinned as he looked back towards the ranch house. "I got a hunch they ain't no one watching the hen house."

Vivian was out on the front porch watering her flowers while Sitting Dove hung up freshly ironed clothes. She was finishing the last pot of flowers when Zell and his two partners rode up. "So, you're Paula's sister. I'm sorry we haven't had a chance to get acquainted sooner."Vivian dropped the water pail and ran into the house. She yelled to Sitting Dove to lock the back door and hide. She locked the front door as she heard shooting outside. She looked out and saw the three ranch hands Pap left behind to look after the place lying dead in front of the bunkhouse. There were four other hands, but they had ridden out to check the northwest section cattle. She turned and ran to the fireplace. A long-barreled shotgun was hanging above the mantel. It was all she could do to reach it, but she managed. She broke it open and found it loaded.

Suddenly, something flew through the French doors to the side entrance of the house. It was a sledgehammer. She turned and fired. She then ran to the cabinet where the shells were supposed to be. Zell and his men suddenly burst through the doors and rushed her as she fumbled with the gun. She was desperately trying to get another shell in the barrel before they overrun her. The shell slipped in and the barrel clicked shut.

Sitting Dove had walked to the entrance of the big room. She carried a knife on her always. She threw it and stuck Pepper deep in the left shoulder. He fired at her as she disappeared into the other room.

Vivian came around with the big shotgun and fired, but Zell had caught hold of the end of the barrel and turned it towards the ceiling.

"Ole Pap, he's got a fiery one! It must run in the blood! Paula, she put up a hell of a fight, too."

"You bastard!" Vivian swung hard and caught him on the side of the face with her open hand. He laughed. It was then she heard Cran crying. The loud shooting had startled him.

Zell held her arm and stretched his neck listening at the baby crying. "That kid in there come damn near being my grandson, instead of Pap's. Had his granddad not beaten me to his grandmother by a day or so, he would have damn sure been mine. I wondered all these years if Chalk was my kid. When I seen him, I knew he was Pap's."

"You barbaric filth." She was so angry she could feel herself shaking.

"Now, now, you need to get hold of that tongue of yours. Paula wasn't a name caller. She fought in silence, tough one, that girl. It was a funny thing about her. It wasn't until after I had her the second time that I realized she was more than a whore. She laid there in bed while I pilfered around through her things. She had a lot of things that lent itself to, well, that told me she wasn't a whore at all. She was a hard-working girl trying to make her own way. I hated what I done, but hell, it was an honest mistake. The more I looked at her the more I wanted her for my own." He stopped talking for a few seconds. "Pap, he didn't see it being a mistake. He also didn't like the idea of me falling for his girl. I don't know what he whipped me the hardest for, the falling in love or the tasting of his woman."

"You poor pitiful excuse of a man. The idea you can stand here and say the things you just did... tells me you don't know what love is. You never have, and you never will. You don't love anyone or anything other than your scorn and revenge for Franklin."

He slapped her and then looked at her somewhat amused. "Franklin? Hell, it's been so long since I heard him called that I forgot what his name was. Me and Franklin played together as kids and fought in the war together as young men. Zellard and Franklin. I was the poor bastard up the street, and he was the rich one down the street. Oh, I don't guess he was rich, but he sure had everything, a horse, his own rifle, clothes, boots and plenty to eat. Me, I had to scrap and fight for everything I got. Mom and me lived in a shack by ourselves. In the winter the wind would blow snow in on my bed. I'd lay awake at night thinking about Franklin up there in his nice warm house. I hated him. I didn't let him know it until the incident with Paula. I almost shot him once in the back when we was fighting the North."

"You're one brave man. From what I can see you didn't deserve any more than you had."

Zell hit her in the mouth, causing her to fall to the floor. "You'll watch your tongue, woman. I'll knock those pretty teeth out of your head."

Raff and Pepper came back in the big room, their guns trained on Sitting Dove. She was carrying Cran.

Zell took hold of the blanket and peeled it back. "Good looking kid."

"Boss, I've got a damn knife sticking in me, fairly deep. Hurts like hell."

"Raff, get me some whiskey."

"Where?"

Vivian picked herself up from the floor and with some degree of difficulty she walked to the cabinet to get a bottle of whiskey for Pepper's wound. She handed it to Zell without looking at him.

"Pepper, this may hurt. Raff, grab hold of the top of his shoulder. I got to pull that knife out. It's damn near all the way up to the handle." He pulled the knife out with a strong quick jerk.

Pepper groaned loudly and then eyed Zell over. "I thought you were supposed to pull a knife out of a man slow like."

"Slow, fast, what's the difference? It's out."

Zell looked around at Vivian. "Get some cooking done. We're hungry. You try one thing, and this Indian squaw is going to have three times the problems Paula had. Be thinking about breakfast, too. I plan to be here awhile."

Zell had given up on making Pap crawl until the opportunity

suddenly presented itself to buckle him at the knees. He figured to kill his wife or the baby, either one would do it. He knew Pap would do anything to keep his wife and grandson alive. He'd make him crawl and beg. He wanted to rule over Pap, be God over him. He wanted him to beg for their lives. He now had the power to give life or death. He smiled, and Raff saw it.

"What's funny?"

"I'm going to make Pap choose which one lives or dies, the baby or the woman." He had an evil grin on his face.

"Damn, Zell, ain't that going to..."

Zell's eyes had fire in them. "Don't say anything you can't live to regret."

Raff shut up quickly. He knew Zell would shoot him dead.

Zell looked at Vivan. "You as good as your sister was? Ole Pap, he just can't seem to keep his women from me." He smiled. "Nothing like family."

Darkness came with frightful uncertainty for Vivian and Sitting Dove. She fixed supper and wondered what would happen after they ate. She knew anything could. She worried about Sitting Dove. She was Indian, and these men had little respect for their own kind, let alone a Comanche. She also feared for little Cran. She had to protect her baby. She smiled at the thought. Cran was her baby. Sarah had left him to her, and she promised to keep him safe. She knew she had to do everything possible to achieve that end.

Zell watched Vivian as she and Sitting Dove cleaned the table and washed the dishes. "Vivian, you let the damn Indian wash the dishes. You can come over here and sit on my lap." Zell had found where Pap kept his whiskey. He and his two partners had a bottle a piece opened. "I said lay the damn dish down!"

She let the dish slide into the soapy water as her hand followed it in. When she felt the butcher knife at the bottom of the wash pan, she wrapped her hand around the handle. Raff and Pepper went upstairs to rummage through things to see what they wanted to take with them. That was luck she hadn't counted on having.

Sitting Dove watched Vivian and knew instantly what she had her hand on. She moved over behind Vivian in an act to get a cloth to dry the dishes, giving her time to slip the knife into her apron pocket.

Zell was getting dizzy drunk. He turned the bottle up and drank two big swallows. "I said come here, bitch!"

"You're drunk."

"Yeah, well, so what? I can give you a good time drunk or sober. This is part of it, little girl, me taking Pap's woman a second time." He took another drink and wiped his mouth. "I'd say the tough Pap Dockin ain't all that much of a man. Hell, he can't even keep his women from the other studs." He turned the bottle up again.

Vivian made a gesture for Sitting Dove to follow her into the other room. She walked slowly towards the kitchen door leading to the living room.

"You going somewhere?"

"We are retiring to the living room."

"No! That damn Indian bitch can leave but you got business in here with me!" He was loud, and his voice slurred as he spoke.

"You aren't touching me."

Zell tried to stand up. In his attempt, he fell and hit his head on the table and was knocked unconscious.

Vivian and Sitting Dove quietly slipped into Cran's room and wrapped him in two blankets. Sitting Dove had a bottle of milk and corn starch that she shoved in a cloth bag. Vivian grabbed a handful of cotton linen binders and a jar of salve. They quietly slipped to the living room. They could hear the other two upstairs throwing things against the walls. The big living area seemed even larger to Vivian as she led the way across it. She dared not look up for fear she would cause them to be there. It turned out it didn't matter. Zell had come to and began to yell for Raff.

"Raff! Get in here! Where's the damn women?"

Vivian had stepped up on the three-inch half-moon entry into the big room when Raff fired his pistol at her. The bullet broke the doorknob as he started down the stairs. "You hold on, woman! I'll blow your head off!"

Pepper was much slower coming down the stairs. His arm was in a sling from the previous knife wound, and he was drunker than Raff.

Cran was crying from the loud gunshot and Vivian was trying to remain calm.

Zell came and stood at the entry to the kitchen. He was holding on to the door facing, too drunk to turn loose of it. "Get that bitch, Raff!"

"I've got her!" He grinned as he came closer holding his pistol on her. "Nice try, honey." Raff was within fifteen feet of the two women when he stopped. He looked back at Zell and saw him sliding down the door facing. He was out. He turned back to Vivian. "I think you need to get out of that dress. I want to see what's under it." He was still looking at Zell making sure he was out. He looked up the stairs at Pepper. He had sat down, as he too was too drunk to move. "Damn, looks like I get you all to myself. I want to see what ole Dockin has been havin' for dessert." Pain exploded in Raff's stomach as he turned to find Vivian standing within a foot of him. She thrust the butcher knife all the way up to the handle just below the rib cage. He dropped his gun and fell to his knees. He took one hand and managed to sit down on the floor and looked up at her. "You've killed me. You no good whoring bitch! You've killed me!"

Vivian picked up his pistol and walked out the door with Sitting Dove and the baby. She knew the man she stabbed would live awhile with a stomach wound, but he would be in misery. They ran out into the yard past the deceased Dockin ranch hands. "Sitting Dove, we have to hitch up the buggy."

Sitting Dove handed the baby to Vivian and went into the corral for the buggy horse. She bridled him and brought him out. The harness was hanging inside the barn. When she came back out her face was pale. She tried not to lock eyes with Vivian who was standing beside her as she rigged up the harness. She had seen something in the barn that made her angry and sick.

"Hurry, Sitting Dove! If Zell wakes up, he'll come looking for us!"

"I hurry." She finished and had just turned to Vivian to get the baby when Zell came staggering across the yard to the barn. "Run! Vivian, take child and run!"

"Come with me!"

"No! I give you time to get away! Go!"

Vivian ran into the barn. There was a back door that led out to a small patch of woods. She had to get there. She stopped and caught her breath when she came through the door of the barn. One of the beautiful stud colts lay in the hallway of the barn. He was dead. He had been shot in the head by Zell Davis. She was grateful the other colt was with Huey or he too would be dead. She turned and listened. She could hear Zell yelling at her.

"You come out or I'll put a bullet through this damn lice-infested Indian!"

Vivian started to run but hesitated. "You come in here and get me!"

When she saw him stager to the barn door she yelled at Sitting Dove. "Go! Get help, Sitting Dove, find Franklin and Pooh!" She heard the buggy whip and then the sound of the buggy wheels racing away.

Zell turned and fired six times in the direction of the buggy. It swerved sideways once, he thought he hit her. He turned back to Vivian and walked in the barn and stood beside the dead colt grinning. "I killed his best damn breeding stock. He's begun to pay up. Me and you, we got some settling to do for ole Pap, too.

Me and you, we... we're going to take us a roll in the hay."

Vivian's mind was racing as she held Cran. She had to do something, but what?

"Set that little rat down." There was a stack of loose hay over in a stall area. He planned to have her in the hay, and she knew it. He sat down on what looked like a short milking stool, and then pulled his shirt and boots off. "Once you've had a real man like your sister did, you'll leave town like she did looking to find another one like me. But hell, they ain't one. I'm it. I tried to raise me a couple of boys that could match up, but they didn't make the grade." He grinned. "You're one damn lucky woman getting to have me." He reached down to pull his socks off and fell over headfirst.

Vivian saw her chance and ran past him. She had made an error. Raff's gun was in the bag with the baby's things. The problem with that was, the bag was in the buggy and it was gone. She ran as hard as she could down the road away from the ranch house. She looked back to see if he was coming. It was too dark to tell. She had to keep moving. "Hold on, little Cran, we'll make it. Just hold on."

She ran until she came to the small stream that crossed the road. She carefully lay Cran down on a flat rock and took one of his binders stuffed in his blanket and soaked it. She squeezed the water down over her head. It ran down her neck and over her shoulders cooling her down. She listened for horses and heard none.

Cran began to cry and just above a whisper she talked to him. "Hush little man. We have to be quiet. You and I are playing a game. We're running from the bad people." He stopped crying but kept whimpering. "You are a smart one, aren't you, Cran? You and I will talk about this, years from now." She took her finger and put it in his mouth. He began to suck on it, and slowly drifted off to sleep. She sat there looking up and down the little stream, debating on what to do. Go up stream or down, or maybe stay on the road.

Suddenly she heard horses. They were coming from the ranch. She had to hide in a hurry and do so quietly.

She gently picked the baby up and waded up the stream. When off the road she eased up on the side of the stream bank and curled-up around Cran. She prayed he wouldn't cry out.

Three horses went racing by, splashing through the stream as they went. She lay still until she could not hear the horse's hooves. "Come on, little man, we're getting out of here." She picked Cran up and continued up the small creek, not having any idea where she was going. It didn't matter as long as it was away from Zell Davis.

Chapter 33

Sitting Dove was pushing the buggy horse harder than she liked, but she had to catch up to Pap. She had two reasons to hurry, Vivian was in trouble and she was wounded herself. One of Zell Davis's bullets hit her in the right leg. She was beginning to feel a little weak and sick. She was thinking aloud. "The shadows run together. I feel sleep."

She came to a rather wide creek and decided to take advantage of it. The horse needed to rest and possibly drink, and she needed to tend her leg. She had all of Cran's binders in the bag and could use one of the binders for a bandage. In the process of getting one out her hand felt something cool and hard like metal. She pulled it out and discovered she had the pistol Vivian had picked up. She laid it on the seat of the buggy and went about cleaning and bandaging the wound. After tying it off the bleeding slowed down considerably.

She had been stopped for about ten to fifteen minutes when the sound of running horses came to her ear. Her heart pumped wildly as she picked up the lines and slapped the buggy horse lightly. Then a gunshot. The running horses were coming fast and right at her.

"I am Sitting Dove, Comanche. I not run from these dogs." She pulled the buggy over to the side of the road and turned around in the buggy seat. Once turned, she laid the gun barrel on the back of the seat to steady it. The hammer came back easily. "Come white man, come." She waited. The riders fired two times, exposing muzzle flash which presented a target to shoot at. She fired three times at the oncoming riders. Two of them pulled up, turned around and headed back the way they came. The other one rode towards her for another ten yards and fell from his horse. Her first shot was the one that did the damage, because she was sure the man nearly fell with the first round. She got out of the buggy and limped to where he had fallen. It would be too much to hope it was Zell Davis who was lying there. The man was lying on his side with his back to her. She walked around to see his face and saw it was the one Vivian had stuck the knife in. "You tough dead man. I saved you trouble of gut agony. You would die in two days from knife wound." One of her three bullets had hit Raff high in the chest near the neck.

Sitting Dove made her way back to the buggy, climbed in, clucked to her horse and headed for the cattle drive. She had bought some time for Vivian but finding Pap quickly was a must. If Vivian got away, she would have one less to contend with when they return to the ranch. She spoke aloud. "Help me Great Spirit. I must get to Pap."

Zell and Pepper rode back to the ranch house after losing Raff. He sat in Pap's big chair while Pepper stretched out on a settee. The killing of Raff and nearly getting killed himself had sobered him up. Pepper was getting feverish with his shoulder wound from the knife Sitting Dove had thrown into him. It had begun to have heat and swell.

Things had not gone well with the two women. Zell sat thinking about Vivian, and then it came to him. "I think I know how to find the woman and baby."

Pepper half turned to look at Zell. "How?"

"That ole hound out there on the porch. He knows the woman. We take him down the road and let him pick up her trail. There's a nice big dew on. Hell, he'll pick her scent right up."

"It might work. I'm afraid you got to go it alone."

"Why?"

"I'm running a fair-size fever. If I don't see Doc Zimmer soon, I could be in as much trouble as Raff."

"Alright then, you stay here and nurse that shoulder. I don't need you to track down a woman and baby."

Pepper didn't hear him. He had fallen asleep from exhaustion and the trauma of the knife wound.

Zell got the hound to come along after giving him a chunk of meat. Duke didn't act too friendly at first, but the meat made him accept the stranger.

He took the hound and walked down the road a short distance and Duke began to whine. He was picking up a familiar scent. He was soon on Vivian's trail. "That's it! You go, boy! Go get her!"

Zell took in after the hound as fast as his long legs would take him. "Go get her boy!" He was laughing every step. He was running Pap's woman down with his own hound. Zell always felt he was smarter than Pap, but it was Pap who got all the breaks. He now thought it his turn.

Duke came to the stream of water in the road and stopped for a moment. He raised his head high in the air and then back to the ground. He picked Vivian's scent up to where she had turned in the road. She had gone in the water and the dog was confused. Duke was a good hound, though. He went up the creek just a short distance and found where she had lain on the creek bank. That was it. He could not find any more scent. Vivian had stayed in the water. Still it was enough for Zell to know which way she went.

Zell checked his rifle and side iron. "Okay, hound, you done good. Now git!" He threw a rock at him. Duke jumped and dropped his tail between his legs. "Git! I don't need you trailing along. Git out!" Duke ran back down to the road, stopped and looked back. "Git!" He dropped his tail again and went trotting back toward the house.

Sitting Dove came racing into the Dockin camp with a tired, lathered up horse. She had pushed him to his limit. She stood up to step off the buggy and fainted.

Bailey was still sitting at the fire while everyone else was sleeping. He was missing his partner, Art Teague. He jumped up from the fire and was at the buggy when Sitting Dove fell. He reached and caught her before she hit the ground and then laid her down gently. By the time he had laid her down, the rest of the Dockin crew had gathered around.

"Pap! better get over here! Bring some water, boys!"

Pap felt sick inside when he saw Sitting Dove. Vivian was in trouble.

It happened it was Pooh who brought the canteen. Pap was down on one knee examining her. He looked up at Pooh who handed him the water. Pooh, realizing it was Sitting Dove fell to his knees beside her.

"She'll be alright. She's lost a little blood. I'd say from the looks of things... she's put in a hell of a night ride. Boys, let's give her some room." They backed away but not too far. They were cowboys and cowboys like to know what's going on.

Sitting Dove opened her eyes. "Pooh." Then she remembered where she was and what she was doing. "Pap, Viv... Vivian in trouble. Zell Davis come to ranch. He bad man. Try bad things. Vivian, she try get away. I not know what happened to her. She tell me to run, run for help. They follow me little ways. I shoot one. Two left."

Pap stood up. "Speck... get two horses saddled. Pooh, I'm leavin' the herd with you. You take care of Sittin' Dove and drive these cattle on to Amarillo. Make a bed in the chuck wagon. The wound doesn't look to be too bad. The bullet didn't hit the bone. I think she'll be alright once you get some food and water in her. When you get to Amarillo, get her to a doctor and see a Mister Gerald Zoric." Pap went to his saddlebags and pulled out the sealed agreement price that Ellison Jones had negotiated for him. "These are the papers you will need to present to Gerald." He turned to Bailey. "You're the new ramrod on this drive." Tanner, you scout ahead for 'em. Check the creeks, rivers, and watch for any trails that have been washed away. Remember, this is outlaw country too. A man rides up on you, don't take his word on anything. Everyone rides in pairs and deal with everyone in pairs. Take no chances." He looked around the men as Speck came back with the two horses. “Well, good luck boys. Have a drink on me once you get there.”

They all grinned. One of them answered him. “We’ll do-err, Boss.”

“Pap.”

“Yeah, Pooh.”

“This is it. This is the day we’ve all knowed was coming. Us boys can’t help but want to be with you. Since we can’t, don’t you let that bastard get the drop on you.”

“Pooh, boys, I...” He stopped and stared at all of them standing around him. “Yeah.” He turned and took the reins from Speck and mounted up. He and Speck left the Dockin men standing around Sitting Dove, watching them as they disappeared into the night.

Chapter 34

Zell eased up the creek being as quiet as possible. His head was throbbing from all the whiskey he had consumed. He sat down on a rock and listened. He wasn't going to be able to see Vivian, but he thought he might be able to hear the baby cry. He was betting it would start crying before daylight. It would get hungry, and nothing would quiet it then. He decided to sit and listen. He sat there for just over two hours when he heard something up the creek that sounded like a baby. He grinned and spoke aloud. "I'm coming for you honey." He got up and very slowly made his way to the sound of the crying baby.

"Shush... don't cry little one, don't cry." Vivian looked down the creek as much as she could. It was still dark. She listened but with Cran crying it was hopeless. She tried rocking him, but he was too hungry. She found a rock that dished out some and filled it with water. She wet the baby's tongue and he instantly stopped crying. The touch and taste of liquid was enough to quiet him for a while. It wouldn't last long; she must keep moving and get out of earshot if possible.

After a bit, it looked to her like she was walking under overhanging cliffs. She waded up the creek and found an opening in one of the bluff rocks. With a little balancing effort, she managed to climb up on the rock and step to the next one. She then was able to maneuver around until she was on the end of the bluff overlooking the stream of water. The moonlight shined on it and ripples of water could be seen from the way she had come. At least she now had an advantage with a view for quite some distance down the little creek. She stretched out on her stomach and watched, hoping to lay there until daylight. She wondered if, and hoped, Sitting Dove got away. The sound of the gentle stream below along with her ordeal of escaping Zell Davis made her sleepy. Slowly sleep overtook her.

Pap Dockin
By Royal Wade Kimes

Pap and Speck made it to the ranch at dawn. The first thing they saw was the three men they left to watch the place lying dead by the bunkhouse.

"Speck, I should have left more men and had the other four stay around the ranch house. They'll be up at the line shack another day." He glanced at Speck. "What was I thinking? I should have stayed here. You offered to take the cattle for me."

"We're human, Pap. I didn't figure on this either."

Pap pulled his gun and let his eyes take in everything, what was familiar and anything that might not be.

Speck too, drew his six-gun and stepped down from his horse. He eased up to the door of the bunkhouse and stepped in.

Pap was in the process of dismounting when suddenly, Duke bawled out in that coon hunting voice he had. Coon hounds don't like to be snuck up on. He was sound asleep dreaming about some big boar coon he had treed sometime in his past. Suddenly a stranger opened the screen door from inside the house.

Pap dropped to one knee behind the well. A bullet slammed into the cross member the rope pulley hung on. He could hear glass breaking and was sure they were breaking out the window to shoot through. He turned to see where Speck was and saw him flanking the house to the left.

Speck signaled Pap to open fire. He would make his move then. When he started shooting, Speck ran to the side of the house.

Pepper was in more trouble than he knew anything about. All Speck had to do was make his way to the French doors on the other side of the house. If they weren't locked, he could walk in unheard.

"Zell, give it up!" Pap thought he would try reasoning.

"Zell ain't here!"

"Say again?"

"You're kidding, right?"

"About what?"

"I said... Zell ain't here you hard-hearing bastard!" Pepper fired another shell in the direction of the voice.

"Throw your gun out whoever you are!"

"Go to hell! I've heard what happens to them what gives it up to you! You hang 'em, or whip 'em half to death!"

"Hang, you say? Yeah, you'll hang! Depends though! If you have harmed my wife or grandson, I won't hang you!" Pap paused for a long second. "I'll cut you like a pig and drag you all the way to Mason City behind my horse. I'll ask if anybody recognizes you when I get there. If they do, I'll drag you until they don't!"

Pepper shot three times at the well. He looked around for more guns and spotted the cabinet on the far wall. There were at least six rifles in it. He ran and grabbed one off the rack and then ran back to the window.

"Come on, Dockin! I've got more than a pistol to shoot at you with in here!"

Speck made his way around to the double doors and turned the knob ever so slightly. He whispered to himself. "Pap, do some shooting." It was like Pap heard him. He fired four rounds slow and spaced. The shooter on the inside fired back five times. Speck entered the room and slowly walked up behind the shooter, recognizing him right away. "Pepper."

He whirled around and tried to fire the rifle. He was too slow. Speck shot him in the stomach not fifteen feet away.

He dropped the rifle to the floor and slid down the wall by the window.

"Damn, Pepper, you've come to a bad end." Speck kicked the rifle away. "I've got him, Pap, come on in!"

Pap entered the front door in a hurry. He went through all the bottom floor rooms. He looked up the stairs and bounced up them like an eighteen-year-old. He wasn't up there long. He came back down and walked over to the man lying propped up against the wall. He reached down, picked him up and slung him out the door. Pepper rolled off the porch into the yard with Pap right behind him.

Speck followed. He watched as Pap went to work on the wounded man. He kicked him in the face and then in the ear. "Where's my family? Talk!" He kicked him in the face again. Pepper began to cry and whimper. "That's right, cry! What was you doing when my wife and baby was being mistreated? Maybe you was doing some of the mistreatin' yourself."

Speck took a step closer. "Pepper, I'd talk if I were you."

Pap turned to Speck. "You what? You know this man?"

"Yeah, I'm afraid so. He works for Zell. I met him in a little town in Arkansas... Chester I think it was. The Butler Saloon to be exact. He was on the run. I heard he killed a man in Missouri. You can hear anything. One thing I do know for a fact... he's a horse thief. He took Fargo Mimm's horse that night. Pap, meet Pepper Smoots."

Pepper was beginning to come to his senses. "Drink... I need a drink of water."

"You may need, but you don't get... not until you talk!"

"Water."

Pap kneeled down in front of him. "You tell me where my family is, or I'm goin' to make you wish the Comanches had you instead of me."

"I don't know where they're at, honest, I don't."

"Say again?"

Pepper was getting weaker from his stomach wound, not to mention he was feverish from his knife wound.

"I don't know where they are, I've been asleep. This knife wound is dirty and needs tending. I'm... sick from it." Pepper looked up at Pap the best he could. "I'm done for... looks like. My stomach... aches like hell. I'm dying. Speck done shot my guts out. Guess I can stop worryin' about my... my knife wound."

Pap was under the persuasion that he was telling the truth, he didn't know where Vivian and Cran were.

"Speck... watch him. If he twitches for any other reason than to die, shoot him."

Speck nodded and watched as Pap walked to the barn.

"You know, Pepper, I can't remember a time I've seen Pap Dockin this mad. There'll be no reasoning with him today. You think dying with your stomach wound is bad. Be glad you're dying, because this ain't slow at all compared to what he might have thought of, no sir. The one thing you don't mess with is his wife and that grandson."

"Why didn't you... shoot me dead?"

"You needed to talk. Had I known you was so damn dumb, I'd of shot you in the head."

When Pap came out of the barn, he was walking extremely slow. He never looked up from the ground. He walked in front of Pepper and stared down at him for a couple of seconds. "Which one of you dirty sunzabitches shot my colt?"

Pepper looked up at him. "Zell did, laughed about it. He has a terrible... hate for you."

Pap saw Pepper was growing weaker at a rapid pace. He knelt down close to him. "I figure you got all of two-minutes left before you expire. If you have anything you want to say to me or to the Maker... I'd be doin' it."

Pepper looked up at Speck with scared eyes. "Never was no count. God forgive me." He made an odd sound and fell over on his side.

Pap stood up and looked over at Speck. "Good Book says God is a merciful God. It's a good thing, because I sure can't forgive him. I could if these were men we were dealing with here. They're not. They've invaded my home. They've burned my crops, killed my men, killed one of my stud colts. They've killed my son and his beautiful wife. God only knows what Vivian is going through. I'm not in the forgiving mood right now."

Speck eyed Pap. "Ole partner, I understand. Sometimes a man has to be reminded of what the hell is really going on." He eyed Pepper one more time and then looked at Pap. "Well... now what?"

"I don't know. Let's look around. See if we can pick up any tracks."

"Won't be any other than what might be in the road. There's too much grass." Speck was walking down the road when he said that and was surprised when he saw a small boot track. "Pap! I got something!"

Pap looked where Speck pointed. "A woman's boot print, looks to be running."

"Yeah." Speck was slow to say what else he picked up. "Here's another track. A man's track... Zell Davis I figure."

"Yeah, look here, Speck. Duke has been down here."

"Shore has, don't mean nothing though. He comes down here all the time."

"Maybe not, but he'll probably go back to where he was if it had something to do with Vivian."

Pap called to Duke. He came running, waging his tail, happy to be asked to do something. "Ole boy, you got to help me out here. Let's go, come on, let's go." Pap took off in the direction all the tracks were going. That was all Duke needed. He had already played this game once and he liked it. He took off and even bawled a couple of times. "He's on 'em, Speck, let's get a move on."

"I'm not able to run as fast as you, Pap, I'm overweight. I ain't got the wind you have."

"Say again?"

"Go on! If you lose me don't worry about it!" Speck didn't know if Pap heard him or not. He was already turning at the little creek and heading up stream.

Zell heard the shooting back at the ranch house. It caused him to move out with more urgency. He figured the Indian squaw had brought Pap back.

He waded up stream watching and listening. He knew his way of finding her was to be within earshot of the baby. He stood and listened under an overhanging bluff. He listened and then smiled. He cocked his head sideways. He was sure he heard a baby noise. They were overhead. He now knew Vivian had watched him come up the stream. He began to look for a way up and found it. He climbed up on the first rock and jumped to the next one, soon he was at the top. He found where she had lain with the baby, and he grinned as he peered in the direction of her tracks. Then he spoke in a taunting voice. "It won't be long now. Let ole Pap come... I'll kill the both of you."

The day Zell had been waiting for was here. He figured he had Pap right where he wanted him. He knew he would not shoot at him if he was holding his wife or baby.

Zell got down close to the ground and saw where she had run through the tall grass. Again, he spoke out to her. He figured her close by. "I'm right behind you honey, wait up. I ain't had but one old whore since my old lady died. I'm due a classy looking woman like you. You being Pap's woman sweetens the deal." He grinned at the idea of the whole thing. He was a man consumed with hate, a hate that carried all the way back to childhood.

"Cran, you have to be quiet, please be quiet." Vivian had watched Zell as he made his way up the stream. She lay as quiet as she could above him on the bluff. Her attempt at being quiet didn't last long. Cran made a noise and to Vivian, it was loud enough to wake the dead. She tried to muffle him, but she knew out in the woods it was futile. Sounds just seem to carry better. She laid as still as possible and listened. Then she heard him and whispered under her breath. "He's climbing the bluff!"

She scooped Cran up and took off. "We've got to run! We've got to hide. You have to be quiet, son. It's not your fault. You can't help being hungry. I've got to get you fed real soon, or I'm going to have another problem. You could become ill. I sure hope Sitting Dove found Franklin." She was talking to Cran. She knew he didn't understand but she needed to talk.

She ran through a small patch of tall blue stem and stopped when she came to a few hackberry trees. One was bigger than all the rest and had a large hollow trunk. It was just big enough to squeeze into. She stood as still and quiet as possible. All she could do was pray little Cran stayed quiet.

Speck was about to leave the road and follow Pap, when something truly unexpected happened. In fact, his jaw dropped when he realized who he was looking at. "Well, I be damned. I thought you were visiting a cousin up in Kansas... Bear Creek I think it was. I guess the newspaper business didn't work out."

"Yeah, well, I didn't exactly tell the truth about my intentions." Baldy Cooper shifted his weight in the saddle. "Your boss didn't have much respect for me or the law. I gave that some thought. He treated me mighty shabbily. His wife wasn't very kind either. I decided I would not live with that... that I would come back and prove myself. I've come back with these five deputies to let him see how lawin' works. Maybe this time he'll have a different opinion. I'm here to give him a taste of real law." Baldy had leaned forward in the saddle with a smirk on his face.

"You don't say. Well, don't let me keep you from going on up to the house. I shore don't want to get in the way of a damn good lawman." Speck had a twinkle in his eye.

A frown appeared on Baldy's face. "What are you doing down here this early in the morning?"

"Oh, I like to take a morning walk about every morning. I like to dip my feet in this stream. It's cool, even cold some mornings." Speck looked at Baldy and decided that everything Pap thought about the fool was right. He smiled as he looked at the rest of the men.

"What are you smiling about?"

"I smile at miracles. How God has kept you alive is nothing short of a miracle. You may be the biggest feeling idiot I ever met."

"Mister, you need to watch your tongue. I might arrest you along with Pap Dockin. I mean business this time." He clucked to his horse and rode towards the ranch house.

Speck watched as the well-dressed deputies rode by him. They all wore nice vests, pearl handled pistols and dusters. He mumbled to himself as he grinned. "Bunch of show. Cowboys have their dusters tied on behind their saddles when it ain't raining, or the wind ain't blowing. They're sure going to get a hell of a surprise when they get up to the house."

Speck turned up the creek leaving the deputies to find their own way. He knew they would try to follow. He grinned, but then stopped suddenly. "Duke has treed. I can hear him over on that next little holler. That ain't Zell or Vivian he's got treed. I know that treed bark. I bet he's got a big boar coon up a burr oak."

Chapter 35

Pap made his way up stream not too concerned with hiding his coming. He wasn't worried of Zell trying to ambush him. He knew this was going to be face to face. Pap began to talk to himself, and it was fairly loud because of his hearing problem. "He'll flaunt Vivian and Cran in front of me. I can't see Vivian getting away from him with her carrying the baby."

He went about another sixty yards up the stream when he came to an overhanging bluff. He listened. He could hear nothing. Moss was hanging off the bluff, water dripped from it into the stream. It made it hard to hear and he couldn't hear it thunder anyway. He waded over to the bank and saw what looked like a track of a boot heel in the edge of the damp bank. It was going through an opening to the bluff he had been under. He climbed up on the rock and jumped to the next one. He could see that he could climb out on top of the bluff from there. He kept looking for another sign. He found it. Another boot track and he wasn't sure, but maybe a smaller one. He hurried for a few steps and then slowed down. He crouched as low as he could when he got to the tall blue stem on top of the bluff. He knew the terrain well. There was an open meadow ahead of him. He was betting she hid in the stand of hackberry trees.

Suddenly.

"You looking for us?" Zell Davis had his arm around Vivian's neck. "Looks like judgment day has come... don't it?" He ran his nose through her hair. "I was going to have me some of this pretty little thing, but you showed up too soon. I probably wouldn't have found her, but ole Chalk pulled the same trick. He crawled up in a tree trunk when he was hiding. She tried the same thing. By the way, Chalk... he was an accident. I didn't mean to kill him. He did kill Ted, though."

"Let her go, Zell. This is between you and me."

"She's part of you now... ain't she? You two are hitched."

Pap was straining to hear what he was saying. "Where's the

boy. Where's Cran?"

"Little lizard is laying here at my feet in this tall grass."

"Let 'em go, Zell."

"Can't do that. This good-looking thing is what's going to get you killed. She's my hold card. Besides that, I plan to have her once you're gone. No way in hell this goes to waste." He was smiling the whole time, but then he began to grin, showing the gap between his front teeth. "I've been giving something some thought. Once you've left us all behind for that make-believe place in the sky, I'm going to kill that damn kid. They ain't going to be no Dockin blood with your old mama's blood mixed in with it. She hated me, and I hated her."

Pap stood looking at Zell Davis knowing the end had come.

Speck was giving second thought to following Pap up the hollow. He pulled off his boots and stuck his feet in the cool water. He figured he might as well wait on Baldy and his deputies, because as soon as they seen all the dead men at the ranch house, they'd be back.

He was watching for Baldy, but heard horses coming from the other direction. It was Huey and Ben Watts. "Dang, this little road has more traffic on it than Main Street in Mason City. Morning, Huey, Ben."

They pulled up. They both sat there looking down at Speck setting on a rock wetting his bare feet. Ben chuckled. "What the hell are you doing?"

"Cooling my feet. I come down here ever morning about this time and cool 'em off."

Ben looked over at Huey. "When we worked here, Huey, did you ever see Speck cool his feet off in the morning?"

"No, don't believe I did."

"Me neither. Now what's going on, Speck? I figured you'd be with the cattle drive." Ben looked towards the ranch house and saw six men coming on horseback in a hurry. "You better make it snappy. Riders are coming. Strangers, I make 'em." He dropped his hand next to his gun and thumbed the cord off the hammer.

Speck grinned and began to put his socks on. "That's Baldy Cooper and his deputies. You know Ben, that boy ain't got any sense, none a-tall." He slipped his boots on and stood up. "We got trouble. Things have been a happening right along here on the ranch. Huey, Pap is up this holler looking for your pa. He's killed two of our men, killed the sorrel colt, and has Vivian or is chasing her."

Ben frowned "How long has Pap been up in there?"

"Not too long."

Huey looked at the hollow the little stream ran up. "Ben?"

He knew what Huey was thinking. "Yeah?" His voice had dread in it. Not for the task at hand, but for Huey. "Maybe you ought to stay here?"

"No Ben, I know who my pa is. Now I have to face it."

They dismounted and handed their reins to Speck. "Boys, I'll hold Baldy Cooper and them glory seeking deputies off long as I can."

Ben smiled. "Much obliged." They took off at a trot up the middle of the stream, knowing they had to hurry.

"Whoa! Whoa up here!" Baldy and his men rode up in a gallop and slid to a halt. "Who the hell was that? And where are they going? What happened back at the ranch house, there's dead men lying everywhere!"

"Some of Zell Davis's work."

"Who was the two cowboys that left their horses with you?"

"Oh, them? Well, that is Huey Davis and Ben Watts. I think you know Huey."

"Yeah, I know him." Baldy showed his first sign of irritation. "Could I trouble you with asking where they're going?"

"I don't know. They might be going fishing. Wouldn't that beat all? Minnows and maybe a perch is about it in this spring. If it were me, I'd go..."

"You might be going to jail if you don't start giving me some straight answers."

"You know, you're a tad on the side of too ignorant to be an idiot."

"I'm what?"

"Stupid. You're just damn stupid." Speck splashed the water with his boots. "I'm not, nor would anyone else tell you a thing, especially regarding their friends. Ain't no one telling you a damn thing. Why don't you take your boots off and cool your feet like I did? It's a pleasurable thing. I'm going to start doing it more often."

Baldy looked at Speck with disgust and then had his deputy's dismount. "Pull your rifles. We're going up this little creek and see if we can find out what's going on."

"You'd be better advised to stay here and cool your feet." Speck grinned real big for Baldy.

"We'll see." He hit the water in a big splashing hurry and his men fell right in behind him.

Speck looked them over as they ran past him and called to the last one. "Son!"

He stopped and looked around at Speck. "Yeah."

"Is any of you young bucks shaving yet? I'd guess there ain't a one of you over eighteen. You'd have to hurry to be sixteen."

"What's it to you?"

"I just hate to see boys die because they were pulled too green."

He looked at Speck with questioning eyes and then went splashing up the stream to catch up with his friends.

Zell held a pistol against Vivian's back. He bent down and picked Cran up, while holding his pistol to her and watching Pap. He couldn't hold everything, so he dropped his rifle. He pulled Vivian up tight to him as he held Cran over his head. The baby began to cry loudly, which annoyed Zell. "Shut-up you little tit sucker." A crazy twisted smile appeared on his face. "Your end has come. You can see it, can't you, Pap? Not a damn thing you can do either. All you can do is die."

Pap made a step to his right, looking for an opening... something... any kind of mistake. If he shot Zell, and he could, he would drop Cran. A drop like that would kill him or cause head injuries. Zell also had his pistol cocked, and the barrel was now at the base of Vivian's neck.

"You alright, Viv?"

"Yes." She looked up at Cran who was now screaming at the top of his lungs. That seemed to bother Zell even more, but there wasn't anything he could do about it. Pap also noticed how calm Vivian was. She was a strong woman.

"Zell."

"Shut-up. I've always had to play second fiddle to you. Well, not anymore." He began to back up, looking back as he went. When he was closer to the edge of the bluff overlooking the stream of water, he stopped. He turned halfway around leaving Vivian full in front of him. He lowered his arm letting Cran extend out over the edge of the bluff.

"Who has the damn reins now, Franklin 'Pap' Dockin? I got the spurs and the reins!" He laughed. "You make one damn move with that fast gun of yours, and I'll drop this little tit sucker over the bluff." He laughed again. "Hell of a thing, knowing you killed your grandson. Maybe your wife because you couldn't keep your head. How does it feel knowing I have the winning hand on the last game played?"

"I can't hear you, Zell. The boy is crying too loud."

It infuriated Zell that Pap hadn't heard him. He didn't want him to miss one thing. The telling of it was as important as the doing. "Come closer you bastard!"

"Say again?"

"Closer, damn you, closer!"

Pap walked straight at him. He was within fifteen feet. "Stop! Now you'll be able to hear me."

Cran was still crying loudly. "Say again?"

Zell was becoming angry. "Come closer. But you watch your damn self."

Pap stood there like he didn't hear him.

"Move damn you! Come closer!"

Pap walked to within ten feet of Zell before he ordered him to stop again. "That ought to do. If you can't hear me now, I'll just drop this little bastard."

"Zell, you ain't leavin' the top of this bluff if you harm my family."

"Family! I'm family! What about me, brother Franklin? Me and you got the same daddy! What about me?"

Vivian tried to look at Zell. The news that he was Franklin's brother stunned her. It all made sense now. That's why Franklin had let Zell get away with so much. She wondered why but would never ask. It was up to Pap to tell her the why when he was ready.

"Zell, I didn't have anything to do with how you came into the world, or what happened afterwards. Dad tried to do right by your mother and you. She was sick, mentally. She hated him. She wouldn't let him help you. She didn't want him around. Dad married my mother a year and a half after he gave up on the idea of your mother and him havin' a life together. He would have married her, but somethin' was wrong with her. Zell, it wasn't Dad."

"The hell it wasn't! I tried to have a relationship with the bastard. He wouldn't have it. He had you on his knee."

"That's not true. Your mother would come down to the house after you were asleep and raise hell with Mom and Dad every time you spent time with me playin' or workin'. She accused Mom of tryin' to take you away. She threatened to kill her. Dad had to physically remove her from the place. Another thing, how did you repay Dad when he did try to talk to you? You stole from him. Things he would have given you, but your mother wouldn't let him give you anything. She would bring back stuff you stole, until she found out you was stealing them. Then she quit."

"You're a damn liar!"

"You've had this consumin' hate all these years for Dad and Mom, when it was your mother all along. I tried to tell you, but you wouldn't listen. Mom tried to talk to you about it, but you were blind to your mother. It wasn't dad who didn't love you, it was your mother. She didn't care what happened to you. She used you to make Dad and Mom's life miserable. Mom didn't hate you. She just didn't want trouble from your mother. When you and I went off to war, that was when your mother completely lost it. Zell, she didn't die of heart failure. She was put in an asylum."

"Lies!" Zell titled his head and frowned trying to comprehend what was being said to him. His eyes darted here and there, as he tried to think of something to say, something to dispute what was being said.

"Zell, your mother died in the asylum just before the war ended. You weren't to know. Mom and Dad tried to spare you the heartache of the knowing. When they died of the fever, you were the only blood kin I had left, same as I was yours. I thought if we could leave Alabama, maybe we could start over. Maybe we could forget all the bad things and have a new life. I knew during the war how you felt about me. I saw the looks you gave me every now and then. I saw when you didn't know I was watchin', but I'd hoped the new country, Texas, and a cattle operation of our own would change that. All the wild cattle gave us a start. It took some time gatherin' those brush wise beeves. We drove them north to Dodge City and was on our way to becoming cattlemen. But your misguided jealousy and hate for me destroyed it all. You raped Paula. You raped so many women in the war, what was one more to you? I never knew if you did it because you knew she was my girl, or she was just there to be had."

"I thought she was a whore! Once I had her I wanted her. But there you were getting first choice again, always in my way. The whipping you gave me for that, I wouldn't give to a damn dog!"

"Bein' good to you, Zell, didn't work. I was through. You should have been hung. I would have hung anyone else. I just couldn't hang the last breathin' relative I had. I regret that now."

"You whipped me with that bullwhip of yours until I bled my boots full. Then you took 'em off me and made me walk until my feet were bloody stubs. No man, kin or not, whips me like that and doesn't pay for it. I've waited a long time to get even with you. Oh, there's a many a time I wanted to walk up behind you and blow your brains out during the war. I lost count of how many times I've wanted to put a bullet through your damn heart. But that would have been too quick. I wanted you to suffer first, suffer like I did."

He stopped and got a better hold on the crying baby. The little fellow was starving, and Zell was holding him too tight. "I could have killed you several times, but I was patient. I wanted you to build up your section while I built the Sliding D." He looked at Cran, then back at Pap. "I wanted you to have plenty before you watched it all go away. I wanted you to crawl like you made me crawl back to Mason City. I wasn't able to walk. I crawled the last four or five miles. I was a solid year getting over that whipping, a solid year!" His voice rose. Then he grinned.

Pap had seen that one before, several times in the war. It usually came just before he did something terrible. "It's time to pay you and our old man back."

"Nothin' I've said to you matters does it? The hate is more important to you than the truth."

"The only thing that has ever mattered to me is you finally getting yours. I lived with you being the one with the silver spoon, the spoon that should have been mine. And then you whipped me like I was some kind of stray bitch dog. You whipped me for what? A damn woman you bedded?"

"No Zell, for your raping her." Pap paused, trying to think of something that might get through, that would cause him to think. "Zell, what about Huey? Doesn't he matter? He favors our dad to the letter. He's even got his ways."

"Huey went against me, sided with you. He's dead as far as I'm concerned. Him looking like our old man may make you feel all warm inside, but he just reminds me of an old bastard."

"The boy wants you to love him."

"He needs to act like a man if he wants special attention from me."

"You said you tried to have a relationship with dad, but he wouldn't have it. Maybe Huey is trying to have one with you, and now it's you that won't have it."

"You've always had the answers, haven't you little brother?"

"You need help, Zell."

"You think I'm like my old lady... crazy?"

"I didn't say that. You just need someone to help you."

"No! You're the one! You need the help!" He raised Cran up higher over the bluff.

"Don't do it, Zell!"

He cocked the hammer back on the pistol held to Vivian's neck.

"Can just anyone come to this little party?" A new voice entered the intense and deadly showdown between the two brothers, Zell and Pap.

Zell turned quickly towards the new voice, and then back to Pap. It was Ben Watts. He was standing thirty feet from Zell on the other end of the rock bluff, which gave him an open shot. The only problem was, Zell had Cran hanging out over the bluff, and Ben could tell his arm was getting tired.

Zell now had a dilemma he hadn't planned on. "You stay back, Ben! I'll drop this kid! I swear I will! Stay back... hear me? This ain't your affair! Stay back! You hear?"

"Oh, I hear, Zell. We've got a big ole problem though."

"What's that?" Zell cut his eyes at Ben, and quickly back to Pap.

"I don't work for you. Quit taking orders from you some time ago."

"Yeah, well that may be, but the Checkered Kid told me something about you awhile back. He said you had a heart. You ain't going to be the cause of this crying baby falling to its death, now are you?"

"Don't plan on it. Zell, the Checkered Kid didn't know me as well as he thought. He was of the mind he could take me too. You know how that turned out. Cost him his life." Ben looked at Pap. "Sometimes you have to make hard choices." He then looked at Vivian. "I'm going to count to three. One." It felt like an eternity and a half before he said... "two."

Pap knew he was right and saw no other alternative. He saw no way to save Cran. It had come down to him having to make a choice as who would live or die. Then suddenly it became clear. Zell was going to drop Cran either way. He wouldn't want a Dockin left walking around on earth with Franklin 'Pap' Dockin blood running through its veins. He said that already. The only thing left to do was try and save Vivian. Pap knew if they waited, Zell would drop the baby and get a shot off into Vivian too. They had to move first. Pap looked at Ben and said something odd. "I might need a little help from a Saint to get out of this." He let him know he was ready to make a play.

Zell was getting extremely nervous. His eyes cut to Ben. When they did, Pap took another step closer... just as Ben said "three."

Speck had tied Huey and Ben's horse to a small brushy tree and eased up the creek behind the greenhorn deputies. He figured things could get a little exciting with Baldy Cooper being in the same ravine with Pap and Ben Watts. He didn't think Zell would be a factor. Pap would take care of him. He had only gone a short distance when he ran upon the deputies. "You boys going for a swim? Water ain't deep enough, is it?"

Baldy looked at Speck with a tub full of scorn. "Hell no, we ain't going swimming. Blake here has fallen and broken his ankle."

Speck smiled. "I'll be. These rocks are slick, green algae on flat rock bottom makes for some careful walking. Another thing, this creek is known for nests of cottonmouths." Speck didn't crack a smile and just kept walking.

Baldy looked at the rest of his young deputies. "I can see you boys are scared of snakes. We'll get Blake back to Mason City and let the doc set his ankle."

One of the deputies spoke up. "I'm not afraid of snakes, Mister Cooper."

"Yes, you are." Baldy and one of the other deputies picked up the crippled deputy and started back down the creek to the horses. Speck shook his head, grinning as he watched them pick up and go. Then he hurried to catch up with Ben and Huey. They were the last two to head up stream.

Zell dropped the baby over the side of the bluff, causing Vivian to scream and twist loose of him. She tried desperately on the count of three to reach Cran, but it was all in vain. He went over the side and out of sight.

Pap had drawn, fired and leaped for Vivian at the same time. His bullet hit Zell as center of the forehead as could be measured. Ben fired at exactly the same time and kept firing. Pap fired two more times as he grabbed Vivian and shielded her with his own body.

Zell's gun went off, but the bullet went skyward as Ben and Pap riddled him with bullets. His body jerked with each hit, and then buckled over the side of the bluff.

Pap held Vivian as she sobbed uncontrollably.

"My baby! Oh Franklin, our baby!" She cried even harder.

Huey Davis stood below the buff watching as his father held little Cran out over the jagged rock. It was twenty-five to thirty feet to the top of the small bluff, and Huey was waiting to catch the baby if his father actually dropped him over. He positioned himself exactly where the baby would fall. He waited and listened. Zell was talking loudly so Pap could hear him, and in doing so, Huey heard what he was saying. He now knew Pap Dockin was his uncle. He remembered Pap saying he put him in mind of someone he had a lot of respect for. I must look like Pap's dad. Like... like my grandfather on the Dockin side. That means I look like the Dockin's, not the Davis bunch. I'm half Dockin... and half Davis. Dad was half Davis on my grandmother's side but was a Dockin on my grandfather's side. He was a Dockin. That means my grandmother gave Zell, my dad, her maiden name... Davis. She didn't let him have the Dockin name. Now I see who dad got his hate from.

As he listened to his dad talk a million things ran through his mind. He now knew the whole story behind the rage and madness boxed up inside his father. He turned when he heard water splashing. It was Speck coming faster than he probably wanted to. He slowed up when he got closer so as not to alert Zell that he was down below. He waded up beside Huey. Speck saw what Huey was going to try and do. He also saw the beads of sweat on his forehead.

He whispered to him. “Here, take my coat. It was kind of cool this early morning and I always wear a thin jacket. I'm fair size. Let's spread it out between us. If he drops the little dude, we'll catch him in my coat. It's the best chance he's got of surviving.” Speck winked trying to reassure Huey what they were attempting to do would work.

They waited... and watched. Speck was also learning the mystery as to why Pap hadn't killed Zell Davis a long time ago. He looked over at Huey. “This is hard on a neck looking straight up like this.”

"Yeah, I just hope pa comes to his senses."

Speck eyed Huey, knowing that wasn't likely. "Huey, if he drops little Cran… when he hits the jacket, go with the drop a little. That way, it won't be too sudden a stop. It'll be a softer fall."

Suddenly the baby was falling, and it sounded like a war on top of the bluff had started. The baby was falling backside first. That was a break for Speck and Huey. "Here he comes, Huey! Here he comes!"

"Are we under him?"

When he hit, they let the coat give a little to soften the fall like Speck suggested. They had done it! Baby Cran was safe at the bottom of the bluff.

Not more than six feet from Huey the water splashed over his head and Speck's, too. Zell Davis had landed in the water beside his son. Blood began filling the stream immediately.

Huey turned loose of the coat once Speck had the little bundle secured and knelt in the water beside his father. "Pa. Why? You had the world. You had me and Ted… and we loved you. Why couldn't you love us back and let your hate go?" Huey looked up at Speck. "I guess pa was just too sick to have right thinking."

"I'm sorry, Huey."

"Well, at least it's over for him now, for all of us."

Speck looked down at little Cran in his arms and smiled. "Huey, you helped save your cousin today."

Huey stood up. "Yeah, that's something ain't it, Speck?"

"It sure is son." Speck knew Huey needed something to make him feel better. "I bet you and Cran will have some good times together. You can teach him how to handle horses."

"Yeah." He looked at Cran in Speck's arms and smiled. Speck turned his head away from the baby. "His mother better get here pretty quick. He needs fed and by the smell of things he needs changed."

"I'd probably need changed too… had I been dropped from a bluff and all was going to save me was two cowboys holding a jacket stretched out between them."

Speck stared at Huey and it took a second for Huey to recognize Speck was laughing. He hadn't made a sound, but his stomach was shaking visibly. Huey smiled and chuckled at that. He was doing his best to concentrate on the positive that came out of it all.

Ben stepped over to the edge of the bluff and looked down. He smiled and waved to Speck as Huey removed his father from the water. "Vivian, Pap, don't worry about the baby. He learned how to land before he got there."

Pap was distraught and then confused by Ben's comment. Vivian was sobbing and Pap was holding her while tears ran down his own cheeks. They got up from the ground and looked over the side of the bluff. Vivian started crying again. This time she was shedding joyful tears. Pap put his arm around her. "Beats all. I never heard you so much as whimper around me. Today you're boohooing all over half of the Texas Panhandle." All three of them laughed at the joyful outcome.

"Guess we need to get down off of here, Pap."

"Yeah, we do. Ben, wait a minute. I want to thank you for what you done. I couldn't figure what you were up to. I just hoped it would work. When I learn a man, I trust what I know about him. You had an ace in the hole. You had Huey down there the whole time."

Ben smiled. "Yeah. Well Pap, you said you might need a saint to help you with this one." They grinned at each other, and then made their way off the bluff and down to the stream where baby Cran awaited them.

Chapter 36

When everyone finally came out of the narrow gorge onto the road, Baldy Cooper and two of his deputies were waiting. He had left the others in town with the one that had broken his ankle.

"Pap Dockin, you're under arrest for murder and no telling what else."

Pap handed Cran to Speck and asked him to take Vivian and the baby to the house. It was imperative that the baby be fed. "Huey, you go with them."

"Pap?" Huey wasn't wanting to go.

"You're my nephew, do as I say." He smiled at Huey and then nodded for him to go on.

Huey liked that and walked up the road with Speck and Vivian, looking back now and then. Pap turned his attention to Baldy while Ben stood beside him.

"Did you say I was under arrest?"

"I did."

"You don't give up easy." Pap took a long deep breath. "Here's the short of it. You three roosters will have to pull those irons and go to shootin', because that's the only way, and I mean the only way, you will take me anywhere."

It wasn't hard to see the lack of self-confidence the badges suddenly had.

Pap shook his head. "Baldy, you must carry a rabbit's foot in your pocket. It's the only thing I can think of that's kept you alive this long. The Good Lord would have thrown up His hands long ago. You survived one gunfight that you should have been shot dead in. That alone would have been enough for me to take my sign down and quit the lawin' business." It was then that Pap got an idea. "Ben, show these youngsters what us washed up cowboys can do."

"I'm washed up?"

"You weren't until these featherless chicks fresh out of the eggs showed up."

Pap took a silver dollar from his pocket and pitched it. Ben drew and fired, hitting it center enough to send it further into the sky. "Now it's my turn. Ben, can I borrow your gun. I haven't had time to reload my own."

Baldy rolled his eyes when Pap asked to borrow Ben's gun. Pap had just told him he would have to pull irons and go to shooting to take him in, and he was standing there with an empty gun the whole time.

"I'd admire it if you would use my gun." Ben grinned and then pitched a silver dollar high into the air. Pap drew and repeated what Ben had done. When he was through shooting, he was standing there with the gun on Baldy. "Now, there's four shells left in this sweet, hair triggered little darlin' I have here. Shall we dance?"

One of the deputies spoke up. "Baldy, I told you I wasn't afraid of snakes, but I've got sense enough to keep 'em from striking me." He turned his horse and rode off.

"You come back here! That's an order!"

The other one turned and rode after him. Baldy started to yell after them, but then let it go. He looked at Pap and Ben with embarrassment written all over him. "I'm pretty much a fool I guess."

"Well, recognizin' what you are and not likin' it, is a start to workin' on what you would like not to be." Pap handed the pistol back to Ben.

"I'd like to make a lawman, but when I get around you, I know it'll never be. I've got too much to learn. I'm the dumbest man to ever wear a star. Maybe I'm too stupid after all. You give me a lesson and a thrashing every time I see you."

"Life is full of lessons. I take it you've give up on the idea of arrestin' me?"

"For what and how?" He smiled and even chuckled for the first time.

"Already you're wiser. You need to apply commonsense with your law. You might turn out." Pap wasn't saying, but he wondered if the boy had any commonsense.

"You think I could turn out to be a lawman?"

"I said... might."

"Yeah..." There was disappointment in his voice.

Pap gazed at the young lawman with bafflement. "Baldy, you need to find some happy middle ground. One minute your quittin' the law business, the next your lookin' for encouragement to stay in. We live and die by our decisions... guess you aren't any different than the rest of us. Just greener."

"Yeah, guess so. By the way, is Zell Davis up in that holler?"

"Say again?"

"Is Zell Davis up in there?"

"No. His body is."

"I think I'll round the boys up and get him out. We'll call this case closed and go home."

Pap smiled and cut his eyes over at Ben. "You know Ben, if Baldy can live long enough to get a little age on him, he might settle down to be a fair law man. I don't have any use for 'em, but he might make one."

"He might... yeah, he could. Age is a good thing sometimes. Long as people don't go around calling you an old man... before you're an old man."

Pap smiled at Ben knowing he was jabbing him. "Let's go to the house." He untied Huey's horse from a small bush Speck had him tied to and then mounted up. Ben grabbed hold of the saddle horn to his own horse and swung up in the saddle.

Pap started to ride off, but hesitated. "Baldy, if I could say somethin' here."

"You've never held back before."

"A lawman needs to get the lay of the land, watch what's goin' on, listen, and talk little. When you have to use force, don't wait on the cows to come home doin' it. Make your play, you'll live longer."

"Thanks, Pap, I'll remember... I appreciate that. Oh, one thing. Do you want me to tell Marshal Thorp hello for you?"

"I don't care. I don't know the man anyway." He clucked to his horse and headed to the house.

Baldy sat grinning. Then he looked down at his mount. "Horse, he told me he knew Marshal Thorp." He stared once more after Pap and smiled. "I hope we don't run out of his kind. Just maybe, just maybe I'll make a lawman one day. I can hope." The horse had one ear back listening to Baldy like he knew what he was saying. "Come on boy, let's go."

Chapter 37

Ten Years Later

Two horses with riders sat under a shade tree up on a hill overlooking the Dockin spread. Pap had taken Cran with him for the first time, to the same place he had taken Chalk. His grandson, who felt more like a son, was becoming a fine rider at just over ten years old. He was riding Night Train, his daddy's horse. They sat looking out over the ranch at all the pretty country, horses, and cattle. Pap had a tear in his eye and a smile on his face at the same time. He had hoped Chalk would be sitting here with him. In a way he was, his son was sitting in for him.

"Me and your daddy came up here. He was ridin' ole Night Train just like you. I wanted to show him what the ranch looked like from up here. It was all goin' to be his. Now, it's goin' to be yours if you want it. We ain't there yet, but we will be one day."

"Daddy Pap, maybe in a year?"

Pap chuckled. "Maybe a little longer than that."

"Daddy Pap. I love Night Train, and I love the house."

"You mean the ranch?"

"Yes... the ranch." Cran grinned. He felt big sitting up there on Night Train with his Daddy Pap. It was the first time he had let him ride up on the hill with him. He had watched him for the last six or so years ride up on the hill and sit for long periods of time. He would be playing out in the yard and wondered what he was doing when he sat there.

"Daddy Pap. You like coming here, don't you?"

"Yeah... guess so."

"What do you do when you come here and sit so long?"

He knew Cran was maybe a little young to understand, but he would try to explain it to him if he could. When he started to speak, he found he couldn't. He had a sudden lump in his throat and watery eyes. "Oh', son, I see things."

"What kind of things?"

"I see what was, what is now... and wonder what's goin' to be." He hesitated for a moment. "I see your dad down there sometimes. I see you in another six to seven years ridin' the bluestem, workin' cattle. I see your Mama Vivian ringin' the dinner bell for us to come and eat. You didn't know him, but sometimes I see Art Teague working alongside Bailey Harris down there. Those two were the best together when working cattle." Pap paused to gather himself. He was becoming emotional and needed a moment. He cleared his throat and continued. "I see old Speck checkin' the cattle and tellin' Pooh what to do. I miss Speck, miss him bad. He was my best friend."

"I miss him, too. Daddy Pap. What was wrong with him?"

"Oh... he come on to a bad ticker, his weight maybe. Don't seem like he's been gone three years already, but then sometimes it seems like a hundred." He reached up and wiped his eyes.

"Are you crying, Daddy Pap?"

"No... I'm just." He thought about what he was about to say and decided to be straight up with his grandson. "Yeah, Cran... I guess I am cryin'."

"How come?"

"Well son, I'm sad about not havin' my friend around, but happy at the same time. I'm sad that the man I rode the high plains with is no longer with me. I miss talkin' to him. On the other hand, I'm happy about the fact I have you and Vivian around. Happy about the life I've lived and what I've built up doin' it. I just get to missin' my old friends that have gone on while the buildin' was bein' done. You know, like Speck, your dad and mom, and your grandmother, Paula."

"Daddy Pap. What was she like?"

"Say again?"

"What was she like... Grandma Paula?"

He smiled as he thought about her. "You ask a lot of

questions."

Cran smiled really big.

"Your grandmother was a quiet, sweet, soft spoken lady. She worked hard and didn't bother anyone. She liked to be alone mostly. She was a woman with a lot of pride. She loved your dad more than anything in the world."

"Wish I could have known her and my real mom and dad."

"I do too, son." They sat there in silence for a while.

"Daddy Pap. How many cows we got?"

"Oh, I don't know... several thousand grown head. We'll have a few more once we get the other four sections bought."

"Do we got to milk them all?"

Pap chuckled. "No, we don't have to milk them all."

"I see Mama Vivian coming, Daddy Pap!"

"Yeah, she sure is." Vivian was riding a sorrel horse that shined like a new penny in sunlight. Cran had a big grin on his face when she made it to the top and sat beside them. Cran was feeling even bigger sitting there with his Daddy Pap and Mama Vivian.

"You boys having a good time up here?"

"Yes. Daddy Pap has been telling me about what he sees up here."

She smiled at him, and then looked over at Daddy Pap. "He has, has he?" She knew what he was seeing up on this hill. He didn't have to tell her. She looked into his eyes and they were watering. "Well, I thought I would ride up and visit with you two for a little bit. I waited until the two of you had talked and told a few lies first."

"Oh, Mama Vivian, we ain't got to the lies yet... you'll have to come back."

She and Daddy Pap laughed. "Well, I might just do that, with your permission of course."

"Okay." Cran grinned, for he felt big and was happy.

Vivian turned her attention to her Franklin. He sat silently looking at her, his chin quivering from suppressing emotion. A tear was half hidden running down his cheek through white stubble whiskers. “I love you, Vivian, I...” His voice cracked and he couldn’t speak. He looked off the other direction.

She reached over and wiped a tear away that was running down his cheek. “You’re a wonderful man, Franklin Dockin. Just enjoy what God has given you. Chalk is here with us... him and Sarah.”

“I know.”

She looked at Cran and smiled. “I don’t think you boys need me at the moment. Dinner will be ready at one o’clock. That gives you two little boys an hour.” She kissed Pap and then kissed Cran.

“Mama Vivian. Someone might see.”

“Oh? You worry about that?”

“No... I guess it’s alright. I just don’t see any of the other cowboys kissing out in the open.”

“I’ll watch that from now on.” She looked over at Pap. “Guess I’ll go.”

“Viv, me and Cran, we’re going to take a swim.”

She searched his eyes. “I understand.” She reached out and put the palm of her hand on his cheek. “I love you, Franklin.”

He couldn’t answer her. His throat wouldn’t let him, and he dared not look at her at that moment.

Vivian rode down the slope in a slow walk.

“Cran, you see that pool of water kind of over to our right?”

“Yes.”

“Me and your daddy rode down there and went skinny dipping one day.”

“You mean... with no clothes on?” His eyes got great big.

“Yes, with no clothes on. You want to go?”

His eyes got even bigger. “I sure do!”

“Me and Chalk was going to go fishing there, but things got in the way.”

"Can we go fishing there sometime?"

"I don't see why not. You think you're ready to catch some big whoppers?"

"Yeah!"

"Okay, we'll see." Pap became quiet.

"I'm ready, Daddy Pap."

"Say again?"

"I'm ready to go swimming."

"Ok, we'll ease over that way here in a second."

Pap looked out across the ranch one last time. He watched as Vivian made her way to the ranch house and he could see Pooh, Bailey and Tanner over on the west side of the place. They were bringing in a small herd of cattle to be worked. He still had his Amarillo deal in place, but times were changing. He scanned the horizon. He knew there would come a day when ranches like his would be a thing of the past. When courts and lawyers would rule the land. With that would come limitations, and the need to make and pass more laws. He knew his day would soon pass, when a man was his own law. He looked at his grandson.

"Cran, one day you'll take the reins to this place. When you do, you'll have to deal with a new way, one you'll understand... one I could never understand, or fit into."

"Daddy Pap. You're already here, you already fit in."

He smiled at him. "One day you'll look back at this day and understand what I was tryin' to say. The time I came up in was wild, nothin' like it is now. No tellin' what it will be in ten or twenty more years, give or take a few. A man can't hold back time. All he can do is remember the good times he had in his time." He looked at Cran with love in his eyes. "If a man is lucky, he won't live long enough to see the changes he couldn't abide. I'd like to think I left my mark while I was here. One thing's for sure... I come to dance."

"You like to dance, Daddy Pap?"

"Depends on the dance and who it's with... I guess so. You

ready for that swim?"

Little Cran smiled big, exposing a missing front tooth. "I sure am."

Pap took one last look out across the wide-open plains known as the Dockin Ranch. For a fleeting moment, he could see Speck riding up the narrow road to the ranch house. He glanced at Cran. "Let's go get that swim."

"I'm ready." He looked at him and smiled. "Daddy Pap"

"Yeah?"

"I love you."

Pap smiled, turned and rode down the hill with his little partner riding alongside him on old Night Train.

THE END

CPSIA information can be obtained
at www.ICGtesting.com
Printed in the USA
LVHW010554260420
654449LV00001B/167